ELENA CHIZHOVA

The Time of Women

Glagoslav Publications

The Time of Women
By Elena Chizhova

First published in Russian as "Время Женщин"

Translated by Simon Patterson
Edited by Nina Chordas

Front cover illustration by Ivanna Mikhailenko

© Elena Chizhova 2009
Represented by www.nibbe-wiedling.com

© 2012, Glagoslav Publications, United Kingdom

Glagoslav Publications Ltd
88-90 Hatton Garden
EC1N 8PN London
United Kingdom

www.glagoslav.com

ISBN: 978-90-818839-0-6

CONTENTS

CONTENTS

To my grandmothers

My first memory: snow.... A gate, and a haggard white horse. My grandmothers and I are plodding along after the cart, and the horse is big, but dirty for some reason. And there are also long shafts dragging in the snow. There is something dark lying in the cart. My grannies say it's a coffin. I know this word, but I'm still surprised, because a coffin should be made of glass. Then everybody would see that Mama is asleep, but will wake up soon. I know this, but I can't tell anyone ...

When I was little I couldn't talk. Mama would take me to all sorts of doctors, and showed me to various specialists, but to no avail: they never found the cause of it. I didn't talk until I was seven, and then I started to, although I don't remember it myself. My grannies didn't remember either – not even the first words. I asked them, of course, and they'd say that I had always understood everything and drawn pictures – and to them it was as if I'd been talking. They got used to answering for me ...They'd ask, and then they would answer.... My drawings used to be kept in a box. It's a pity that they weren't preserved: then I'd remember everything. Because without them I don't, I don't remember anything. Not even my Mama's face.

Grandma Glikeria said we used to have a photo, a small passport-sized photo, and it got lost when they ordered the portrait. A metal one, for the cemetery. It got lost too. Maybe my stepfather never got around to going there, and Zinaida threw

5

it away — along with my drawings.

I didn't like winter for a long time after that: I'd get anxious when it snowed. I thought about Mama... I worried that she'd get cold — in her summer dress... Later I got over this, but the anxiety remained, as though in my childhood, which was erased from my memory, something horrible had happened, and I would never find out what it was...

I

THE MOTHER

I chop the onions and nod: the old ladies know better whether it's time. What can you say to them? They're strict. Who am I against them?...

I'd lived in the dormitory long enough, and there it was the more the merrier – there were eight beds in the room. And now I've got plenty of space... Thanks to the local committee... Like Zoya Ivanovna said:

"Not much you can do now, is there?... Is it the kid's fault? Once you've given birth, you can't shove the child back inside. How is it with us, after all? The mother is most important: she gives you food and drink. Who cares if you have no husband? Even people like you get help and respect nowadays. Sytin, the foreman from the sixth, has a new baby: they have two now. So they'll get a two-room flat. And you can move into their place instead."

Nine and a half meters – and I'm my own mistress. If only my late mother could see me...

They don't care:

"You're not the first, and not the last. And remember, the kid is ours, it belongs to the factory. That means it belongs to everybody. The authorities don't have stepchildren. So don't you worry: there'll be a nursery, a kindergarten and a summer camp when she's older. And you're not alone, you're part of the collective. And there's no need to shield him. After all, it didn't come out of nowhere. We'd sure put the screws on him if we found him!"

I didn't say anything. They didn't ask anymore.

I thought that it was a good thing that I was in a city. There are thousands and thousands of them out there walking the streets. Not like in the countryside. They'd know all about it there – men are few and far between...

Maybe if he were from the factory, I would have told them... Zoya Ivanovna is so kind. But he isn't from the factory, so what I can say? All I know is his name. Not even an address or surname...

Yevdokia lifted an eyebrow:

"We're running out of vegetable oil."

I look at the bottle, running out is not the word... There's nothing left. A few drops on the very bottom. Do they drink it or something? I only got it last week.

"What about the onions?" I look around. "I've got to brown them, don't I?"

"Use margarine," she advises me.

He was handsome, and well-built. But I couldn't quite figure him out. He expressed himself strangely, like city people do.

"Have you been waiting long, young lady?" he said to me. I nodded, and didn't say anything: it's awkward with a stranger. He looked polite enough, but you never know. He was silent for a while and then asked: "Are you on your way to see Santa Claus?"

"What do you mean?" I said in surprise.

"Your bag," he says, nodding his head

towards it. "It's big. Is it for presents?" How silly. "What presents?!" I smile. "I'm going to the market to buy potatoes."He lifts his eyebrows: "To the market?' he asks. 'With a bag?"

"It's Sunday," I explain. "I've got to get potatoes for the whole room." – "For the room?" he shakes his head. "And what about the hall? Is it going to starve? Or is your room kind enough to share with everyone?..."

I brushed the onion tears away with the back of my hand. I smiled to myself.

I stir and stir... The margarine is not so good. It spatters everywhere. My hand is scalded already. Yevdokia has some advice for that too:

"Rub it with laundry soap."

He stood there for a few moments, then went over towards the street-lamp. His legs were long, like a crane's. He walks around, stamping his feet. He looks at his watch; "Now how much longer do we have to wait?" He's lost all his patience, he must be freezing. And his shoes are very thin, with no warm lining. "It must be soon," I try to comfort him. "I've been standing here for quite a while now..."

"No, no. It's hopeless," he looks around. 'We wait and wait, and nobody comes." – "But everyone's asleep." – "Asleep?" he echoes. "That's right. That's what I should be doing, silly me..."

Yes, I think to myself. And his face does look a bit mangled. Must have been out drinking all night. Doesn't reek of alcohol though. Our guys always do till lunchtime the next day.

"And you," I plucked my courage to ask, "up so early... Got to be somewhere?" – "Of course..." - he narrowed his eyes. "I woke up and went off to the market. To buy potatoes." – "Oh!" - I brighten up. And he looked me over from head to foot, and says: "You surprise me, young lady. Did you study in America or something?"

"Why," I was frightened, "Why in America? In a village. Malye Polovtsy." He furrowed his eyebrows: "In a Soviet village? But you don't remember the most important thing: where the collective goes, I follow."

"What collective?" - I'm confused. He laughs. "What about you and me? – Citizens gathered at the bus stop... Under the present circumstances I suggest we hail a taxi..."

He brought me to his place. A big roomy flat.

"Where is everybody?" - I ask. "Everybody is at the dacha," he says. "I mean the old folks."

How come they're at the dacha? I wonder. It's winter...

"And where are the neighbours?" I look around. – "Alas," he lifts his hands in dismay. "We don't have that kind of stuff. We live like under Communism."

I go in. And it's true. They live well. There's a desk and books lining the walls.

A picture of some bearded guy in a knitted sweater above the sofa. In a frame. "Who's that?"

"Yes," he waves his hand – "there is this one person." Perhaps, I guess, it's someone from the family. It's hard to tell with the beard...

We sat in silence for a while, and then he made coffee. In very fine white cups, which I was almost afraid to drink from. God forbid the handle might break off. "Take some sugar," - he moves the sugar bowl towards me. I took a sip and grimaced. I put two teaspoons of sugar into it, but it was still bitter.

"Black coffee," he says. "Not everybody likes it. It has to grow on you. Don't be upset, you'll get used to it." He took a sip, and put the cup aside. It didn't look as though he was all that used to it himself...

And though we didn't have any wine, I felt as if I was drunk. I listen to his voice. I don't even know how it happened... It was as if I were in a fog...

I jerked the drawer open, and felt for the grater. Now to grate the carrots... The onions are sizzling. I turn off the burner. But my hand is still aching. I turn the water on – stick it under the tap...

He took me out to the cinema during the week. I was happy. I'd always envied other girls who went out with guys. "We can't go to my place," he says. "The old folks rushed back from the country after they heard the radio." And he looked a bit grim himself.

We went to the cinema and there was a comedy showing. "Carnival Night".

"That's great," I say. "All my friends liked it." He shrugged his shoulders.

We leave the cinema. I'm happier than ever, but he's as gloomy as a thundercloud. "What," I say,

surprised, "didn't you like it? I did, very much...
I wish I lived like that... It's a nice life they have, like
in a fairytale."

"They won't be any fairytales anymore," he
sneers in reply. "Have you heard about Hungary?..."
– "What about Hungary? You mean on TV?
Of course, I have. They told us all about it at the
political information hour: hostile elements... They
conspired against us. You have to wonder what's
wrong with them!"

I saw his mouth jerk as though from a whiplash.
His eyes suddenly looked dull – neither dead nor
alive. The eyes of a fish. He waved his hand at me,
and walked away.

Should I run after him?... But I stood still. And I
kept standing there until he disappeared...

"Oh, I forgot! I've got some sugar candy for
you".

They like this. It's colourful, homemade. You
dissolve it with jam and let it cool, and it thickens
into something like caramel. I snagged it up with
the knife. They can pick at it.

It's always like this with lump sugar. God
forbid I serve granulated sugar at the table.
The tongs are small and shiny. Antique. They
don't make them like that anymore. The tongs
crack sugar with a nice clear sound into very
small pieces. They take a piece and put it in their
mouth. Take a sip of tea and suck. I used to think
they were sparing it because it was expensive.
Wasn't I earning enough to buy sugar? But they
said it tasted nicer like that. And what's more

they even taught the girl to like it. She pushes the sugar bowl away, if you move it towards her...

When I moved in with the old women, the girls tried to scare me: "How will you get on with neighbours!" At the dormitory it's all family. Over there I'll be a stranger, a country bumpkin with a baby. Go talk to Sytin's wife, they say, maybe she'll give you some useful advice.

I found her. "Don't be afraid of the old women," she says. "The main thing is to make them respect you. Don't let them think they're in charge. You'll take my place in the kitchen – I got myself a good one, by the window. Just shout at them, if they give you any trouble: they'll crawl into their corners. It's a shame you haven't got a man – they sure were afraid of mine"...

I moved in with them. They turned out to be all right – quiet old women. But I was still afraid. Sytin's wife was a big, strapping woman. She could shout loud enough to make the saints blush.

At the beginning, I tried to be very quiet. In the morning I'd wrap the baby in a little blanket, and the pram is under the stairs, with a lock on it. A heavy lock, with a chain. The pram was given to me by the factory, and I bought the lock myself. I'd run down the stairs, open the lock, put it under the little mattress and hurry back upstairs to get the baby. All done, and, blizzard or no blizzard, we go to the nursery. I leave her with the nannies and off to work. The nursery belongs to the factory. But all the same, my soul aches. Sometimes I have to work the second shift, if the foreman wants me to. Then, when it's already late at night, I get back to the nursery. There's a nanny on duty. She wakes the baby, wraps her up and brings her to me. And it would all have been all right if she hadn't started to get sick. Zoya Ivanovna would comfort me: "Children all get sick, yours will recover too".

The nursery is on the balance – the factory pays the difference to the staff. The mothers also give the nannies things on holidays, like candy or stockings. I did too, but I was too shy to ask them to do anything special for her. There were a lot of new babies and only one nanny. She'd cry herself sick because she stayed in wet nappies for too long, or have a stomach ache. I got tired of having to take sick leave all the time. And on sick leave they only paid me the average, of course: it was nowhere near the money I earned normally.

It was all right at first. If her temperature rises, you just give her some drops and that's it. And it goes down in a couple of days. It wasn't until later that the convulsions started. She'd get blue all over and go into a fit. Her eyes would go cloudy and white. And my heart would stop: I'd think it was the end of her. So I made up my mind to send her to the country. My mother was still alive. And that's where the old women came in. They wouldn't hear of it..

They didn't have any family themselves. Their husbands and children were all gone, dead. No grandchildren either. "Go and work," they said. "Surely the three of us can raise her!"

And so it all started that at home I became something like a servant. I'd go to work, then to the shops to wait in various queues. Then, I'd do the washing, the cleaning and the cooking for everybody. They were retired, and their pensions were tiny. I had to pay for a lot myself. Still, the girl lived like a princess. And no wonder, three nannies for one child – she was well looked after. They took her for walks, and read to her. They taught her French, if you can believe that.

She was growing up smart – not a bumpkin like me. She drew pictures a lot. She learnt the alphabet at four. She understood everything. But wouldn't talk. She turned five, then six, and still wouldn't talk.

It was all my fault anyway. I kept silent until my belly started to stick out.

They transfer pregnant women to other shop floors at the factory. You can bring a certificate from the health clinic and they'll transfer you out of the hazardous jobs. Give you a position as a cleaning woman or at the storehouse. The married ones don't mind telling. Why would they? They're in the right. But people like me... how can you admit it? It's shameful...

Before the decree came out, you weren't even allowed to think about an abortion. If you get knocked up, you have the baby. But no one could keep the girls from doing it. At the first alarm, they'd get rid of it in secret. One, they say, really took to it. The guys joked that she tired out a whole team of workers, bitch. Well, she wasn't bothered – she lies in bed for a little while, gives it a rest and she's at it again. Two girls died, though, they say. From blood poisoning, it seems. Now the decree came out, you can do it every year if you must. It's still scary, of course: they make it hurt as much as possible. But there wasn't much to be done. So I made up my mind.

I went to the hospital, but the doctor said: "It's too late now. It's too far along. You'll have to have it".

So I got some pills from the chemist. I thought I'd miscarry if I took them. I took them for a week. But no...

She turned three, and I took her to the clinic. The doctor examined her mouth, spread some pictures on the table. It seems that everything is all right, she said. She hears, she understands. It's some kind of developmental delay.You've got to wait, she may start talking.

She said there was a professor in Moscow. That means I have to take her there. And where do I get the money to do that from, I wonder? As it is, I can hardly make ends meet from one paycheck to the next...

At first I cried a lot: I thought she'd grow up to be a freak... I can't send her to school or summer camp. And the worst thing is, she won't have a family. Who'll marry a mute? She'll die an old maid. Unless she finds a mute like herself.

The grannies, thanks a lot, tried to comfort me.. Everything is in the hand of God. When the time comes she'll talk. But sometimes, you're just walking along the street. And all around, you hear other people's children talking. Your heart contracts and you turn away, swallowing tears.

The grannies advise me: don't you talk about it at work. If they ask you, say everything is fine. People have long tongues, evil tongues. All woes come from tongues. They'll tell you they sympathize with you to your face but behind your back, who knows? They may slander you.

"Would you like some cabbage soup?"

They would. Soup is good for you. I got a nice piece of meat yesterday at the grocery store on the square. Brisket. With fat on it, the way they like it. And with the bone. It's a good marrowbone. "Leave the marrow for the little one," they say. "We'll do without it..."

I have basins in the corner, with linen soaking. I'll leave it there until the evening now, until after the shift.

No one knows about the grannies. I said I had sent for my mother from the country, and she is the one looking after the child. Zoya Ivanovna asked me about it too. No, I say, she doesn't get sick at home. And she says: it's all right while she's a baby, but when she grows up a bit you should send her to kindergarten, to be among other kids. Because, she said, she'll have a bad time at school if she's not used to being with other children. I thought about it. Maybe she will be more at ease with other kids after all. She might come out of her shell and play and start talking. The grannies never let me, though. Leave her at home, they said. There'll be plenty of time for her to suffer later on. And now they've thought up a new one: they want to take her to the theatre.

To a New Year show, I ask them? I got the ticket already. They were giving them out to everybody with kids. I got the ticket out, showed them. A coupon comes with the ticket. Santa Claus gives out candy, sweets of all kinds, wafers. Santa Claus is all very well, of course, but it's really the factory that pays. On the shop floor, they say that it's a good present. They put in some chocolate too.

We never buy it. She doesn't know what it is. I get soy bars or caramels from time to time...

The grannies looked at the ticket and said – No. You'll go get the present yourself. But *she* won't go. She's going to another theatre, the Mariinsky. And she doesn't need a ticket, they'll let her in without it. They have a friend there. They go to church together. She'll let her in, find a seat for her and look after her. The friend doesn't have anybody either: no children, no grandchildren.

They told me to get her a suit: a woollen, Chinese one. A jacket with buttons, tights and a hat. All children have them, they say. It must be expensive, - about six rubles. And ribbons for her braids. Silk ones, of a matching colour.

Can they be nylon, I ask. No, they say.The nylon kind split at the ends. The ribbons she wears at home are soft, the grannies make them out of old rags.

We gathered for early tea in the kitchen. Here, before the child wakened, we discussed all the important matters, and made our plans. The day started with a dark dawn, like a long age. Daytime was a long road that rolled on, glancing back at striped milestones that fell behind – once and for all.

At nine it's time to get up, get dressed, and wash. At ten, there's a story on the radio. Lunch at two. After lunch, it's naptime: you don't have to sleep, but you've got to lie down for a while anyway.

Between the milestones, depending on the weather, there were things to do. The most important one was to take a walk. Here time would slow down and resign itself to the yearly cycle - like it does in the country.

In the spring we'd go to the little park near the Lviny bridge. They close the gardens at this time of year to dry them out, because it's too muddy. In the autumn, to the park near Nikolsky Cathedral: to walk under the oaks by the railing where there are a lot of acorns. In October, the maples shed their leaves. You walk, and the dead leaves rustle under your feet... In November, the first snow falls.

In winter, also to Nikolsky Cathedral, or to Soldatsky garden. The slide there is so high... Children line up to go down the slide – on a sled or without it. We have a sled, and it's old and good. But we didn't let our little girl ride on it much. And we learned to walk along the edge, away from other people. With other kids, it was a real pain: "Is your girl a deaf-mute?" It was easier in summer, as there weren't so many of them – some went to the country, some to summer camps.

Here, at the table, just after they got the baby, they all came to an agreement: the first thing was to baptise her. In secret, without the mother's consent. She didn't have a word in these matters. Thank God, they knew the bell-ringer at the Nikolsky cathedral. He's deaf, but understands everything. He agreed to talk to the priest, and ask him to come to the home.

She was called Suzanna in the birth certificate. What an unchristian name, God forgive us. In the olden days, they called whores that, so as not to dishonour the names of the patron saints... And now her own mother called her that – a name for a dog...

They thought and thought, and leafed through the church calendar. There are too many good names to count, but you can't just take the first one you come across. Father Innokenty said: search for something resembling the birth certificate. You can choose by meaning, or by the first letter.

Glikeria came up with Serafima.... No. They decided to call after Sofia.

In the evening when her mother was present they avoided calling her by name: *her*, for *her*, *she*. In the daytime they called her lovingly – Sofyushka. Among themselves – Sofia.

Father asked: is anyone called Faith, Charity or Hope? She would be the godmother then so they could celebrate the Saint's day together. They shook their heads: no. No Charity, no Hope, no Faith. While deciding, they almost had a fight over it. There can only be one godmother. And she's the one that answers to God. The godmother is family, and so the rest of them will be...what – strangers? Father Innokenty made peace between them. God, he said, will hold each of you responsible in turn. The one who goes to Him first will be the first to answer.

And then it was hard to know whether to laugh or cry: they started comparing their illnesses. One had a bad heart, one could barely walk. Father Innokenty said: people cannot know when their time will come. Sometimes it happens that God takes the young and healthy but leaves the old and sick. Can one see into His design? They agreed. They remembered the young and healthy. Their own young and healthy.

As it turned out, Yevdokia Timofeevna had a baptismal shirt in her chest of drawers. It was amazing that it was still there after so many years. It had belonged to her elder son, Vasiliy. Even his bones had decayed long ago, but the shirt was still there.

The fabric was thin, as light as air: an angel's garment. The lacework was a little crumpled though, like fallen-out feathers. The grandson had had not been able to use it. Her son and daughter-in- law didn't let her baptise him. They had their own religion, they said.

The son became a big shot. "The people today are no match for me," he said proudly. "I've been with the Bolsheviks ever since the Civil War".

She didn't dare to do it secretly. She was afraid of getting them into trouble.

We're building a new life, they laughed at her, and you still long for the old times. You want to drag us back to the Tsarist past. Back on the old road. There's no way back, and your religion is opium.

The things they'd come up with! Opium is sold at the chemist – the doctor prescribes it for pain. And the daughter-in-law chimes in with him. Look around you, mother. It's too late for me to look around, I say. You look around. You'll have to live this life. Then, before they had time to look around, they were taken away. And that was it, they disappeared in their Communism. Thank God, they didn't take the grandson: the *other* grandmother took him.

A couple of months went by, then on Trinity Sunday she took a present she'd managed to save up, and went to see her grandson. And, stealing a minute when the boy went out to play in the courtyard, she brought the topic up. Let's go together, she said. He'll grow up to be a heathen. What a sin! The other grandmother grew frightened : "Don't you even think about it! If somebody finds out, they'll come for him straight away. And they'll lock him up in an orphanage. He'll never come out of it".

And this other grandmother went together with him in the evacuation. They were killed by a bomb somewhere close to Luga. So she was the first to stand before Him – and the first to answer.

They prepared the shirt, washed it. The lacework was worn-out, and they spread it on a towel. It looked as though it got whiter when they washed it. But when it dried, it was all yellow again. Maybe if it was put in boiling water... But they didn't dare to do this: it was at the end of its life – it would come to pieces in their hands.

They heated up some water beforehand. The priest said: well, make up your mind and dress your little girl. They brought the shirt, and put it on Sofyushka. Yevdokia stood there with a frozen expression: how could it be easy to see her baby son resurrected... After that she was all right, and got a hold of herself. I can't be the godmother, she said. My heart turns black when I look at this shirt. You be the one, Ariadna. It all happened the right way in your family: your husband died in the First War, your son in the Second, and your grandchildren died along with your daughter-in-law in the Blockade. It was all proper.

How can it be proper, she says, if they're all lying in ditches. Let Glikeria do it: she never had children. The count, her unwed husband, fled from the Revolution. Who knows, he may still be alive.

They agreed to that. After all, Ariadna knew better. Who are we to second-guess her... She's the educated one. She even lived abroad when she was young.

Glikeria was the godmother, and the other two sang along with the priest. Father Innokenty says: sing quietly so that no one hears. Who would hear, we say, there isn't anybody around.

He performed the ceremony well, didn't miss anything out or hurry. Sofyushka, smart girl, blinked her eyes, and listened attentively, as if she understood.

She only cried once, when Glikeria denied the demons. Yevdokia looked at Ariadna as if flicking her with a knife.

Everybody sat down to tea. The priest smiles: I must admit to this fault, I'm a inveterate tea drinker. I like to soothe my soul with tea and sugar lumps. They remembered the bucket samovars. It's not the same on stove burners. The boiling water is weak, without any taste. It boils up nice and thick in a samovar.

As for the communion, he says, see for yourselves. It's all right, we say, it's all the same now, we'll bring her.

23

The weather is good. Frosty and dry. When it warms up a bit, that's the right time to go for a walk. We look out into the yard – it's white as white can be. And the yard-keeper is nowhere in sight. In the old times they used to come out before dawn with a shovel. They've got very slack since then. We sat and talked about the old times.

Ariadna came to herself first. She went to the pantry to take the dry stockings down from the washing line. Yevdokia went to get the kasha: the mother made it at night, and put it under the pillow. It's nice and crumbly from under the pillow. Every buckwheat grain is like another. And she won't have any other kind: neither semolina nor porridge. Yevdokia grumbles: they give them God knows what in kindergartens. Buckwheat is expensive, hard to come by. Lucky that Antonina gets it at the factory. Two kilos a month they give her, one for her, one for the child.

Ariadna dressed her and brought her out to the kitchen. Sofyushka is used to the routine, and goes to the tap herself. Glikeria is waiting with the ladle in her hands. In summer the water in the pipes is warm. But in winter we've got to heat it up to pour over her little hands.

"You can relax now," Yevdokia orders. "Let the child eat in peace."

She ate and had her tea after that. She drank and set aside the empty cup. We don't teach her to cross herself, God forbid. We're scared of the mother. What if she sees it.

After breakfast, Glikeria sits her down with the embroidery hoop. She's too young to sew, but it's just the right age for embroidery. Satin-stitch, knots, and chain stitch. The morning lesson is a little yellow petal. She won't give it to us until she's done.

She works on it, and Glikeria tells her about the Saints, or the Holy Virgin.

Then, it's Ariadna's turn: she reads a story. She has her own stories, in French. The book is plump, with lots of pictures. Whatever stopped them from burning it during the blockade... She reads until the end, then starts with some questions: she asks, she answers herself. She talks strangely – in French. And from time to time she deliberately makes a mistake: she wants to check whether the girl understood. Sofyushka frowns, and shakes her head. She points in the book – it's not right, she means.

Yevdokia saw it once: "Is she really reading, or is she pointing at random?" Ariadna got offended: "Why at random? I move my finger along the lines when I read so that she can follow too. And she's known the alphabet for a long time. I showed her back in spring".

"Come," Yevdokia says, amazed, "ask her some word. Let her find it in the book".

Sofia smiles archly, and runs her eyes over the lines – she finds it twice.

"Oh, get along with you! - Yevdokia cries out happily. - Who can test you literate people – you must have arranged it together!"

Sofyushka wrinkles her nose. That means she's laughing.

The big, black radio is in Yevdokia's room. Sofia comes in, and gets on a chair. She turns it on, and presses her ear against it. Quietly, so that she doesn't disturb the grannies.

"I couldn't sleep at night, and remembered things: the sweets used to come in boxes. Some were plain, some were wrapped in gold. And when you open the box, you find silver tongs. Ivan Sergeich often bought them for me – he liked to spoil me."

Her eyes are happy, and she smiles, as if she has gotten younger.

"Yes, I can see that he spoiled you," - Yevdokia purses her lips. - "Fancy the things you remember: sweets wrapped in gold..."

" It's not the sweets I miss," - she screwed up her face.

Yevdokia's lips are dry and thin. As thin as a thread.

"Yesterday on Ofitserskaya I saw them digging again. They dug an enormous hole, and clouds of steam were coming out of it. There were footbridges and tripods on the side. So I'm walking past them with Sofia, and, good gracious, there are evil spirits: voices coming from under the ground. Who could be there in the boiling water? I looked and saw some men. Two of them, their mugs all dirty, digging around under the pipe. And they had the nerve to laugh at me: 'What are you afraid of, granny?' Of course, I'm afraid. Devils, God forgive me! They dig and dig. They'll soon dig right through to the other side. They can't sit still on this earth."

"Where on Ofitserskaya?" - Glikeria cracks

sugar, and pours it into the saucer. She's as tiny as a sparrow.

"Here, round the corner. What do they call it again? Dekabristov."

Glikeria is sucking her sugar and thinking:

"Those Decembrists, when did they get famous? In the revolution or the war?"

"God bless you." - Ariadna shrugs her shoulders. – "It was back in the last century. The December uprising of 1825. Against the law of serfdom."

She's learned. Reads a lot. She has a whole shelf of books.

"Ah," - Glikeria shakes her head, - "that's when it was... That's why I can't remember. It was when they gave freedom to my mother. We were all serfs. But mother wasn't too happy about it. It was better with the masters, she used to say. The ones who went to the city to work made out the best. Though they had always done it freely. In the old times they paid you everywhere. It was enough to pay the master and still have some left for the family."

"And before the war," - Yevdokia nursed her cheek, - "they also used to dig. I remember I went for a walk once and thought to myself – what are they digging for? They'll dig up some evil. I said as much to my daughter-in-law. And she pouted: they're laying pipes, she said. Under the Tsar they didn't see to it that all the houses should have water."

"And mother told me, our master was good. Never made anybody marry against their will. My father was a blacksmith, you know. So he and

27

my mother came to the master. But he didn't mind. He blessed them. Young couples went to ask for blessing for a long time after. There was freedom already, but still..."

"It's not true that they didn't see to that, I said. We've had a tap since the old times. And the water was good and never stank of anything. But my daughter-in-law says, we'll change the pipes everywhere. And we'll put trains underground. She laughs..."

"People laughed often before the war..." - Glikeria remembers.

Yevdokia screwed up her face: - "They're good at that, they are. They either laugh or dig up the ground..."

"God," - Ariadna sighs, - "so many nameless ditches... When I think of how many of them were left after the blockade..."

"After the blockade!... What about the Canal?"

Glikeria crossed herself:

"Too many people around. Some dig, others lie in the ground."

"That's if they're lucky..." - Yevdokia banged her cup on the table. – "They think they dug it for somebody else. And then it turns out it was for themselves... All right then." - She smoothed the oilcloth. "One turns into a sinner, sitting here with you. Oh, my tooth hurts, damn it. My mouth's empty, no teeth left, and they still hurt..."

Tights made of thick wool. Glikeria undid an old fleece cardigan and knitted them in double strands. Felt boots, white, with rubbers. Nowadays they make them black. And you can't bend them at the knee, so it feels like you're walking in stocks. Under the hat — a cotton scarf: they tie it up and ask me if it's too tight. The coat's new and warm. Yevdokia turned her own inside out. It's thick cloth, and she put in a double layer of wadding. She's got another one – it'll last the rest of her lifetime.

"We'd better go to Nikolsky," – she tied up her kerchief and tucked in the ends. – "Don't give us the sled – we'll walk."

Ariadna shuts the door behind us:

"When you're walking past it, have a look: maybe they've brought Christmas trees..."

The stairs are wide and not steep. There are two apartments on every landing. The house is old, but there's nothing left of the past apart from one grotto. The Bolsheviks never got to it. Tritons, sea shells – everything is untouched. Sofia always turns around to look at it when she goes past it. She likes fairy tales.

Ariadna noticed it a long time ago. It used to be like that: she sits and listens, just so someone is reading to her. It didn't matter if it was Little Red Riding Hood, that Buratino, or the witch Baba Yaga. And now that she has learnt something – she brings the book herself: she opens it and gives it to Ariadna. As though saying : read about the girl, about the Little Mermaid. Ariadna can't stand it any more: she's exhausted. How many times can you read the same thing?.. You know it by heart, don't you, she says. And Sofia frowns,

29

her eyes fill with tears: she points at it with her finger – read. Ariadna even tried to cheat her: she'd leave out one thing or another sometimes. But no! She's older now. You can't fool her like that any more...

Glikeria figured it out first. It's because, angelic soul, she understands it to be about her muteness. And the Little Mermaid is like her. Only the Mermaid knows why she's been deprived of speech. And ours, what does she know...

There's a little park in front of the house. Behind it is a monument: it faces the square and turns its back to us. On warm days children climb on the rails. The rails are slippery and slick with ice in winter. We pass the monument and turn the corner – and here they are, the domes.

Grandma grabbed her back. We'll stop for a minute, she says. It's been getting numb since morning, as if it weren't mine. She stands there, looking around.

"I wish," - she whispers, - "I could have twenty more years..."

And I'm walking by her side and thinking: she's old, why would she want so much?

"To see what they'll come to in the end.

Who are they?

Yevdokia mutters gruffly as if she overheard:

"They... the Bolsheviks. Never mind," - she says, - "you keep your mouth shut. And don't listen to the old hag. Look under your feet so you don't stumble... First to the church, I've got to light a candle. It's a bad day for me today – a bad anniversary. Then we'll walk to the belfry. Do a circle along the canal – and home."

It's gloomy below. The upper church is bright. It's incredibly beautiful if you climb the little stairs: decked with gold wherever you look.

We'd take her to communion when she was a baby. Now we're scared. They're knocking down churches again. They can't sit still, those snakes. It looked like they'd calmed down after the war. Now they're at it again...

Grandma Yevdokia is very strict in church.

"That's the altar," - she instructs me. In front of it are the holy gates: when they open you can see everything through them." Priests walk inside the altar like righteous men in Heaven. When the service starts in the evening – they light chandeliers. The light is soft and lovely. You look around and your heart rejoices: the gold sparkles and glints – as if it were bathed in fire.

She leaves me and comes back with candles, then takes my hand and brings me closer.

"Melt the candle at the bottom a bit," - she says, - "Fix it well so it doesn't fall over. And don't look around. Look straight at the holy face. Now cross yourself while no one's looking. Not like that, you

31

oaf: put your fingers together tightly. Entreat the Holy Virgin for the lost souls, sinful souls. She never listened to me, but maybe she'll have compassion for one who is wordless...."

The holy faces are stern and dark. The flames are dancing and flickering on the candles. Grandma Yevdokia says: "They are living souls glimmering. When they burn out, the old woman in black comes along; she'll brush the stubs into her apron. And that's how we live: we burn for a while and then we go out. The candles burn to the end, but as for people, they don't even burn down to the stubs sometimes."

Grandma Glikeria's more fun to go to church with. She takes me to Saint Nicholas.

"Pray, Sofyushka" - she instructs me, "for the wanderers and travellers."

She keeps him in her room too. And under him there is a flame in a red cup. Grandma comes up to him. She stands there and talks. Whispers and whispers. And he remains silent. Apparently he doesn't know how to talk.

"Saint Nicholas," - she says, - "protects everybody. Those who travel the seas, who are lost in the woods – he sets them on the right way. He visits those who are in prison and cures those who are lying sick...."

She takes me to the icon and explains. "Here, look. All human life is shown here. In this world and in the next. There beyond it's light. Our Lord sits in the middle, and on both sides are the righteous. They don't remember their former life: they enjoy themselves in a new way. And why would they remember? They have it all different there now, not like we do..."

"And below," - she frightens me, - "is hell. The tortures: weeping and gnashing of teeth. And in hell, no doubt, are the sinners. Only He comes down to them – he descends to them. Sinners are all different: some are inveterate, some sin through folly. Life," - she sighs, - "can go in strange ways – especially when you're young..."

We came out of the church and went along the canal. And there's that scary house; those enormous guys. Grandma says: idols, blockheads. We're walking past them, I steal a glance: what huge legs they have. They'll crush you if they step on you.

We walked in a circle, and now we are home.

"Well," - Grandma Glikeria helps me to undress, - "where have you been, what have you seen?"

"Where have we been?" - Grandma Yevdokia answers. – "We were at the church, tell her, then we went along the canal."

"Well, how is it out there? Is it freezing? Froze right through, did you?"

They took off the galoshes, and put the felt boots against the heater to dry.

"Why are you so gloomy?" - Grandma Ariadna appeared and leaned against the lintel.

"I know why. She's afraid of those idols," - Yevdokia says, unwrapping her kerchief. "No use trying to talk her out of it. It's like talking to a brick wall."

"But they're statues," - Ariadna shakes her head. – "How can you be afraid of them?"

She takes me by the hand and leads to her room.

Elena Chizhova

"I told you, didn't I? They're called Atlantes. Sculptors made them out of stone. There's a story that says they're holding the earth on their shoulders. And they're hollow inside. Empty. There's nothing but wire inside to hold them firmly."

There's a pencil on the table, a grown-up's book, open. A pile of paper sheets next to it. Grandma Ariadna gives them to me one by one to draw on.

"Draw a bit, while dinner's heating up."

She leaves.

There's a cloud above. Under the cloud is a big house. Below it is a long canal. A fence runs along it. And in front of the house they stand – enormous. Their heads are black and scary. There's wire inside them. Their big fingers stick out – it looks like they may move from their places at any moment...

I put the pencil aside, and listened: no, no one's calling me. I took up the pencil again. The letters are big, crooked. I wrote:

BOLSHEVIKS

"Why are you so quiet? Are you drawing?" - Grandma Ariadna peeps in to call me to dinner. – "Well, show me, what have you drawn? ...Oh my God..." - She covered her mouth with her fingers. She snatched the sheets and left the room.

Grandma Yevdokia comes in and looks at me angrily:

"What are you thinking, girl? Have you lost your mind? You'll be the ruin of us all. To write such nonsense!"

She frowned and shook her finger at me: - "You watch it, girl!"

"You mind, Yevdokia Timofeevna, watch yourself. It's you she's been listening to. And what if she starts talking?... At school, say, God forbid..." - Ariadna is picking up stitches, and thinking aloud.

"Oh, our sins are grave," - Glikeria sighs.

"What have our sins got to do with it?"

"I don't know what's better" - Glikeria counts stitches, - "with a life like ours: chattering or silent like her.

"What's there for her at school anyway? She's already literate," - Yevdokia puts in guiltily. – "I myself did three years of school - it lasted me my whole life. And our girl knows both Russian and French. She'll learn to count, and that'll be enough for her too."

"Think, Yevdokia, before you say something: how can she do without school? If she doesn't start talking, they'll send her to a *special* one," - Ariadna whispers as if she were afraid of somebody.

"I won't allow that," - she raised her voice, - "no way. Over my dead body. There's nothing for her at a school like *that*."

"Your dead body will scare them a lot, that's for

sure," - Glikeria looks at the door over her shoulder. – "They'll come and drag her away by force..."

It's quiet outside the window. Flowers spread over the window panes. The mirrored wardrobe is in the corner. I close my eyes – I'm scared. I feel as if somebody's creeping after me, threatening to drag me away...

The voices are dry and weak, and they barely get through to me. Grandma Glikeria is knitting a fleece cardigan – she promised me one for the New Year. The cardigan is warm and blue. "You've grown out of the old one, - she says, - so we'll unravel it. We'll add some red wool. And you'll be all ready for school then"...

Unravelling is fun: the yarn runs, winds, and slips out of the stitches. Glikeria tugs at the yarn, and Ariadna sits opposite her and spools it in. When it tears, she finds the ends and ties them together in a knot. The wads are plump, soft, and curly with old stitches. After they wash them they hang them on the line, and put a little bag of sand under each of them. That's to straighten out the stitches. Otherwise, you start making a new garment, and the old stitches won't settle. And this way the yarn is smooth, although it's ripped in many places. Once they've knitted it they turn it inside out – and the inside is all covered in knots...

I got back from work.

"Well, I've been to Gostiny. I asked them. They say they had small suits, but they were all sold out. And there were orders from the factories too, so I think maybe our union committee also ordered some."

I took some potatoes, and spread out a newspaper to peel them on. My hands are so tired from the work day, they can't even hold a knife. I've been unwell of late, I think to myself. It's sort of all right in the morning when I'm on my way to work. But later it comes over me suddenly. And I can't look at food, I feel sick...

"Don't forget – come to the office on Sunday, there'll be flour to queue up for again. I'll drop by and find out for you: they may start putting people on the waiting list the day before. They said that they give two kilos to each person in the queue. And we mustn't forget to make some nails red-hot. Last year I didn't bother and the flour went bad. So you get ready for Sunday, get wrapped up warm. You may have to queue for two hours, maybe all three.

I didn't say anything about the child. They won't let her go anyway: what's the point of her jostling around in a queue, they say. Others don't care about that: they even drag newborn babies along with them. And why not take them there? They do give two kilos to each person, and a baby counts as one.

I rinsed the potatoes, and put them on to boil. Now to throw away the peelings. A cold draft is coming from the back stairs.

On the stairs there are rubbish bins standing in the corners. Mama takes the potato peelings out and throws them into a bin. The bin is full already and they fall out to the floor. If I peep out, grandma Yevdokia gets angry: "Where're you going, - she shouts, -curious cat? Aren't you afraid of the Raven? Watch out, or he'll get you..."

The Raven comes at night, pecks the rubbish. It turns everything over, pecks at the peelings, and flies away...

I went and rummaged around the shelves.

"There aren't any nails," - I say. That means I've got to drag myself to the scrap-heap again. – "Mind you, look for the thicker boards" – Yevdokia explains, - "the thinner ones have small nails in them, they won't do."

"I don't think I'll go today – it's dark already. There's plenty of time until Sunday."

The stove is black, and huge. There's a little iron door on the front to stick the logs into. The little door has a wrought-iron bar. They stuff the stove full of logs and bar it up. The fire roars and groans inside. If you peep inside through a slit, you see spurts of flame winding up, breathing heat out. It's too scary to come any closer: Baba-yaga will sneak up on you and shove you into the stove alive....

They make the nails red-hot and take them out with a pair of tongs. The nails are all crooked and red: they put them into flour jars so that the flour doesn't go bad.

I drain the potatoes - and we sit down to supper. We have the potatoes with vegetable oil, and Suzanna has some cottage cheese. They say she shouldn't gorge herself on potatoes. She'll have time to do that when she grows up.

"You're bringing up a lady, aren't you," I laugh: "Maybe we should buy her some caviar?"

After the supper they leave the kitchen. Now they'll read to her. That's fine by me, I think to myself.

Grandma Glikeria puts the book aside.

"My eyes hurt." - she says, - "They've become weak. By evening they get very weepy. Tonight I'll tell you the way I remember it."

"Once upon a time in another kingdom there lived a king and a queen. They were happy together, but cruel fate gave them no children. They lost all hope, but God is merciful, and they finally had a girl. They were very glad and chose a beautiful name for her. They invited guests..."

Oh, I just noticed that I put the kid's clothing to soak in the grown-ups' basin. Good that the old ladies didn't see that – they tell me to keep it separate. "Grown-ups' dirt is acrid. It's amassed over an entire lifetime. No matter how much you wash it, it doesn't come off". Let them have their way. They probably know better. They worked at the Maximilianov hospital for so many years, as nursemaids in the reception ward.

Yevdokia was the first to get a job there. Then she lured the others. So they worked shifts there together every third day. They liked it at the hospital. The work was good and easy: you receive a patient, give out the linen – and sit down again. And you're full all day. They feed you from the hospital kitchen. You can wash if you need to. And you get clean linen every time you want to change it. You don't have to wash anything yourself, you just take it to the matron. It's a pity it wasn't like that at the dormitory, we did all the washing for ourselves...

"And the sorceress was very mean. She hated it with all her heart when people forgot about her. The moment she found out about this, she started to play dirty tricks on them: she only wanted it all her way and no other. The king and the queen bow to the fairies, and thank them for their generous gifts. Scarcely have they sat down to the tables, than they hear a thunder-clap: a black carriage comes along, drawn by a crow. The crow rolls his shameless eyes, and squawks in his crow tongue. The sorceress comes out of the carriage and goes straight to the cradle. You thought you'd do without me? I'll show you! And she shook her finger at everybody. I've prepared a present for you too: let her live, she says, until she's grown up, and when she's grown up, she'll jab her finger with a poisoned knitting needle – and in the blink of an eye, she will die..."

I rub and rub... The soap is slippery, as if it's trying to jump out of my hands. The white washing needs to be boiled: I drag the heavy tank to the stove. When it cools, I rinse it, then soak it with laundry blueing. All this dragging makes my stomach cramp. It used to be all right: I'd lie down and it'd go away. But lately I've been bleeding. Not much. Just for a couple of days. Still I have to use rags to soak up the bleeding. I wash them separately.

The public laundry is in the basement in the yard. Some of the housewives go there. I used to go there too. But then I gave up. The heat and the stuffiness, and those huge boilers were all too much for me. Let the people from the communal flats use it. You can't do much washing in the communal kitchen. I'm lucky, because the old ladies go to bed early, so I'm my own mistress at night...

"...The king began to cry, the queen began to cry, but the first fairy lifted the curtain and came out into the light. She was hiding there from the start to stop the evil witchcraft. Don't cry, my queen and king, she comforted them: she won't get her own way in any case. I haven't got enough power to cancel out her witchcraft, but I won't sit back and do nothing either: I'll cast my own spell. Let your girl grow up and prick her finger on a poisonous knitting-needle - there's no way around that. She'll prick her finger, and fall down as if she were dead, but she won't die – she'll only fall asleep for a long time. And when the hour strikes, she'll open her eyes and wake up for good..."

Grandma Yevdokia looks into the room.

"Read enough? It's time to go to bed now. Shall I turn the light on for you?" - she feels for the button on the night light. – "You won't go to sleep without the light, will you?"

The night lamp is white with a red pattern - it looks like a little house. There are fairies on the sides and a golden rooster on the top...

I did all the washing, and wrung out the linen. I filled the entire kitchen with laundry hung up to dry. It's nice at night, I think. It's quiet. You look out the window – there isn't a light anywhere. As if there were no one around...

I once thought that I saw *him* near Gostiny. My heart skipped a beat. I was just surprised: he looked like such a big shot. In a deer-skin hat. I caught up with him, and glanced into his face so as he wouldn't notice. I look, but no. Whatever on earth came over me... He's different. But how is he different? It's hard to say. I haven't got the right words for it.

So many years have passed – I've started to forget the face. They say you'll see it in your daughter, and then you'll remember. Especially if she takes after him. It's hard to tell so far: it seems she looks more like my late mother. And other times, when she sits down and props her cheek against her hand, and lifts her eyes to the ceiling – she's the spitting image of him. Her face is different, but she has inherited his manner. She's never even seen her father, but it seems that she remembers. And what if she starts talking? Will she talk like him too? I won't understand half of it again, will I?... I checked myself: let her speak any way she likes, pure French even, as long as starts speaking at all....

Everything is strange in these matters. When I was a young girl, I marvelled at it. How come that children are different when they have the same mother and father? One turns out to be hardworking and slaves away all day, but the other is a lazy bones... I asked the village teacher why it happens like that. I don't know, she said. It all comes from nature.

When I was pregnant, I thought about it too. I tried to talk to Zoya Ivanovna. "It all comes from upbringing," she said. "You reap what you sow. If you miss the boat, she'll grow up to be like her scum of a father." - "What's the point of blaming anybody now?" I said. "Whatever the father is like, it's my fault too." Mother warned me so many times. She never taught me to go to bed with the first man to come along, that's for sure...

And I also think it depends a lot on the name. Take mine, for example: Tonya is all they call me. So I decided that if it was a boy I would call him after my granddad – it doesn't matter so much to guys. And if it's a girl – let her hear a beautiful name from the start. Perhaps she won't repeat my life then.

After all, the law says: you can write down any patronymic you want. Zoya Ivanovna said: "Use the grandfather's name, or your father's". Well, I thought: it's not right somehow, not proper. Let it be her own father's name. And so I wrote down his name.

The grannies have their own ideas on the matter: "Whatever is born is what will grow up. An apple may grow on a fir tree, but then a pinecone may grow on an apple tree too." - "Well, then, what's the point in trying to take good care of the child?" I asked. "For example, a cone will never turn into an apple." - "No, it won't," they agreed. "But if it's an apple, then it still depends on other people: whether it stays wild and sour, or becomes a sweet garden apple"...

I close my eyes tight: balls of coloured wool roll around... All the threads are tangled up. The grannies pick up the ends and tie them together... The curtain at the window is flapping: a fairy is hiding behind it – waiting for the evil sorceress. And the sorceress has saddled the Ravens, and is riding along the streets: past the church, past the canal, up to the blackest of the houses... The Bolsheviks rejoice at seeing them... They move their empty fingers...

"Yesterday I couldn't sleep at all," Ariadna complains.

"I certainly heard you walking around. You can hear everything through that wall."

"I was very thirsty," - she apologises. – "My throat gets dry. I had to get up twice. I drink a little, and go back to bed. It was no use."

"Just water by itself? You should at least have put some valerian drops in it. Or corvalol."

"I was lying there and thinking... If my grandson, Aloyshenka, had lived... Sofia is of an age to be like a daughter to him."

"Oh," - Glikeria put more sugar lumps into the sugar bowl, - "so she's not talking yet. When she does she'll ask about her father."

Yevdokia pursed her lips:

"Let her ask her mother – what's a mother for?"

Ariadna looks around for the sugar tongs.

"It's been so many years... He hasn't turned up once. Obviously he's not a decent person."

"Maybe he's dead?..."

"Dead?! In your dreams," - Yevdokia dips her cracker in tea, - "Dogs like him have long lives."

"Oh, come on," - Glikeria comes to his defence. – 'What if he's looking down from heaven and is delighted to see his daughter growing up.'

"Delighted... I bet he is' - she purses her lips. – 'He should help the girl, instead of being delighted: he should persuade them… let her start talking.'

"What is this?" - Ariadna is upset. – "You don't know what you're talking about. That's just some wild gibberish."

"It's easy to turn wild here," - Yevdokia chews her lips. – "Lucky for us that you're so cultured... What would we do without your wit?"

"Antonina says he disappeared... Went and disappeared,' - Glikeria looks down into her cup. – "So I think... Why would he disappear like that? Something must have happened..."

"You're talking a lot of rubbish," - Yevdokia looked daggers at her. – "When was that now? Those were the years when they were letting them out. Those who survived, many of them came back. Not like..." - She was too angry to speak. She put her cracker aside.

What father? Who were they letting out? Came back to whom?

"Well," - Grandma Yevdokia turns to me, - "is your story finished? Get down from your chair then. Just look at you, a little pitcher with big ears! There's nothing for you to listen to. Go and stay in your room for a while."

I ran to my room.

It must be about that girl. The one who lives in the wardrobe.

You open the door, and she comes out; stands there and looks at you. And we have the same dresses – grandma Glikeria makes them. And the room is like ours: a table, a curtain, and yellow walls. But only one bed – there is no other. But then they have a door. And a small stairway. Her father comes home by those stairs and looks from behind the door. He looks at her lovingly and leaves again.

They have a small flat: why would they need a bigger one? - they have no grannies. The grannies live here with me. And her mama doesn't sleep and doesn't cook. She only combs her hair in front of the mirror. And leaves too when she's done with that...

"Well, what are you up to?" - Grandma Yevdokia looks in, - "twirling in front of the mirror again? Take care you don't grow up to be a hussy..."

She came up to me and closed the wardrobe door:

"Time to go for walk. Grandma Ariadna will take you."

We come up to the railing and there's a lock hanging there. And the slide is empty – no children around. And the people in the park look all the same. They walk around and scoop up the snow with their shovels.

"God Almighty!" - Grandma Ariadna peeps in. – "What an awful lot of soldiers… Let's go to the bridge, my little dove, and admire the lions. The lions are kind and gentle. They sit there and guard us. My grandson Alyoshenka liked them too. Nikolenka, the youngest, was too small to remember. But the elder should. We went there with him very often, as often as we do with you. He remembers everything about us. When you grow up, remember him. When I die, he won't have anybody: just you…"

We got back home. We ate and drank, and it was time to have a rest. Grandma Glikeria tucked in my blanket:

"Go to sleep, my little dove. It's holiday soon. We'd better check the Christmas decorations, what if they're broken. But if they are, that's not a big deal. We'll take some wool and knit baskets of different colours. Mama will bring a present, and we'll put candy in the baskets. What do we need those balls for, anyway?…"

It smells of potatoes. I can hear the frying pan sizzling in the kitchen.

"There are soldiers there. They're shovelling the snow away today," - Ariadna stirred something

47

in the frying pan and turned away from the stove. – "We had an artillery battery placed in our garden too. And I was happy to start with: I thought he would continue to serve next to the house. He'd drop by at first. He brought canned meat. They supplied them well at the start. But then in September, that was it. They transported the battery to the Gulf, to the forts. And he'd comfort me: 'That's all right, Mum... It's not far from Leningrad. They'll soon let me go on leave.' He wrote to me often. Then he stopped. The last one came in February: my younger son had already died. And the elder lived a bit longer after that – he and the daughter in law died the year after that...."

They nod and listen. She is telling the story for the thousandth time, but it's still new somehow.

"And if no one had died," - Yevdokia has finished cutting bread, - "what would they have eaten? It's been so many years since the war now and we still haven't got enough flour. See for yourself – there are four of us, so they'll give us eight kilos. And if you put all your family together and added mine – how much flour would we need? That means hunger again."

"Oh, don't even talk about it," - Glikeria took some bread. – "Last spring, remember, many people saw their flour go bad. It became infested with bugs. You walk down the street and see bags of flour lying around. The whole rubbish dump is covered with them. It's white as white can be... They don't know how to store it, evidently. They buy it and then they don't put nails into it. It would last as long as three years if they did."

"Before their revolution," - Yevdokia puckered

her lips, - "nobody would put nails into flour, would they. There was enough for everybody."

"Before the revolution," - Ariadna bent her head, - "common folk suffered too. Not like they do now, of course... In a different way. But lots of people did."

"Suffered. I'll say!" - Yevdokia shook her head. – "Suffered from idleness, that's what they suffered from. Those who worked didn't suffer."

"Enough," - Glikeria waved her hand in desperation, - "that life is gone. What does it matter now?..."

"Well, it's doesn't matter to me" – she quiets down, - "I won't need any flour in the other world. I'm just sorry for Sofia... She still has her life before her."

"And I sometimes lie there and think: what if they hadn't bombed out those warehouses, maybe we would have had enough flour to last until the end... They said on the radio that the store was enormous..."

Yevdokia collected the plates in silence.

I can hear the water running – that means they're doing the dishes. They'll go to the room now, to spool the yarn.

"Well, look here, first you do the bottom."

The fingers are nimble, and the crochet hook jumps up and down – how can you follow it?

49

"Now we lift the sides and knit them together in a circle."

There's a blue edge at the top, and a handle attached to it. They hang it on the Christmas tree by the handle.

"Remember," - grandma Glikeria asks, - "what decorations we have?"

Coloured balls, little fishes, all sorts of beasts made of cardboard. Also birds made of glass – doves. And instead of claws they have hooks. So they can cling to the Christmas tree. There are doves next to the church too: those are different though, lordly. They walk waddling sideways. People feed them grain, and throw them millet. They flock together and peck at it.

There by the church is a scary old man. He drives a sledge. The sledge is broken, and has no backboard. He's short, his legs are empty, and instead of hands he has iron hooks. He bent them himself out of wire – he rests them against the ground and pushes himself along. Grandma Glikeria got angry: "What are you staring at? Look away. It's an invalid. He came back from the war like that. There used to be a lot of them. Now he's the only one. They must have died, the others. They've suffered enough now, the doves. They're having their rest in the other world."

Oh... I see... They're only scary here, but up there they turn into doves. And they put up a Christmas tree for them in the other world. And the doves perch on it. They don't suffer any more, they hold on to the branches with their hooks. Doves don't need hands. They have beaks now and they peck at sweets from baskets.

Grandma fixed the thread, and stretched it between her fingers.

"Well," - she says, - "it's all ready now. We can starch them. And I'll sit down in the evening and knit another basket."

She put the basket aside, and took up her own work. If you look closely, you can only see little crosses of all colours.

"And you – step back a little," - she orders me, - "It's easier to see from a distance."

And so it is. I look and see a horse, and a rider carrying a spear on his back.

Grandma says:

"Here he is, Saint George, my father's patron saint. Sit here by my side, embroider your flower and I'll tell you about him."

"It all happened in Jerusalem, the sacred city. And around the sacred city there were three lawless kingdoms: the city of Sodom, the city of Gomorrah, and the third one was nameless. And so our Lord grew tired from looking at their wickedness and sent Sodom and Gomorrah into the ground. And to the third kingdom he sent a fierce dragon. The dragon would creep to the cathedral square and shriek in a terrifying voice: give me a man from each city! And so there were soon very few people left in that kingdom..."

She bit off the thread, and looked at her work.

"Here," - she promises, - "there will also be a dragon. I'll give it to you when I finish. And when I die, this memory of me will remain. You'll hang it up in your room."

Grandma Yevdokia listened to that and said:

"And I will leave you a tablecloth from the old days. The fabric is strong, it's damask, and there are roses along the hem. Guests will come to you, you'll set the table and they'll be surprised. And you'll say then that it's from your grandmother's dowry."

Grandma Ariadna heard that, and beckoned me to her room. I ran after her. And she says, looking at the door over her shoulder:

"I prepared a present for you too. Antique earrings, diamonds. It's a souvenir of my parents. We bartered everything in the war, and they are the only thing left. We'll put them in your ears. No one else will have earrings like that. When you're grown up, you'll look in the mirror and remember me."

When they die, they'll go to that other girl and live with her. The girl will meet them and be happy to see them. Although her room is very small, it has too little space to live in. Let their rooms die too, so that they can all be accommodated...

"Why are you sad?" - Grandma Ariadna says, - "It's too early to grieve yet. We'll keep on living yet as long as God lets us. And you, while you're young, live well, don't think of us. We'll think of you ourselves, and admire you. And you life will be a long one... Well, go on to the kitchen. It's time to drink some milk."

So I went into the kitchen and thought on the way: where will they have their meals in the other world? The kitchen should die too.

Grandma Ariadna has poured it through a little sieve: here, she says, drink it. And she gave me a piece of gingerbread. The glaze is dry, it crumbles into little stars, like snow.

Gingerbread is made out of flour. There's no flour in the other world – so there's no gingerbread... What do they eat there, I wonder? Probably soup...

The door bangs in the hall, and the lock scrapes. Grandma Glikeria peeps in:

"Run and meet your mother."

But Mama comes in herself. She sits down at the table looking sad:

"I'm exhausted... I've searched all the rubbish dumps: I only found two boards. I should have done it yesterday – today everybody snatched everything, and took it away... And the nails are crooked, rusty – I could barely pull them out. Just give me a minute," - she adjusted her hair, - "I'll get my breath back... And I was going to get kidneys. Make rassolnik. I got to the grocer's, but forgot that the pay check is due on Friday. I would have had enough, but I'd set six rubles aside in case they brought the children's suit. Zoya Ivanovna promised me... And also: next week it's going to be very busy at work, they've got to meet a deadline. I said to the foreman: if necessary, I'll work overtime. And they'll pay me for that by the 30th. So I'm thinking: it would be nice to have wine for the holiday. We'll get flour, I'll bake pies. Potato pies, or maybe cabbage pies. One of the girls at work said she'd get a cake at 'Sever'. And I thought: maybe we should too? But then I thought: no. We shouldn't indulge like that. It would be better to buy some sausages or cheese. It is a celebration after all. And I'll make vinaigrette too. And herring with onions. And we'll see it in properly, no worse than other people do."

Yevdokia says:

"You don't mean to leave the child without soup? At least make her a vegetable soup: chop up some potatoes and carrots. And we'll put some milk in it. It's a long time yet till Friday..."

"We'll get our retirement benefit on Thursday," - Ariadna apologises.

"Lord," - I even got upset, - "Is that what you think I'm talking about? It'll be about eighty rubles with the overtime. We'll manage. Ok," - I said, - "I'll go lie down for an hour. You have dinner by yourselves. I'm tired..."

"Herring would be good..." - Glikeria peeps into an empty pan. - "Gets some salt into you."

"You're a famous spendthrift among us," - Yevdokia is angry. "All you want to do is squander money."

My head is not right, it feels heavy. Have I caught a chill from a draft?

I lay down. It's bad, I think. I've been feeling like I'm dead or something lately. I walk around, and do things, but it's all empty inside me... The winter has dragged on for too long. I feel almost like I won't make it till summer...

I found Zoya Ivanovna during the break, and asked her about the suit. And she says: "I've got something to talk to you about. Drop into my office after the shift".

On my way back, I see Sytin's wife.

"Well, how are you doing? Have they kicked the bucket yet, the old witches? How are they getting on with your mother?"

"It's fine," - I say, - "we get on."

"Mind you don't cut them any slack. When I lived there, I didn't. And don't you mind that they're old – they'll outlive us alright. They sucked enough of my blood, I'll say. Volodka was a little boy then. Any little thing, they appear. 'Tell your boy not to shout so much in the hall way.' – 'Well,' - I say, - 'maybe I should seal his mouth then?' And that nasty Yevdokia hisses: 'That's right, maybe you should.' – 'Maybe,' - I say then, - 'we should all seal our mouths? And talk with our hands like mutes do? You should have looked after your own children and left everybody else's alone.' I see she's not saying anything. And what can she say? Not much. I know all about her, the neighbour from downstairs told me: they shot her elder son even before the war, and it was even worse with the younger - he served as a prison guard. Oh, it'd be great if you got married,

Antonina... You have a second kid, the factory will give you an apartment. Otherwise you'll never get out of their swamp. Damn those old regime bitches!... It's been a long time now since we moved out... So many years have passed and believe it or not, but I still dream about them. And I wake up in a cold sweat. Then I lie there and think it's silly, they aren't there anymore. We live alone now. And something's constricting inside me: God, I think, this is paradise..."

She's a bitch, this Sytina woman. She lives in clover, and still bitches... Prison guard... Just to slander somebody else's son. And she's not afraid. She has her own sons growing up. What if somebody slanders them?

The shift was over and I went up to the Union committee room.

Zoya Ivanovna asks me in:

"Sit down, Antonina. So what do you think you're doing to your kid? The little wench is six soon, she'll go to school in a couple of years. I understand she'd get sick all the time when she was little. But now she's all right, it seems, and she's still with her granny. All the normal kids go to the kindergarten. Take my grandchildren: they draw, they sing and recite poems. And your mother is illiterate - how can she prepare her for school?"

"No, no," - I make excuses, - "it's all right: Suzannochka knows all the letters of the alphabet. And she reads a bit."

"Exactly," - she says, - "a bit. And at the kindergarten they have special teachers, they stage plays. Once a week they have a music lesson. No way can you compare that to sitting at home. And they took them to the Puppet Theatre recently, on the Seventh of November holiday. And you should have seen how they prepared for the celebration! They learnt songs and chants off by heart. And the food there is healthy and varied. You must understand: your child is not a country girl. She'll have to live in the city."

"Thank you," - I say, - "I'll think about it."

"Don't think for too long," - she hurries me, - "time will pass, and you'll miss the chance."

"So," - I still ventured to ask, - "what about the suit?..."

"Well, Antonina," - she frowns, - "you're more like a stepmother than a mother, that's what you are. I'm talking serious matters with you here, and you're thinking about trifles. You'll kick yourself when she grows up to be an old regime girl, but it'll be too late then. Well, never mind, off you go now... And as for the suit, they promised. They say they'll see if they can have it by the day after tomorrow. There may still be some at the warehouse. We ordered them for the November holidays – I got them for my grandchildren too..."

I walk home and think: I didn't tell them she's mute. What if they find out? There was this girl in our shop. She worked with acids until the very end, and wrapped up her stomach so that no one noticed. And when the boy was born he seemed to be all right at first. And then they saw he couldn't walk properly, and his head was kind of too big. They comforted her first and said he'd grow out of it. And then it got worse... They diagnosed him with water on the brain, and he's been practically living in hospitals ever since... Once you let them get hold of you they never let you go. They'd do her to death, dragging her around from one doctor to another. That'll be the end of my girl. No, no way, I decide. I'm not giving her up to them. We live well. No worse than other folks do. They have theatres? Our girl will go to the theatre too, to the Mariinsky. They've promised, haven't they? She'll go to a ballet. As to festivals... Well, we'll have a nice one too, we'll decorate a Christmas tree, we'll see whose is better yet... Lord, I think, I'm still scared. What if they take her away from me?

I crossed the road, and my heart was pounding.

The grannies are smart of course... But then Zoya is smart too: she's right in what she says. They've lived their lives. And life now is different – what do they know about it?...

I came home and started on the subject:

"At the shop some people are lining up to buy a TV. It costs three hundred forty eight rubles."

"In old money?" - Ariadna inquires.

"Of course not," - I said, - "In new money."

"Good gracious!" - Glikeria flung up her hands. – "That's three and a half thousand in old money."

"The TV is new too," - I say, - "without a lens, - the image is like in the cinema. Maybe we should buy one too? Why not? They have good programmes: both for grown ups and children. We'll save up for it while we wait our turn: if we just put aside money every month, even thirty rubles. We'll put it in Yevdokia Timofeevna's room: it'll be like our own propaganda room then. You'd sit there in the evening and watch the news: where and what's happening in the world. Say, in America, or... in Hungary... And Suzannochka will watch it too – she's got to go to school soon..."

They're silent.

"Well," - I say, - "think about it in the meantime. Suzannochka likes the radio, and a TV is even better."

Yevdokia grumbles:

"Newspapers, radio – it's never enough for them. Now they've invented the TV. They'll soon get inside a chicken egg."

"Why talk like that?" Ariadna reproaches her. – "What's so bad about watching a good programme?"

"I see you haven't seen enough in your time... Well, I have. My son was like you. He liked to read newspapers: 'We must always keep track of things, mother,' - he said. Well, I thought... I know what track they follow: they'll get you whether you read or not."

"If people listened to you they'd still live in the Stone Age. They'd still be lighting sticks."

"Well, what's wrong with that?" - Yevdokia shrugged her shoulders. – "Were the sticks bothering anyone?"

Mama peeps into the room:

"Come, I've kindled the stove. Have a look at the flame."

I ran after her, and set my little chair opposite the stove door.

Mama says:

"Watch out. Don't move too close. You'll look as long as you like when we have a TV. A TV also has something like a small door, but it's different, made of glass. It's called a screen. They plug it in, and in a moment you see a small flame like a little star, and then it flares up and all kinds of different pictures flash past: it's amazing... They show and tell you: where and what, and how people live. Other people watch it and become wise. And so you will watch, and then you'll go to school. The teacher will say to you: 'Stand up, Suzanna Bespalova, tell me: do you know what a puppet theatre is?' And you'll reply: 'Of course, I do. I saw it on TV. They have such nice dolls there. Some are made of wood, some of rags. People put their fingers inside them and so they start acting: they cry and they laugh. Like they're alive.' Now she'll be very happy with you: 'Sit down,' - she'll say, - 'Suzanna Bespalova. I'll give you an A.' And the children will be surprised too: 'Would you believe it? She never went to kindergarten, but she knows everything'..."

Mama opened the stove door and stirred with the poker inside it. And the heat from the stove is so hot that it hits you in the eyes. She closed the door and wiped her eyes with her hand.

"It's all right," - she says crying, - "don't you fear. We'll be all right. Go to the grannies now..."

"Well," - Grandma Yevdokia undoes the little buttons, - "and where did you stop with Grandma

Glikeria? Oh," - she sighs, - "my head is like a sieve, it doesn't remember anything. Ah..." - she says, - "Now it's all coming back to me. The step-mother turned the step-daughter out of doors. 'Let her die in the woods,' she said."

She put the dress on the back of the chair and sat down on the edge.

"So she lived in the woods, and the step-mother had a mirror and it wasn't like any other mirror, it was a magic one. You could look into it and see what was happening in other places, and what other people were doing. So the step-mother asked the mirror: 'How's my step-daughter? Is she really doing well without me?' And the mirror flared up: 'She's living well,' - it answered, - 'She's living happily. And she's getting more beautiful every day'. Here the step-mother turned nasty, and called for the cook. 'Go,' - she told her, - 'dress up like a pilgrim, and I'll give you a pretty dress, soaked with poison – and you give it to my step-daughter.' The old cook put a head scarf on and pretended she was a kind hearted woman, and went to the forest.

"So the hunters come back home, and there's something wrong there. They come into the house and see their sister lying on the ground lifeless. They looked and looked, but never guessed about the dress, never thought to take it off. They grieved over her, but there was nothing they could do, so they made a glass coffin on iron chains. The maiden lay there as if she were alive. But the step-mother just wouldn't let up, and she looked over her country again – and asked the mirror; 'How's my step-daughter? Has she died forever?'...

"Are you asleep? That's all right, you sleep now..."

"Well," - Yevdokia begins, - "make up your minds about that TV."

It's an early, grey morning. "Now Maria Grigorievna Petrova is on the air". They honor her with her patronymic, but her voice is weak, like a child's, as if she hasn't lived yet. Just the right voice to tell stories.

Sofia is frozen in her chair - she's listening.

"Well, it's a bit expensive," - Glikeria has her doubts, - "I hardly know..."

"Other people manage to buy them, though. Antonina says you have to wait for your turn to get one."

"Well, maybe they've got money to spare. Not that many mouths to feed."

"Where from? ..." - Glikeria waves her hand. – "There aren't any masters any more: everybody lives on their salaries or retirement benefits."

"You don't say," - Yevdokia took the bottle and splashed some milk into her tea. – "Remember, in '44? They'd just lifted the blockade – they brought that woman here. She was fat, quite well-fed indeed..." - She took a sip of tea and her face screwed up as if she'd eaten something very sour.

"Has it gone off?" - Glikeria was frightened.

She doesn't say anything. She keeps her face in the cup.

"And the boy she had, he was barely alive when she gave birth. The doctor said she'd smothered him with her fat. The husband visited her, you could tell he was important. He'd bring expensive parcels. She'd hide under the blanket and gobble it all up."

"I remember," - Glikeria sighs, - "how can you forget: it smelled so strongly of sausage... I was carrying the parcel and my head went dizzy – so I felt like I was about to faint. When they discharged her from hospital and I brought her her clothes, she slipped me a slice of that sausage as if in gratitude. I went out, locked myself up in the bathroom and swallowed it. It was a little slice. But I threw it up in less than an hour. The slice came out whole. What is it with me, I thought? Can't I eat people's food any more? I had got too used to mill cake..."

"People's..." - Yevdokia screwed up her face again. – "Since when is it for people? People ate bread... Or margarine sometimes. And even wallpaper glue. And they were lucky to get glue. It all ran out in the first winter. My neighbour, a little boy, used to nibble coal for that matter. He'd get it out of the stove and nibble. He died with a piece of charred wood in his hand. His hand was stiff and he was still clutching it... They barely managed to unclench it. And the mouth was all smeared black... The sausage must have gone off, I think, so she gave the rotten stuff away."

Elena Chizhova

"Oh, it smelled good!" - Glikeria says as if hadn't heard anything. – "And after the war when it was in the shops again I couldn't eat it for a long time. I'd get queasy at the very smell of it... Oh, I'm sorry," - she collected herself, - "it's hardly table talk..."

Ariadna is cunning, and starts on another topic:

"Remember Solomon Zakharovich?"

"Of course!" - and she giggles and even blushes.

"I'll say she remembers!" - Yevdokia snorted, - "There was something going on between them in the war..."

"Oh, it was nothing!" - she waves her hand. – "We were both living corpses back then. All we could do was talk..."

"And after the war?" - Ariadna stirs the tea in the cup and pretends to look away.

"We saw each other," - she nodded. – "He proposed to me. His wife had perished – she went to visit her mother right before the war. In Byelorussia, I think... And then she couldn't get out and stayed there under the Germans."

"Well, what did you say to that?" - Yevdokia stopped chewing and listened.

"He had kids. Two of them. I thought about it for a while, but didn't have the heart to marry a man with kids. He was a good man, though, and an excellent doctor. But I still couldn't bring myself to do it. I pitied him, of course. He said at the very beginning that if the Germans entered Leningrad, he and the girls would be among the first to be shot. And I was stupid enough not to believe him: I thought that under the Germans everybody was the same."

"Their nation," - Yevdokia gets angry, - "was at least killed by Germans... But ours was mostly killed by our own people. Truly, we are our own worst enemies. Foreigners may only think of something, and we've already done it. We acted like heroes against the Germans. I wish we'd done the same against ourselves..."

"Oh come on, how can you?!" - Ariadna got really upset. – "You don't even know what you're saying. It's a sin to compare us with Germans!..."

"And you'd better listen to other people," she grumbled, - "if you have no sense of your own... Well... Enough of this tea drinking... It's time for the child to take a walk."

The weather outside had cleared up.

"Well," - Grandma Yevdokia asks, - "shall we walk as far as the bridge? We'll see if they've brought Christmas trees yet?"

We get there and see a fence on the other side. Behind it are fir trees with bristling boughs. And some strange man is guarding them.

The fir trees are thin, and lank. The ground is strewn with needles. In the forest they're not like that, they're fluffy like in pictures.

Grandma says:

"Just look at these fir trees! Where do they get them from, I wonder – bare sticks... Now, I don't know what to do," - she says. – "Maybe, we should get one while there's no one around. People will snap them all up after work."

The man opened the gate: "Take your pick".

We walk among the fir trees trying to pick one. Grandma Yevdokia gets angry:

"They're all dead... Did they cut them down last year or something?... - All right, I've chosen one, I think. - Give me this one," - she orders.

The man was nimble: he cast a loop over the tree and wrapped it up. Then he threw it on the sled as if to say "you can take it away now".

"Well," - Grandma says, - "we'll drag it home and hide under the stairs: I can't take it upstairs. Let your mother haul it up when she gets home from work..."

"Well," - Grandma Glikeria says to us at the door, - "where have you been, what have you seen?"

"Say, we got a fir tree, and hid it under the stairs. We barely picked one out. It's shedding needles as if it's been lying there for a year.

I go to my room, and get my coloured pencils out. Grandma Ariadna nods to me in approval:

"That's a good girl. Draw us a nice Christmas tree."

It's a pretty fir tree, fluffy. There are large balls and little candy baskets on the boughs. And between them invalids without legs – on hooks. They don't feel pain in the other world. They just hang there, they don't suffer, they're resting...

There's room left at the bottom. I drew the canal there. The railing is black, and Grandma and I are walking past it. And in the sleigh there's our fir tree, dead and wrapped up: it had lain there for a year. People from the other world gave it to us: they celebrate and then give

them away to us. I closed my eyes tight – I see big letters.
No. I shouldn't write. They'll get angry again.

I ran to the kitchen. Grandma Ariadna says:

"What a beautiful picture! Everything's as it should be: we have the fir tree, and now we'll decorate it."

"Good lord," - Grandma Yevdokia peeps in, - "what is it you have there on the sleigh? It looks like a corpse. What are you smiling at? - she says, - That's how they used to carry them in the blockade. They'd wrap them up in a piece of canvas, put them on the sleigh and take them. You'd go past them and look: if it was small, then it was a child. They carried such an awful lot of them in the first winter..."

"In the second winter, there were just as many" - Ariadna sighs.

"More"- she grumbles – "or less…Who counted them back then…"

"Yes-s" - Yevdokia shakes her head, - "lovely…"

There was another one that was red, but I chose this one. - Mum spreads it on the sofa and admires it.

The Grannies stand around nodding:

"Of course! Red just doesn't compare."

"The wool is soft," - Mum strokes it with her hand, - "just like a calf. We used to keep a cow before the war. Then we had to slaughter it."

"That's the Chinese for you..." - Grandma Yevdokia sighs. – "We never even heard about them before: it was all Japanese and Japanese. And now look how much they've learnt."

"What do mean 'we never heard of them'?!" - Grandma Ariadna stands up for the Chinese. – "The Chinese are an ancient people. They've been around for almost fifty centuries."

"That's right... Give us another fifty centuries and we might learn something too."

"But didn't we use to know!" - Grandma Glikeria throws her hands up. – "We could do everything! We used to make such beautiful things: gold embroidery, and lace... ruffed blouses, ladies' hats, silk shirts, underlays – my late countess preferred Russian work..."

"Oh," - she remembered, - "ribbons! I bought ribbons too."

"I don't even know what to say," - Grandma Glikeria smoothes the ribbons out, - "a proper princess... Well, how do you like it?"

"All right then," – Mama says, - "you try it on and I'll go and peel the potatoes."

"Well, take your dress off" - Grandma Yevdokia orders.

"Here," - Glikeria takes me to the kitchen, - "let your mother admire you."

"Good gracious!" - I cry out in amazement. – "Whose girl is that in the costume?! I wouldn't even recognise you! Is it my own dear little daughter?"

"It's her," - Glikeria says happily. "We'll plait the ribbons in her hair, and then we'll be ready for the theatre."

I drained the potatoes, and we sat down to dinner.

"So," - I ask, -" have you decided about the TV?"

"We have," - Yevdokia says on everybody's behalf, - "we want it."

I opened one of the window frames: it's cold between them, and a good place for keeping butter. – "I was walking through Gostiny," I said. - "They have this drapery there. So many fabrics! Wool and calico and rayon... I wonder if I should make a dress for myself, a flannel one. Mine is very old – the elbows are worn-out."

"Well," - Yevdokia says, - "it's up to you I see you've got rich."

"No," - I collect myself, - "I mean I'll do it sometime in the future."

"Oh, what's wrong with me!" - Yevdokia suddenly recollects. – "It slipped my mind completely. We bought a Christmas tree today. It's under the stairs tied to the sled. You can go down and fetch it."

I washed up, and listened: sounds as if they've gone to sleep... All right, I'll lie down for a little while and then fetch it. I closed my eyes: I see fabrics hanging everywhere. And women walk around and feel them. They aren't particularly young, but they're dressed well. Their husbands must earn a lot of money. One of them was especially rich. She was choosing fabric for a coat. She was wearing a fur coat, and she also needed fabric for a cloth coat. She was there with a relative. The relative was rich too. They were having a discussion. I went up to look at the fabric: good gracious, eighteen rubles per meter. What kind of salaries must they have to buy at prices like that?...

I went downstairs – it was pitch black there. "What bastards!" - I think to myself. They've smashed the bulb again. The boys from the street are always vandalizing things... I went under the stairs, felt for the tree and found it. I pricked my hands on it badly.

Glikeria walks into the room. She just stands there, hesitating.

"I just wanted to ask something... This flannel you wanted – how much is it per meter?"

"Well, it's all different," - I reply. – "if it has flowers on it and it's a bit thicker – it's more expensive. Two forty-five."

"In new money?"

"Of course," - I say. – "It's all in new money now."

She's still there moving her lips:

"Three meters – seven rubles that is... And the thinner kind?"

"The thinner kind is flannelette, at one ruble forty," - I reply. - "It's too thin and soils easily."

"You know what," - she fumbled in her skirt and took out her purse. – "I've only got one ruble eighty now. I'll get the retirement benefit in the next few days. Go and buy two pieces, pick them yourself, whichever is better. I'll make dresses for you and me. Make sure they're the same though: there'll be scraps, I'll also make an apron."

"For Suzannochka?" - I say, - "what would she need it for? Is she going to use a broom from such an early age?"

"What's wrong with that? It'll be too late when she's grown. I was trained as a seamstress almost from the cradle..."

I didn't say anything to that, and thought to myself: those women, nobody trained them, I'm sure. So they grew up to be ladies. Life is keen-sighted – it notices what people are from their very childhood...

I prepared to go to bed, and kept counting the money in my head: that suit cost me a lot. I thought I'd spend about six rubles, but it was nine eighty. So you can call it ten. I'll have to do some overtime again... The foreman laughs at me now: "Aren't you greedy, Bespalova! You get your salary, get your bonuses, and your mother has a retirement benefit – isn't that enough? Are you feeding your girl on gold?" - "That's right," - I say, - "Ignaty Mikhailych, on gold and silver". How can I explain it to him that I have four mouths to feed? "Are you bringing up a princess?" - he says, - "You'll forgive me if I don't choose my words right. You're a young woman. You might get married yet. Something might turn up. And everybody needs a family". - "Who needs someone like me?" - I laugh in reply, - "Not so young, and with baggage like that?" - "Don't you say that," - he frowns. – "Take Nikolai from the

71

galvanizing section. I noticed it a while ago how he looks at you. Why not him? He's a good man, modest: doesn't smoke, doesn't drink much. So I say you should get your hair done, and dress up a bit. Because you go around looking like death warmed over. You two might get something going..."

Exactly, I think to myself: we might.....

I opened the wardrobe door, and the mirror is bad and murky, you can hardly see anything properly. And my face is grey, with blue circles under my eyes. "Which Nikolai could it be?" – I wonder. In my mind, I searched through all of the guys from the galvanizing section. But no, I can't remember...

I opened my eyes – Mama is standing in front of the mirror, doing her hair. She's getting ready to go the other world again. It's nice and pretty there...

She puts the comb down. She wipes away her tears...

"Wouldn't it be better to put it in the ground?" – Grandma Ariadna grunts. "Put on a cross-piece, and then stick it in the sand."

"It wouldn't fit in the bucket with the cross-piece, would it? The bucket is too small," - grandma Yevdokia is holding the tree and figuring out how to position it. – "We'll put some sand on the bottom – that'll be enough. Like we did the year before last."

"Can't you at least stop meddling here," - Grandma Glikeria sends me away. "Off you go now, you'll prick your little hands on the needles."

The tree's shedding needles all the time. I bent down and picked one off the floor. The needle's red, rusty. As if it were a small nail...

"Good gracious!" - Glikeria cried out. – "Look, she pricked her finger!"

"Iodine, it needs iodine!" - Yevdokia darted to the cupboard. – "The tree is dirty, God know where it's been lying..."

They put iodine on it, and wrapped a bandage around it. Grandma Ariadna led me to the sofa:

"Sit still."

I'm sitting on the sofa with my eyes closed. And my pricked finger hurts.

What if go to sleep, I'm thinking to myself. And this needle turns out to be poisonous. I'll wake up in a hundred years...

Isn't that what Grandma said? It'll be over in twenty years. I'll wake up, and there won't be anything around. Only they'll be lying there, enormous, made of stone. They've fallen to pieces, and are moving their empty legs. And the evil witch is driving past in her coach. Still she can't drive around the scattered pieces... She takes up her club and starts flogging the Raven. And he'd be only too happy to go on but the iron wires won't let him.

He's dragging the coach on but the wires cling to his legs... And the witch shouts: "Fly away!" So he spread his wings. And as he was flying he looked down: the girl with the pricked finger was sleeping. And there's nobody near her: everybody has left for the next world, both the grannies and Mama... She'll wake up, and look around: she's all alone now. And she hasn't got a single person in the world...

"Good gracious," - Grandma Yevdokia drops the tree and comes to me. – "Why are you crying like that? Who upset you so? There, there little dove, don't cry. Does your finger hurt?" - She sits down next to me and hugs me.

"She thinks we punished her."

"Why, who will punish you? We just told you to sit still for a little while. When your finger's all right, we'll start decorating the Christmas tree."

Grandma Yevdokia smells dry and sweet. You nestle your face against her, and you're not scared any more. It's all right that I'm alone. I'll join them in the other world. I'll live for a bit longer and join them...

"Well, here you are", - Grandma Yevdokia says, - "your tears have dried now. Get down from the sofa, put on your slippers..."

"Ah," - Glikeria looks around. – "What's she going to wear on her feet? She's got slippers, and felt boots, and old boots – for autumn. But she needs proper shoes for the theatre - they won't let her in with felt boots. You should have seen the shoes my lady had! Embroidered... I was the one who embroidered them."

"Really," - Yevdokia grew thoughtful. – "My daughter-in-law used to wear shoes. She was a lady too... She'd never put on felt boots. They'd get shoes at their special shop for party members. I'd say to her: 'You live well. Like you're special. As if you'd come from a different place.' And she says to me: 'It's for services to the party.' And I say: 'Well, have fun while you can. You're special in everything. Except death.' And she laughs: 'It's not the time now for us to die... To God with it, this death of yours'..."

"If I had an inlay block I'd make them in no time," - Glikeria considers. – "All we need is some leather for the soles. Even a small piece would do."

"Exactly," - Yevdokia is angry again, - "if you had your way, you'd drag a loom here... We should tell the mother. Let her have a look in the shops. Who knows, they might be selling them to everybody now..."

"Gostiny is big" – Ariadna puts in. "My father had a shop there. When a client was interested in something and they didn't have it at the shop, they'd go to the warehouse and have a look. The warehouse was close too – right behind the Duma..."

"It's spoiling the kid, that's what it is," – Yevdokia cut her off. – "She can wear felt boots to your theatre... That's not what's bothering me: Antonina didn't start on all this for nothing! About that dress.What if she gets together with somebody... And then what?...

"What's wrong with that?" - Glikeria sticks up for her. – "The business of the young – you can't sew it up with a thread."

"Well, she can move in with her husband in that case, all that matters is that Sofia stays with us," - Ariadna picked up a silver ball in her hands.

"With her husband!" - Yevdokia shakes her head. - That's only half the problem... What if she brings us another baby?"

"Well, we have to explain things to her. If she does it the smart way, there won't be anything," - Glikeria puts the little basket aside, and starts on the bird.

"How do you know?"

"How? It's easy. Solomon Zakharych explained it all to me."

"Did he really?!" - Yevdokia throws up her hands. - Come on, explain it to us then."

They whispe rand whisper. I can't make out what they're whispering.

"Yes, well... You're a slut, Glikeria, you know that..."

"And you," - Grandma Glikeria blushes, - "have lived your entire life, but for all that I see you're still a virgin."

"Virgin or no virgin, I guarded myself. I had as many kids as the Lord sent me."

"And maybe I'm happy I don't have any kids. Why give birth if they're certain to die?"

"You stupid woman!" - Yevdokia even stamped her foot. – "A childless woman is a sterile flower.

" Never mind now," - she took the shawl off her head, and smoothed her hair. – "The Lord sees everything: he sent me a granddaughter in my old age. Isn't that right," - she turns to me, - "Sofyushka?"

That's right. Like in the story of the Snow maiden... She flew up into the sky when she was playing with somebody else's children. They gather in the forest, and sing their songs. About the little boat and the blue nights. They're always on the radio. And the fire's burning in the pit, the heat is rising. The Snow maiden was also afraid at first: I won't jump, she thought. But the young pioneers shouted: jump, jump! So she did...

Yevdokia dusted the chair with the hem of her dress.

"You may have a point there" – she says, - "We give birth and don't know what death is in store for them..."

She sat at the table and spread out paper notes. And a whole heap of coins. The smaller ones are silver, and the other, bigger ones are red. It's called the retirement benefit. The postal delivery woman brings it. She's large, she has fat legs and a bag across her shoulder. When she comes, she walks straight into the room. She leaves dirty marks everywhere, but the grannies don't scold her.

Yevdokia sits and calculates:

"I can't get used to the new money. They promised us we wouldn't lose anything. And now I look: we used to pay fifteen rubles for a Christmas tree, and this year it's two. We're paying five rubles extra in old money. So I'm thinking: either I'm a silly goose, or they're mighty clever, and know what side their bread is buttered on..."

"Bread is still OK though," - Glikeria says in a conciliatory tone, - "Thank God, it hasn't gone up. It was one ruble forty and it stayed the same. Fourteen kopecks in new money."

"Well, we'll see how it goes," - she says, closing her purse.

They served out milk in the break. I took the bottle and went to the locker room. You go right past the galvanizing section to get there. I peeped in, as if by accident. I remembered him: a plain guy. He saw me too. "Never mind," - I thought, - "What do I care? So I looked in: it's free to look"...

I hid the milk in my bag. Today it's all right, Fedosievna is at the guard house. She's a good woman: she never looks into our bags. Others virtually search them. We're not allowed to carry anything out. They tell us to drink it all ourselves. Those who are without children or the married ones do so. I used to drink it too, but it's been turning my stomach lately. This milk makes me sick..

I came out of the guard house and saw him running after me. "How are things?" - he asks. - "The things," I said. " all depend on me. They won't take care of themselves." - "Why are you so unfriendly?" - "I'm kind of tired," - I say. – "I feel quite exhausted after the shift." - "Well, you've got to get some rest, then." - he laughs, - "Do you like going to the cinema?" - "I've gone to the cinema enough." And I think to myself: to last me to the end of my life.

"You shouldn't be like that with me, Antonina," - he says reproachfully, - "I mean well." - "Well," - I say, - "See you. I'm going to Gostiny".

I got on a trolleybus, and looked out the window: there he is, waving to me. He's not that plain after all I, I think: he's kind of all right when he smiles.

The trolleybus is driving down Nevsky, and I think: if I buy something, it should be bright then. Or maybe with a flower pattern... Like the thing that Nadka Kazankina wore in summer – with big orange flowers. And if you stroke it with your hand, it's pure silk. She bragged that it was rayon. And it had a border along the hem. Good Lord, I remembered, they told me to get the same kind. Glikeria won't wear flowers.

Rayon is more expensive, of course. I saw Nadka today but couldn't bring myself to ask her. She'll make a laughing-stock of me: nearly thirty and still thinking of wearing rayon. Later, I'll talk my way out of it. My mother gave it to me, I'll lie. You can't reject a gift from your mother.

There it is! I'd better go and have a look at the price.

I see a woman in a fancy dress talking to the shop assistant:

"If it's for a dress, then you should definitely take 'Aurora.' There's nothing better than that – it's

79

pure wool. It's expensive, but it'll last well. You'll wear it for a hundred years, and it'll look like you've just bought it. They buy it for dresses, for skirts, for men's suits."

I walked past them, glanced at the price and things went dark before my eyes: twenty-six rubles. It can't be in new money, can it?

And the fancy woman nods:

"I think I'll take the dark green. Two and a half meters."

The shop assistant smiles as if she'd chosen it for her own dress. She brought it over and spread it out on the counter. The material glows as if on fire. Never mind, I think to myself... I'll get rayon.

" Everything's on display," - she turned to me, and shrugged her shoulder: - "Take your pick. Would you like it for fancy or everyday?"

Fancy, I think, fancy.

"No," - I reply, - "everyday."

I come closer and see that the rayon costs three twenty. "All right then," - I hesitate - I won't tell Glikeria, and I'll make up the difference myself. I'm standing there – the choice is making me dizzy: they're all fancy.

"That one," - I point, - "cut it for two dresses, please. With those flowers on it."

I return home.

"Well," - Glikeria hurries me, - "unroll it."

I roll it open, and spread it out on the bed: the flowers are small, poppies on a blue background. Glikeria clutches her heart the minute she sees it.

"Ooh," - she sighs, - "it's too beautiful – it's too die for. I'll start on it tomorrow," - she promises, - "Only I've got to measure first. And you, you know what..."

"What?" - I say surprised, - "Shall I buy some buttons?"

"No," - she shakes her head, - "I've got buttons. I'll get a sewing machine tomorrow, it'll be ready in no time."

"Maybe," - I doubt, - "it's not a good idea to make them the same... It'd be like in an orphanage."

"Good gracious," - she waves her hand at me. – "Did you think I was going to wear it? You wear it."

"Why make it then, if you won't wear it?"

"I can't go before Him in old rags, can I?" - she says, - "No, I'll make it and put it away in the cupboard. Let it lie there for the time being. I have everything ready: a small cushion and an underlay."

"Good Lord," - I think, - "how will I wear this dress?" I wish she'd held her tongue... It's as if mine is for the coffin too. I'd have bought different kinds if I'd known. Oh, - I remembered. – She was going to make an apron for Suzannochka out of the scraps. That won't do! I'll be all right, but she won't do that to the kid. I'll throw it away if she makes it, or better still I'll burn it. As if it had never been there. She mustn't wear coffin clothes.

"There's something I wanted to say..." – she stands there hesitating. – "Life is such that aything is possible while you're young. Who knows, maybe, you'll like somebody, or he'll like you. Anything can happen in life, but don't lose your head over it. We'll bring up one child, God willing, but we can't do more. So listen carefully: if it comes to that, have vinegar or aspirin ready. Dissolve it in water. Take a clump of cotton, wrap a thread around it and dip it in that water. Stick the cotton inside beforehand, but make thread long enough so that the end hangs out. When it's finished between you, remember to leave it there for a couple of minutes and then pull it out. Do you understand?" - she asks me.

I look down and nod: "Yes."

I stand there and think: "Good Lord, how shameful... Who thinks of all these things? Do others use it as well? No," - I think, - "it can't be..."

I go out into the kitchen and still can't raise my eyes.

"Shouldn't you pour the milk out of the bottles?" - I say.

Suzannochka is at the table opening the cake of cottage cheese. She likes them a lot, that kind.

Yevdokia turns around:

"So much hassle with these bottles. And you get so scared while you take it past the guard house. Why don't you, say, take a hot water bottle. Screw a cork in, stick it under the dress – and you go freely. In the blockade, they say, one woman worked at the bread factory and she'd plaster dough on under her breasts. The guards would slap her sides to search her, but they never thought of feeling under her breasts. She saved both her children."

"But," - I say doubting, - "it'll stink of rubber and then you won't drink it, will you?"

"We'll be all right," - she waves her hand at me, - "we're not gentle folk. We'll boil it and it'll air out. It'll do for kasha, and for the little one you can buy some at the shop."

The bathhouse is a long way away in Fonarny Lane. In winter it's all icy and there are horrible snowdrifts - the old women can't make it there... It's all right at home: there's a sink and a stove. We heat the room with gas and put the buckets to boil on the stove. Below there's a pail with cold water. I pour the dirty water out in the sink, that's convenient too. And in the bathhouse I get too tired. After I've washed everybody I feel like I'm dead. No, it's much better at home...

I put the buckets on to heat them up.

"Get ready," - I say, - "And I'll change the linen."

We change it once every fortnight – I can't wash it more often.

Glikeria went and had a look:

"The duvet cover's still clean, I think. Just change me the pillow case and the bed sheet."

I started to make the bed and felt as if something had stung me. She started that talk, didn't she... How can it be that they know? Nothing's going on...

Grandma Yevdokia calls me:

"Come on, little dove, I'll comb your hair, it'll get all tangled if you let it dry after the bath. We're going to the theatre on Sunday – you remember, don't you?"

Grandma Ariadna answers:

"Of course she remembers. About the princess Aurora. Remember the little apprentice cook! How he fell asleep next to the stove..."

Mama brings clean linen:

"The princess... And I didn't get it at first: they're selling wool at Gostiny – it's also called 'Aurora.' They say it never wears out. It lasts a hundred years, they promise..."

She gathered up the dirty linen and left.

Grandma Yevdokia puts the comb down and parts the locks by hand.

"Just you listen to them," - she grumbles, - "a hundred years, they say... They're counting on a whole century now. Well, we'll see... What will they do when they've used up all they've plundered from the Tsar?... What are you fidgeting for? Stand still, don't fidget!"

It's hot in the kitchen – white steam is rising up from the buckets. The burners are on. The lamp under the ceiling is yellow – you can hardly see it. It's swinging on a cord. The shadows on the ceiling are like wings. The windows are dark, fogged up, and little snakes trickle down the windowpanes.

"Well, come on," - Mum takes a ladle and stirs the water in the bucket with it. She splashes some on the stove – the stove hisses like a snake... – "Bend your head forward over the pail. Ooh," - she complains, - "you've got such thick hair – it won't get clean with just one rinse. When you grow up, see that you keep it – it only takes a moment to snip it off. The girls at our shop have cut it all off, had those fashionable waves done: permanents. You do it once or twice and your hair starts falling out in tufts. And short hair holds nothing – neither memory nor power. That's what they used to say, didn't they: short hair, short memory. And why do you need a short memory? You'll have a long one..."

She pours water over me, puts me in the pail and starts to rub me with a soapy sponge.

Grandma Yevdokia peeps in:

"Ooh, you've made it hot in here! Will you two be finished soon? I've prepared all her clothes already."

"We're finishing up... We'll just rinse once again - and that'll be enough. Like water off a duck's back, Suzannochka is so thin!" - she picked me up and put me on the stool. She dries me with the towel, breathing heavily. – "Here's our clean girl – all yours now."

She scooped water out the pail with the ladle and rinsed it.

"Well, make up your minds who's first."

Yevdokia says:

"I'll dress her, and put her to bed – I'll wash later. Let Glikeria go first."

She came in and undressed. She's thin, and all her ribs stick out. When she bends over the pail, her tits hang down like rags. It's scary to look at her, she looks like death itself. I've been washing her for so many years now, but still I can't get used to it. My late mother was sinewy. And these city women all look like they've been wasted by illness.

She raised her head.

"What are you looking at?" - she asks, - "You'll be like this yourself when your time comes. The days come and go, and you don't notice. Then one day you look around — and there it stands, death. I pray God every day to take me in an instant..."

"You should eat," - I try to comfort her, - "Why, you only drink tea, that's it..."

"Well, I eat," - she breathes heavily, - "it's just that my body can't take it in anymore. I've lived too long in this world – the girl's the only thing that's keeping me here."

Grandma Yevdokia folds the bed out.

"Go to bed now," - she says, - "You'll get back from the theatre on Sunday, and soon it'll be New Year. It'll come and we'll have everything ready for it. Your mother promised us pies. We'll get new flour and she'll make them. The pies are soft, they jump into your mouth by themselves. And then another holiday – Christmas... And then the spring's near – we'll bake larks. We'll bake them and take them to the church to offer them to the beggars. Not everyone is lucky like us to die in peace. There aren't many people like that..."

We'll go to the church, and the ones with huge stone legs will come towards us: they're walking and laughing. "See," - they point with hollow fingers, - "that beggar,

*well, she was a princess. We," - they brag, - "stole
everything from her." And grandma will pity her and
give her a lark...*

"I'm a sinner," - grandma Yevdokia complains, -
"I've come to hate a lot of people. So He's keeping
me here, and doesn't let me die. He must be
waiting for my heart to get softer like some kind
of biscuit. Because they only let you into the other
world where you are softened up, but how can you
forget? - she says, - The soul is not like the body:
you can't wash it clean with soap..."

"Tonechka," - Ariadna asks me, - "rub my back,
please, I can't reach it myself."

"Good Lord," - I think, - "her back must be
itchy, - the skin's so tender."

"Don't you scratch it yourself, Ariadna
Kuzminichna," - I say, - "see, there are fingernail
marks..."

She dries herself, wraps her head with a towel
and goes to her room.

Yevdokia comes in:

"We need to air things out in here," - she
sniffs: - "It smells too much of dirt. How I hate this
stench..."

"How can we open the window?" - I ask, - "It'll
get cold in a minute. You'll catch a cough – it's
freezing out there."

"All right," - she waves her hand, - "I'll just wash
like this. I'll scrub myself, you pour water on me."

She undressed. And it's not that she's thin, but I can see that she has become very weak. Last year she was stronger. I pour the water over her and ask:

"How could you put up with it then at the hospital, if you can't stand people's dirt? Sick people stink even stronger, don't they?"

"Well, it's cold there," - she answers, - "It stinks less when it's cold...."

I washed everybody, went into the room and lay down. "When I have that dress, I may go to the theatre too. I've lived in the city for such a long time, and I've never been."

Suzannochka doesn't stir. After all that washing, she's fast asleep.

"Look here," - Grandma Glikeria gives me a little bag, - "here's some sugar, and a piece of bun. Eat them when you're hungry, but do it quietly, don't disturb the others. And if Grandma Aglaya offers you something, don't take it. Who knows what kind of food they've got there at those theatres..."

The hat is soft. The pink tights peep from below the coat. Grandma Yevdokia says:

"I'll take her and come back."

"Don't get it wrong, please," – Mama is worried. – "Last time they were giving it out at the office, now we've got to go to the basement."

The doors are high, and made of wood... We go in, and Grandma Aglaya is waiting there.

"Well," - she says, - "come with me, I'll put you in the best seat – like a princess."

The corridor is long.

"Come," - she leads me by the hand, - "We'll try the director's box. Only we'll go behind the stage first. I've got to arrange something with the manager."

We go up the small stairs.

"Be careful," - she says, - "don't stumble."

I raise my head, and up above I see thick ropes: they writhe like snakes... And a scary guy walks towards me. His beard is red, dishevelled...

"That's an actor" - she explains. "There are lots of them around here."

And then I see a wall moving past. The actors have grabbed hold of it: they're shouting and dragging it along.

Grandma Aglaya says:

"That's what they call a set. See, they've painted trees and a big house. So when everybody goes to sleep, this forest will rise up. And everything will become overgrown – you'll see ..."

A woman is sitting in the corner, wrapped in a shawl.

"Here, Alexandra Dmitrievna," - Grandma Aglaya pushes me towards her – "this is my granddaughter. Grand-niece actually. May I put her in the manager's box..."

The woman looks at me:

"You're a nice girl… Is this your first time in the theatre?"

Grandma Aglaya bends down to her, and whispers, whispers, pointing at her own throat. It must be sore.

The woman looks into a book.

"Good Lord…" - She shakes her head. – "Of course, you can, Aglaya Mikhailovna. We're not expecting anybody in the morning…"

The room is small, with red chairs and a little table between them. On the table is a fancy box.

"Have a sweet," - grandma Aglaya offers. – "Come, don't be shy. These chocolates are delicious. I tried one yesterday when I was locking up after the guests left. It simply melts in your mouth…"

I put the candy into my mouth and chewed it. It tasted sweet. I looked out, and saw lights burning. The chandelier on the ceiling is like a Christmas tree. And the walls are so high… The balconies are all gold, right up to the ceiling. There are people everywhere. They sit there, fanning themselves with pieces of white paper…

The light slowly goes out… The curtain moves and trembles…

A small girl is brought out, and put in a little cradle. The fairies are gentle, transparent. Their dresses are like feathers, and they have wings on their backs. They dance and their wings quiver… And the music around is dark. Here she is… the sorceress… The Ravens are driving her, pushing the carriage in front of them. They have claws on their enormous hands. And she gets out of the carriage - she jumps around, and makes threats...

We went down into the cellar. People are packed like sardines. Some woman makes her way through the queue, writing numbers on people's hands. "Write on both hands," - I say to her – "One of us is late." - "She's late, is she? You've got to come on time: anybody can get their both hands marked..."

The walls are low. The little windows are boarded up. It's so stuffy, you can hardly breathe. A baby starts crying somewhere in the head of the queue. Ariadna has taken her headscarf off – she wipes perspiration off her forehead. "We'll spend about three hours queuing here," - she whispers....

My head hurts as if nails were being driven into it. The voices are loud, and they don't stop...

"But how can I get him here – he's bed-ridden!" - "Well, you should have got a certificate from the doctor saying that he can't get up. I took one out. They promised to serve us if I had it". - "We used to live on 6th Sovetskaya street – there they knew us all right, they would serve us without a word..." - "Never mind what they did at Sovetskaya..." - "We're going to suffocate here – at least there was a bit more room at the office". - "And before the last November holidays we queued in the street – we froze". "Well, now we're going to stew here, it's so stuffy".

I looked in front of me: only heads and heads. And they're crowding from behind too. I turned around, and Yevdokia's fighting her way towards us – her headscarf has almost slipped off her head. "Well, how did it go?" - I ask. – "Did she cry?" - "Why would she cry?" - she's panting, - "She was eager to go"...

We approached the desk – the woman behind it stabs her finger at the paper, counting. "Four?" - she asks again. – "There're five of you in the ledger. A child's also registered. Is she sick or something?" Ariadna nods: "She is." - "Have you got a certificate? Don't you think you'll get anything if you haven't." – "What certificate?" - Yevdokia says, "it's Sunday today. The doctor won't come." - "I don't care... She's not dying, is she? You could have wrapped her up and brought here." - "Well, that's our business," - Yevdokia says, - "You mind your business and serve us."

"Sick, is she?"

The neighbour from downstairs is behind us.

"I saw them today," - she says. "She was taking the girl somewhere." - she points at Yevdokia, - "They're lying... They're total liars. And what for do you lie?" - "And you," - Yevdokia turns around to look her in the face, - "you shut your mouth. No one asked you, did they?" - "Did everybody hear that?" - she jumped at Yevdokia, - "you don't like my mouth, you bitch! Look at yourself and your bastards: they've nailed up their dirty mouths all right, just wait till they get around to yours! They should pull you up by the roots, they should – under the knife with you!" - "And you," - Yevdokia turns black in the face, - "you're ready to go on for a whole century, aren't you? – as if you won't die..." - "I sure will die, but my kids and grandkids will stay, and yours are rotting away in their graves. Well? Where are they? They aren't around, are they?" - She works her fingers loose and wiggles them...

The paper sacks are large. I put them in two bags – it's easier to carry like that. We go out into the street – Yevdokia's lips are blue: she stands there gasping. "I'm nauseated," - she complains, - "it's like something's squeezing my head, and I can't feel my legs..." - "Good Lord," - I say, - "Yevdokia Timofeevna, you shouldn't let yourself get upset by every fool... The main thing is, we got the flour." She's holding on to the water pipe, and she's turned quite black...

The music is faint, and runs like a brook. They've lifted the curtain. It's nice in the other world. They come out and take their places on the porch. They've stuffed themselves with chocolates and feel happy now. Can that one be with them too? Oh, I can't wait for him to arrive on his sledge...

There he is, the dove. He's tall and blue. And his arms are wings. All covered with feathers. And how he jumps! So he's growing legs too. He hasn't got a beak yet... But what would they need beaks for? His hands have grown too...

The guests are dancing and whirling... They wear silk dresses adorned with diamonds. The stones sparkle on the hems. The princess walks among them smiling. She doesn't remember her past life. She woke up and forgot about it....

II

THE DAUGHTER

I was trying to remember something, but my memory ran into a blank wall: gates, a dirty-white horse, and a dark wooden coffin. I don't remember the dress either, but Grandma Glikeria had one like it, and so it seems to me that I remember it.

I was also afraid that I wouldn't be able to become a true artist. That's what Larisa Yevgenievna said: true artists should remember their earliest childhood.

Then I would draw everything differently, but as it is they always scolded me: for the distorted perspective, for the fact that I never achieve a real likeness, for the obscurity of my ideas. Larisa Yevgenievna taught us that the idea should be distinct and clear, so that nobody would have any questions about it, especially not the Admission Committee. I heeded her advice: I believed that she wished me well. And in fact, she did. She taught me artistic techniques, and corrected my competition works – I suffered greatly, but I never dared to object. How could I tell her that her corrections ruined everything, and destroyed the main idea – she was my teacher, after all.. If hadn't been for her I wouldn't have entered the faculty.

No admission committee would have recognized works that lacked perspective and showed the world as if it were divided into two parts: the upper and the lower. Once when they were preparing an exhibition at the Palace, I tried to explain that I could see a line that went across the sheet from edge to edge, dividing it into two halves. What was at the bottom should remain small, that's why perspective was needed to make it recede into the distance. But up there, at the top, everything turns around, it comes closer so that we can see how it rises from the depths to the surface. If you draw according to the rules, as they would have you do, all the important things become flat – they sink into the ground.

Larisa Yevgenievna heard me out and then phoned my Grandmas, and Grandma Yevdokia told me off: why did I have to talk rubbish, they could easily take me to the madhouse at Pryazhka for saying all that. At first I didn't believe her, but then Grandma Ariadna told me that Larisa Yevgenievna was afraid that I had a nervous disorder, and if it didn't end soon, she recommended that I be show me to a psychiatrist, otherwise they would have to intervene themselves.

After that I kept quiet, and drew correct pictures, which allowed me to enrol at the Mukhina Art Academy.

I was afraid for a long time after that, so my real works appeared only later, when I started showing at private exhibitions. There my works no longer surprised anyone.

Back then a lot of people were into icon painting, they argued about the canon, the holy faces and the heavenly arc. They studied old techniques, and tried to understand why the painter used a particular paint: cinnabar, golden ochre or reduced madder lake... It turns out that this was also dictated by the canon: I remember how Grisha told me about it, - I still like his early works.

He was looking for a perspective that would reflect an image of the world – just as precise as the one used by the Byzantines, who regarded the Universe as a temple. It's a shame that he later became interested in installations, but back then we'd talk about everything, and I tried to explain why the canon didn't have anything to do with my life – that it was hard for me to follow a tradition that didn't contain anything personal, anything from my own memory...

Grisha argued with me, he said that I set too much value on the personal, and that this got in the way.

I tried studying ancient traditions, but they seemed dead to me, until I saw one Egyptian picture. A woman on the bank of a brook. This picture amazed me, as usually Egyptian artists painted battle scenes and almighty pharaohs. They intentionally painted them as enormous figures, and kept everyone else small, so that the viewer would get the impression that they ruled over their subjects: over their life and death.

But this picture simply showed a woman on her knees, crawling along the bank of a brook. At first I thought she was a pharaoh's wife too: there was an inscription in hieroglyphics at the top, which I couldn't read. But then I found a translation. It was the soul of a deceased woman drinking water in the other world. I thought of her all the time when I was preparing my first work for an exhibition. I intentionally made it in black and white. Grisha liked my work, he even gave me a nickname: Brook. And I decided it was because of my surname, but he said the surname wasn't the main thing. He simply liked the woman painted in the Egyptian tradition: according to their canon, the body and the face were painted in profile, while the eyes looked ahead... As if they were living a life separate from the body. Grisha said that I had found a precise image.

Once Alesha Rubashkin came to visit us, pale as a ghost, and said that he had heard with his own ears that the Muscovites who had been run over by a bulldozer were going to be sent to prison. Not right away, of course, and it would be kept quiet, but then Grisha had one too many and started to shout that he was fed up with all those old Bolsheviks, and when was there going to be an end to it?...

I don't know what came over me, I guess I wanted to comfort him, so I suddenly said that it would all end one day, although not soon, only in seven years... Alesha was happy to hear that, and counted on his fingers: it turned out to be in eighty-three. And Grisha turned sulky and said: "No, Syuzon... It will never end" - and he soon left for America. Many years later we met at an exhibition and it turned out that he remembered that old story: "Amazing, you only got it wrong by a few years... Own up, Brook, how did you know?..."

Of course, he was only joking: how could I know it? Grisha has always scolded me, he used to say that in our country one had to be interested in politics, but I answered that he was lucky that his parents weren't afraid to tell him things, while my Grandmas kept quiet. Even among themselves they never talked about anything *like that*: only about household affairs.

Grisha wanted me to come with him, he said I was a talented artist and that my talent would wither away here, but I could never find it in my heart to do it. I longed to go with him, but something held me back: I felt that if I went away I'd never discover the truth. Why didn't I have a father? How did it happen that they broke up and Mama married my step-father? After all, there weren't any politics in it, but my Grandmas still wouldn't talk.

Of course, I could ask Nikolai Nikiforovich, but I couldn't bring myself to do it. I thought he didn't know the truth anyway, and if he did he wouldn't tell me. Not to mention Zinaida Ivanovna: every word she uttered was a lie. Didn't I remember her shouting at my Grandmas that my mother had made Nikolai marry her, and my Grandmas, the old witches, cast spells into the bargain, and still they would have failed if it hadn't been for the crafty Jew... He meddled and came up with a plan.

What Jew? Where did she get all those stories? My grandmas didn't have anybody: no friends, or family...

III

THE MOTHER

"Once upon a time in a certain kingdom, not in our country, there lived a Tsar, Ivan Vasilievich, and he had an elder son Vasily-Tsarevich, and the second son was Dimitry-Tsarevich. Once the elder was of age, he had to marry. So they finally found a good, hardworking bride, but the next morning after they were married he disappeared. Dimitry-Tsarevich came to his father and says: "Bless me, Father. I'm going to look for my brother". There was nothing to do — the father blessed him.

Dimitry-Tsarevich saddled his horse and set off. He rode for a day, then for another and sees only the steppe around him. All covered with a sheet of bare snow. He rode on and in a little while he saw a tent: a white tent set up in the white snow. And in the tent, Vasily-Tsarevich, his own brother, was sleeping the sleep of the dead. So Dimitry-Tsarevich thought: "Why don't I kill him while he's asleep, and take all his wealth, and his good bride". And he did as he said: he killed his brother, buried his bones, and went back home. Only before he left he chopped his brother's little finger off..."

Mama sits in the corner and listens.

"Good Lord," - she says, - "what a scary tale. Maybe it's not such a good idea to tell it at night..."

Grandma Yevdokia pursed her lips:

"Scary or not... That's the way it is. I don't know any other. I tell what I was told... All right then," - she got up, - "go to sleep..."

And just when I've fallen asleep, she comes back.

"Get up," - she calls me.

And takes me to the kitchen right in my nightgown.

"Sit down," - she says, - "eat something."

They're all sitting at the table.

Grandma Glikeria raises her liqueur glass:

"May this year be a happy one."

Grandma Ariadna says:

"Just let there be no war…"

And Grandma Yevdokia takes it up :

"At least let no one get sick…

Mama is merry. She's at the table too and forgets all about the evil fairy…

Grandma Yevdokia lifts her hands:

"Why are you crying, you silly? It's a holiday today – we should rejoice."

Grandma Glikeria says:

"We woke her up for nothing. She'd be sleeping peacefully… Come, my little dove, I'll take you to bed."

And the black carriage drives on, with the Raven in the harness. The sorceress comes out of the carriage: "You thought you could do without me? I'll show you! Just you wait! I've prepared a present for you"…

I woke up, and there was no one around. But it was light already. I ran barefoot to the Christmas tree. I grabbed the present and ran back.

Mama is lying in bed and smiling.

"This is a kind of little apartment," - she explains. "It has everything in it – little rooms, and a kitchen, and people. All you have to do is cut them out and glue them together. You'll take small scissors," - she says, - "and cut everything out yourself: the walls, the beds and the little table. There's a whole family there, you know. Leaf through it toward the end. Only practice first, so you don't ruin it."

There's a mother, a father and a small girl. But there aren't any grandmas. That's because it's a different girl. Her mother and father died, and her grandmas live with me...

"Fancy that," - Glikeria came too, and she's amazed, - "it really is a little apartment."

"Everybody was buying them at Gostiny – so I got one too. They promised a TV," - she recalls. "After the holidays. I'll pay it off by instalments."

Yevdokia looks at her, frowning.

"Who was that" - she asks – "who promised?"

"What a crafty old crow!" - I think. – "It's as if she senses something."

"What do you mean — who?" - I pretend to laugh. – "Santa Claus, of course..."

On the 31st, just when I leave the factory, he catches up with me. "You know what, - he says, - "My turn has come to get a TV. I put my name on the list back in the spring. I thought they might give me a room... I was hoping, even before the November holidays. And they say: 'You've got to wait. People with families need them more...' So maybe you'll take it. I'll pay for it now, and you'll pay me back bit by bit. What would I do with it at the dormitory... When your turn comes, then I'll get one..." - and he looked very happy. – "And I'll help you to get it home, and to lay the cable. "

No, I think, thank you very much, that's the last thing I need... The old women are eyeing me with suspicion already. I'll carry it on the sled myself. And I'll get electricians to install it – they'll do it for a bottle.

"Well," - he says, - "whatever — I would do it for nothing."

"I know your nothing," - I think to myself.

We finished our dinner. I tidied up in the kitchen, and put the washing to soak. It's time to go to bed for me too. Suzannochka's already asleep. I came up to her little desk. Amazing, she's almost finished gluing everything – now they're living together, the three of them. And they have so many rooms – a lounge, and a bedroom, and a separate bedroom for the girl too. Where do they work, I wonder, if they get so much space? The father must be a big shot... He's so young – when did he manage to become one? A huge apartment like that would only be given to a boss, or a head engineer. A foreman would never get one like that. She hasn't finished putting together the furniture yet, I see, so they're sleeping on the floor for the time being. That's all right though, as long as they have walls... I remember Sytin's wife. Lord, I can't even imagine it: to be your own mistress. It really would be like heaven...

I lie down, but can't sleep. "Looks like he's a modest guy, doesn't drink. What if Mikhalych's right and he asks me to marry him?... Can't scrape by alone forever." - I imagine his face: a nice face, but I'm still ill at ease. – "It's all right," - I try to convince myself, - "what matters is that he's one of ours: not a city guy. Who can understand them?.."

I closed my eyes but my heart's still pounding. I see that man again, the one with the beard. That hung on his wall... I'm suffocating! I walked around so much, hoped to find him. There was no way to remember the house though... They're all big and look the same in the city. Not like in the village...

I threw the blanket off. My insides are churning. I went to the kitchen to have some water.

I poured myself some, and sat down at the table. The oilcloth feels cold... That's because my hands are burning. I felt a bit better. I sat and thought: "It's also better financially: guys earn more than women do. The job rates are quite different." It sounded as if I was trying to talk myself into marrying. Then I checked myself: "Maybe he doesn't even dream of it. Oh," - I decided, - "When he proposes, we'll see..."

I'm lying in bed but I'm not quite asleep. There's just something I don't understand. It's as if I'm on the outskirts of the village. And I don't remember the way, it's as if there's no road. There's snow everywhere. Everything's white as white can be.

103

I turn around to find my footprints. There aren't any: neither mine nor anybody else's. I look around hoping to see smoke above the roofs of the village. But I see neither rooftops nor smoke. "Then how did I get here?" – I think. I stand there and I'm amazed at myself – because I should be scared but I'm not...

But it's not quite clear what the time is: it's not snowing yet, and I can see a long way in front of me. But it's gloomy – neither morning, nor evening. I'd better start walking, but my legs are heavy, I can't move them. Then I see smoke ahead curling up in a column. So I pull myself together and walk. I recognize the place when I get closer. It's our dugout at the edge of the wood. It's been there since the war. We used to hide there often from the rain when we were kids. The logs in it are all rotten, and they creak. "Who has settled in the dugout and is lighting a fire?" I wonder.

I lower my head and peep in. Instead of a floor it has beaten earth. There's an old broom in the corner. A fire is burning on the floor. The person by the fire has his back to me – he's adding logs to it, warming his hands over the flames.

His voice is dull and hoarse, as if he has a cold. And it sounds familiar, but I can't recognize it. I wish he'd turn around, I think. Maybe it's one of our guys, from the village. So many of them disappeared during the war, and before it too. He's got cold in the forest, so his voice has gone... The sheepskin coat he's wearing seems to be in the military fashion, but it's ripped all over – hanging in rags. I wonder if a bear got him. But there never were any bears around here...

He turns his head around. I look at him – I can't breathe: it's as if the bear has scratched him with his claws. He nods to me: "Well," - he says, - "tell me why you've come. To ask me to let you go? Well," – he croaks – "I'm not keeping you here." I want to reply to him but I have no voice, it's gone, as if I've become mute. The little fire is burning, and the flames are leaping. The shadows on the logs are like wings. I recover myself: "You have a growing daughter and you're in the woods of all places – like a partisan. The war was over a long time ago – it's time to come out into the world." He lowers his head and doesn't look at me...

"Why haven't you turned up, not even once in so many years?" – I complain. "As if you went missing or something..." He's moving his lips but I can't hear his voice - I look at his hands. I forget myself – as if a crooked claw is turning inside me: making me put my face close to his. He grins: he's guessed right. I raise my arms and step towards him.

His mouth jerks open, as if stung by a whiplash. And his eyes are strange: neither alive nor dead. "Your dress is made of rayon," - he laughs, - "you've got to get yourself a new one." And I see that I am wearing the new dress. Poppies on a blue background. "When did Glikeria have the time?" - I wonder, - "I thought she only just cut out the material..."

I felt the buttons – I squeeze them at the throat, and I freeze – what's going to happen? There's nothing in the dugout – neither vinegar nor aspirin... I move away from him and shake my head but the claw inside my heart is aching: I wish he'd stay.

"What's wrong?" - he turns nasty and his eyes grow dull, - "Don't you want our daughter to be born?" - "How do you mean I don't want to?" - I say, - "She's been born already. I don't know how to bring her up..." - "No," - he frowns, - "that time doesn't count." Perhaps it really is like this, I think... Maybe nothing happened, if I'm here in the village?

My legs are weak. I sit down on the plank-bed. "Wait a minute," - I say. How can it be, I think, that it didn't happen, if I remember it all? – "Why don't you want to recognize your daughter?" – I ask him. "Your own blood."

He grins, the devil, and laughs again. "Blood," - he says, - "has gone into the ground. One can't build kinship on blood." - "On what else," - I say surprised, - "if the girl looks like you. Only you were such a great talker, and she doesn't talk at all. I used to hope," - I complain, - "but I don't any more. It looks like she'll have to suffer as a mute all her life. I don't know where you spend your time, but can't you find out if there's any way to help her? Others bring up their children, buy TVs: look what a huge queue they have ... "

A great heat is coming from the fire, and the smoke makes my head spin. He moved closer to me. "Don't be afraid, don't," - he grumbles. – "I'll help you, I'll do everything for you, anything you wish..."

I feel so heavy, I can't get up, I can't escape, as if a bear's fallen on top of me, with his singed fur. I have no strength or will. He's muttering and muttering, as if he's asking for something. I should scream, but my voice is gone. I smell the bear's flesh getting closer and closer... The smell is sweet and sharp like a red-hot nail. I cling and cling to it, tear it to pieces. The fire's burning, moaning, blazing up... I'm hot, so hot... I screamed, as I fainted…

I opened my eyes – it's dark around me. It's as if there's no fire but everything's smouldering: it blazes up, and sparks fly. I feel with my fingers – a bear's fur: sticky, wet... I threw the blanket off and sat up.

My heart's pounding. The nightgown has gotten twisted so that I can't get up. I hardly managed to free my legs. My lips are dry and prickly. A chill is coming from the floor.

"What was that?" – I think. – "It was like paradise..." - I remembered Sytin's wife. – "Good Lord, can it be that she meant *that* too?..."

Grandma Glikeria comes in:

"You've done enough gluing. Do something else. Come on, come with me – we'll get the sewing machine out. If you learn to use the machine, you'll be able to sew whatever you like: a dress, an apron. It'll come in very handy when you grow up. You can't buy much in the shops. It's so expensive..."

The dress, all cut out, is lying on the table. Scraps are on the floor everywhere.

"Here," - Grandma explains, - "I cut it out already."

I picked one up from the floor, and looked up at Granny.

"It's all right," - she encourages me. – "You can take the small scraps. I can't use them for anything.

And you'll gather them and put on them a pin. Only be careful with the pin, don't prick your fingers... Here," - she explains, - "we have a side stitch, and here is the back. First you make a pattern out of paper, then you cut it out. Now we'll iron it, once we've pinched the tucks. The iron's our chief helper, without it you can't even start sewing..."

The machine's black and varnished, with a red pattern on the top. There's a needle stuck at the bottom. Grandma turns the handle: the machine whirs and pecks.

"Well," - she cut the thread off. – "Sit down, try it yourself... What's wrong? You don't want to? You're some kind of rebel… Well then," - she ushers me out, - "you go to your place then. Play at your paper kingdom."

I got out the scraps – I took the pin out. I brought the mama from the kitchen, and put her on a sheet of paper. I traced it like a real pattern. The hem's wide and bell-shaped, and on the shoulders there are little paper squares, so that the dress doesn't fall down. I cut it out. Now I've got to cut it along the scraps. I started to draw, but the pencil gets stuck on the poppies: they hunch and hunch, as if the wind were blowing them. Then it dawned upon me: I've got to glue it on first. Then cut it out...

The mama's beautiful, she's happy to have the dress with poppies on it. It smells of sweet glue. I ran to the kitchen to show my work.

"Isn't that wonderful?" - Grandma Yevdokia says admiringly. – "It's as if she had her own workshop... I'll find you some scraps too – you can dress them all: the girl and the guy too...

They got it all wrong again. He's the father.

"How clever you are!" - Grandma Glikeria's not angry, she spits on her finger. The iron's hissing, it's angry... – "I've only just started and she's already finished everything. She's got it all ready. Well, run and dress her."

I dressed her. I move my lips. It doesn't matter if no sound comes out. They're dead – they must hear everything anyway.

There once lived a father and a mother and they had no grandmas, they only had a little girl. The one in the mirror. They lived very happily. The mother and father would wash, comb their hair and go to work and they'd tell the girl: pick up some scraps, make a few dresses so that everybody can dress up. They come back from work and she's got everything ready – suits, coats and dresses...

There's some noise in the hall. I peep out, and grandma Yevdokia waves me away:

"You stay there, you have no business peeping out. They've brought the TV. You can come when it's been installed and turned on..."

The box is big, a hundred rooms would fit into it. Mama and some strange guy are carrying it – they hold it on both sides. Mama sucks one of her fingers. "Well", - asks the strange guy, - "where shall we take it?" - "There", - Mama points. That means to Grandma Yevdokia...

So they'll come home, change and sit down to their dinner. Their table's big there in the other world – it stands in the middle of the room. And on the table there are plates and saucers of all kinds. Soup in the pot. And a frying pan with potatoes. And no one has to cook. Because everything is made out of paper: eat all you want.

Oh, I checked myself. They don't eat soup. Why would they need it? They've got chocolates in a red box. It's not just any box but a magic one: you take some sweets out of it, and it's still full.

So they have their dinner, and drink their tea and off they go. Only they forget to wash their hands. And in the street the evil fairy is waiting for them, stalking them. When she sees their chocolate-smeared hands, she'll get angry and jab her staff into the ground – and threaten to ruin them. "Why," - she hisses, - "are you enjoying lovely sweets while others are eating soup?... Just you wait till I cast a spell on you!"

The father began to cry, the mother began to cry, but the girl comforts them: don't cry, father and mother. She won't do anything to you. You'll just prick your fingers on a pin and fall asleep – for a hundred years. And then you'll wake up, look around you and there will be no evil sorceress... And no one will even remember about her, as if she had never been. Only your little rooms will be untouched – where they used to be. And your girl. Sitting there, waiting for you. You'll all start living again...

I took a pin and pricked their fingers. Their bed's wide – I put them both in it. There they lie, but their eyes don't close: it looks as if they're not sleepy...

They're walking up and down and talking in the hall. I can't make out the words, but Mama sounds happy.

She opens the door and calls me:

"Come, I'll show you something... You've never seen anything like it before..."

I run out and see a little house. With a little glass window in the front.

"Well," - Mum says, - "Look."

She presses a button and waits...

The little window's dark. Then suddenly a light blazes up like a spark. Wider and wider... And music comes out of the little house. How can that be? Swans are standing side by side, flapping their wings...

"Good Lord!" - Ariadna raises her hands and presses them to her breast. – "It's 'Swan Lake'... The ballet..."

Their dresses are feathery and they've got head-dresses on their little heads. They stand and sway. A whole flock. And in front of them all is a white swan. She flaps and flaps, she's about to take off...

"It's late," – Mama whispers. – "Why don't we have dinner first and watch a bit more before we go to bed?"

"Let her watch until the end" - Grandma Yevdokia comes to my rescue. – "Look how her lips have gone white. As if she's seen a miracle... You won't tear her away from it now."

"Well, all right, then," – Mama nods. – "I was amazed when I first saw it too. We had one at the dormitory. With a thick lens. You couldn't see much through it. It's much better this way.

"Do they mostly show ballets?" - Glikeria can't take her eyes off the screen.

"No," - Mum answers, - "not just ballets. Different things. They show news at night. The custodian would always turn it on. I listened sometimes. It's very boring though. They just sit there and take turns reading. They also have concerts. Sometimes you can hear good singing..."

The music trembles and moves, and it feels sweet inside my head...

A well-dressed woman appears: "We broadcasted scenes from the ballet by Pyotr Ilich Tchaikovsky, 'Swan Lake.'

"Well," - Mum gets up, - "the potatoes must be overcooked. That's the end of the program."

She pressed the button: it shrinks and shrinks until it's just a spark.

It's dark in the little window. Here it is - the button... It'll blaze up again if you press it... I snatch my hand away — I'm afraid. I stood on tiptoe and closed my eyes tight. And it's as if I can hear the music again. How wonderful it is there... They die and are transformed: some into doves, some into swans...

I'm washing up: no, I think, he must have got offended. He came up to me in the morning: "So, are we taking it to your place today?" - "Well," - I say, - "I've done it all with our Sergeich. He helped me to get it there and to install it."

I worked all day but my heart was troubled. Why did I have to hurt the guy? He meant well. He'd have done everything and left, and I wouldn't have held him back. At a pinch I could always explain: "That's how it is. They're old women, they don't like guests very much. I've got to consider them, we live like a family." That's all right, I think, you can always swallow an insult...

I wiped the table, sat down, and I still couldn't recover. Unbelievable... We've bought a TV. In the country we used to sit by the light of a splinter, and now... They wouldn't believe it, if I told them... But I couldn't help telling the girls in the shop. "How come?" - they asked. –"You only just put your name on the waiting list." I didn't know what to say. "I swapped with a girl from the assembly line," - I lied, - "she needed money." That poisonous Nadka managed to put in a word here too: "And you? Have you become rich or something? You don't know what to do with your money?" - "It's my mother's money," - I answer. – "She's been saving her retirement benefit."

So I bragged about the TV and now I regretted it. Why did I have to open my mouth? Well, never mind, after all I didn't steal it. It's not for me, it's for my child.

I took the basin off the hook and remembered: Mikhalych, our foreman, said that they'd invented a machine for washing clothes. He says he read it somewhere: "You put the dirty clothes in, and it whirls around. And it's all clean when you take it out." The girls laughed: "How do you mean it whirls? It's like Baba Yaga's hut on chicken legs, is it?"...

And I thought: who knows?...They sent Gagarin into space, didn't they? A washing machine isn't like going into the cosmos. It must be simpler...

That's how they explained it at the political information lecture: "Everyone will work as much as they want – it may be a whole shift, or a half. Once they've finished work, they go to the shops. And it'll be unlimited bounty in the shops: there'll be plenty of everything. And there will be no need for money. They'll abolish money – you'll be able to take as much as you want." Nadka couldn't contain herself then either: "As much as I want, you say? What will come of that? They'll snap it all up in one day. Say, I'll take ten dresses at once, and shoes... And not just any shoes, but Czech or Hungarian shoes, for example. Why not?" - she winks to the girls. – "Haven't I got the right?" – "You," - Mikhalych gets angry with her, - "You'll learn to be responsible by then". "Responsible..." - she laughs. – "Not so much responsible as old, in twenty years. I'll be forty-five by then – what will I need shoes for? I'll be happy with felt boots then. What about the young?" - she looks at the girls. – "Or is everybody going to be old under Communism?"

I think it over: I understand about the food. First people will pounce on it, of course: they'll want everything, from fish to sweets. Well, then they'll get full – you can only eat so much... And then they'll be after clothes. Or fabrics, for example. And they won't take rayon, of course: they'll want pure wool...

I'm undressing, and I hear her moan... I bend over her – no, I must have imagined it. I fixed her blanket. What a beauty she is – like an angel from heaven. No one would say she was defective. It is your will, Lord...

Oh, I'm so happy she's good with her hands, from a young age. My mother used to say: if you have good hands, you have them right from the start. Sometimes a kid's knee-high to a grasshopper, and still there isn't anything she can't do with her hands, but sometimes you teach and teach them and it all goes down the drain. And they grow up to be good for nothing...

I see she put her paper dolls to bed, too. They're lying there asleep...

I got into bed but I'm afraid to go to sleep. I lie quiet for a little while. Then I think, maybe it's not him after all? I broke out in a sweat: lots of strange things happen. *Those* who appear to us, don't just give up... My late mother told me:

"It was during the war. There was a soldier's wife living in our village. She was a healthy, sturdy woman, she had never been sick in her life. Her husband was at the front - she aches for both of them: for the man and for herself. Then, later towards the end of the war she received a death notice. Well, she grieved and cried, then went back to work again. A couple of months later they started to notice that she was getting black in the face. Nobody minded at first, because the others weren't very rosy either. And then they noticed that she was getting thinner. So the women talked to her: 'You've got to go to the district centre to see a medical assistant. Let him have a look: he may prescribe you some powder or herbs.' She'd listen to them and look at them in a funny way – she'd grin, and her eyes were evil, mad.

"That woman had a friend. So the others turned to her. 'Talk to Anna,' - they said, - 'there's something wrong with her, she'll leave her kids orphans.' So the friend went to talk to her. She started on one thing, then on another. And the woman said: 'You can all go to hell. You need the medical assistant's help, not me. I've only just begun to live. My husband comes to me every night. There's love between us. Before, I didn't even know what it's like...'

"The friend was surprised and told the others. So they decided to ask the priest for help. They had just opened a church then in the district — it was nailed up before the war. But they couldn't go at once. There were no days off. Every day was a working day. So they collected the harvest at the collective farm and started to dig their own potatoes. They dug them all up and went. Both neighbours. The priest was an old man, barely alive himself. When he heard about the woman, he said: 'The devil's tormenting her. You bring her to God's temple, and I'll perform the service. Only these devils,' - he says, scaring them, - 'are the most powerful that take on a lover's image. It sometimes happens that they don't give in the first

time. There's a special, terrifying name for them.'
And the priest told them the name but they forgot
it...

"They went back, but then it started to rain a
lot and the roads became impassable. How could
they take her anywhere? They had to wait till the
roads were good again. While they were waiting,
Anna died. They bathed her and wondered at how
old she looked. A real old hag. Her arms were thin
and her ribs stuck out, as if she'd been ill for a long
time. The devil took all the strength out of her –
tormented her to death..."

I lie in bed and everything stops still inside me...
What if the same thing is happening to me?.. The
devil is tormenting me. I close my eyes. "It's him,
it's him,"- I think. – "Your heart always knows..."

The white snow lies in drifts... A path winds
through the drifts. There are some footprints – they
look as though they were made by felt boots. I feel
the time is just before morning: the sun is about
to rise. I began to follow the prints. "But these are
mine," - I think, - "from the last time..." I look at
my feet: felt boots. "Where from? I usually wear
moccasins..."

The smoke curls up into the air. Only the
forest is strange – it's dark, and doesn't look like
ours. Around it there's a picket fence. Behind
it is a wooden look-out tower, like the ones the
Germans had. They say there used to be one in
the district: the Germans kept prisoners there in
an enclosure... "All right," - I decide, - "I need

to find the gates at least." I look around – there aren't any. Instead of them there's that dug-out: the entrance lies through it.

I lower my head. The floor's earthen, the same, only now there are benches along the walls. They are in two rows, like plank-beds. And there's no fire, but a little potbelly stove. And the angle pipe goes through the roof. But it's still smoking.

Men are sitting on the plank-beds. It's hot here. The air's heavy, intoxicating. They sit there and play – they throw dice in turns and don't see me. I looked closer: the dice are not regular dice. They are too white – as if they'd had all the colour boiled out of them. The bones are lying in a heap in the corner – they feel for them and take more. I got frightened and wanted to run away, but my legs didn't move. They were rooted to the ground.

Well, I think, it can't be helped. So I greet them: "Hello." They stop their game and turn around. My man is also with them, but he doesn't acknowledge himself. And I think, I won't say anything either then – because who knows...

A bandy-legged guy is in charge here. His beard's bedraggled and red - he looks like a real wood spirit. "Come in," - he grins, - "since you're here. Tell us why you came."

Then one puny guy, also with a beard, turns to him. "Don't you know," - he reproaches him, - "how to receive guests properly? They don't come here every day, do they? You've got to give them food and drink first, then you ask questions." I see that the others support him, nodding their heads.

So they swept the dice on to the ground, and cleared some space. "Sit down," - they invite me. – "Drink our water, and eat a piece of bread." They move an iron mug towards me, and hold out a piece of bread.   I sat down on a plank-bed, and smelled their bread: it's foul. I haven't eaten bread like that since the war – it's made with pig-weed. And the water's also bad, it looks like swamp water. "What?" - he says, - "What are you turning your nose up at? Does our food stink?" - "Thank you," - I answer, - "I'm full, I just had dinner – I only just got up from the table." Now the boss gets angry: "What's wrong with you"- he tells my man off, - "that you haven't you taught your woman how to visit us? She loathes our food, does she? Most likely they eat carrion every day where she comes from..."

The others got angry too. They turn about and grumble like bears. They scratch their beards. I got scared, took a bite of the pig-weed bread, and a sip of the water. I see they've calmed down... And I also feel that I've become bolder after a swallow of their fare. And it looks like the smoke has gone down a bit.

"What do you do here?" - I ask. - "We pray to God, what else!" – they grin. - "Ah," - it dawns on me, - "are you really dead then?..." I ask them and I'm not frightened: as if it's quite usual– to visit the dead. "We're not one or the other," they reply. - "How come? How can that be?" - "That's the only way it can be," - they say. - "Don't you know" - "How would she know?" - my man comes to my rescue, - "she's from there, from freedom..." Here they start laughing: slapping their chests with their hands, and turning their heads: "From freedom!" - they shout. – "You must be joking! - from freedom!" They find it very funny.

They get their breath back. And the boss says: "All right, then. If you're from freedom, you're from freedom. Tell me then, maybe you want something? You are a young woman, and we aren't too old yet." – he winks at me, - "Maybe, we'll help you..." I looked at my man out of the corner of my eye – he doesn't say anything.

Well, I gather my courage and say: "I came here so that the father would help his daughter: she's a wordless invalid. She'll turn seven soon, and she still can't speak. You enjoy yourselves here," - I nod my head, - "you play with human bones, while the girl suffers."

They heard me out –they sit there and think. The brigadier chews his lips: "Don't reproach us for the bones. They're ours, you know, not somebody else's..." And the puny one fidgets and fidgets, as if he's going to turn inside out: "I don't understand. Aren't the rest of you speechless too? Those who were talkative have been here for a long time by now..." The boss also scratches his head: "You silly woman! You don't understand how lucky you are. If we had been born mute, would we be rotting here now?" - "Well, I don't know about that," - I say, - "Yours is the fate of men. Maybe it's convenient for you to be mute, but the girl has to marry. Who'll take her the way she is?"

The boss frowns: "Well," - he decides, - "Let the father have the last word."

My man looks at me: "Have you thought it through properly? Say we give her a voice now, it won't be *for nothing*, not even here..." "Will they ask me for money?"- I think, surprised. - "What would they need it for in the woods?"

"I'm paying off a debt at the moment," - I explain, - "for a TV. Once I've paid it all back I'll start working for you: I'll settle with you." Fancy that, I think, he expects me to pay a debt for his daughter, and he's the father...

"And will it take you long to pay that debt back?" - the boss steps in. - "It'll be a long time," - I say, - "Maybe, six months, and maybe even a year..." - "That's not long," - he explains, - "where we are, a day counts for a year... But mind you – you'll pay us and your daughter will pay us too. So you decide for the two of you..."

They live well, I think to myself. With us it's more like a year for a day... I sat down, and rested my cheek against my hand – the smoke's thickening again. Their pipe must be blocked. And it reeks in the corners. It stinks of rot. I'm afraid I'll throw up... I feel sick again. But the guys don't say anything – they just wait.

I picked up the pig-weed bread, and took a bite. I sort of felt better – the sickness left me. "I've made up my mind," - I say. – "You guys do as you must. My daughter and I will work it off - don't you doubt it..."

The boss hit his palm against the table: "All right then. Hold out your hand if you've made up your mind. Not like that," - he puckers his face, - "not with the palm up. Not like your people do. You stretch it out: we'll chop one of your fingers off – as a deposit." I got scared: "How will I work then? They'll kick me out of the factory if I don't have a finger." "Well, you don't tell anybody - they won't even notice. They're blind, after all."

Then I see he's getting out a hatchet. A big, sharp one... I stretched my hand out, closed my eyes – and he struck. And it hurts so much that I should scream... But I bear it.

My man took my finger and wrapped it in a piece of cloth. "Now," - he announces, - "we're married. This finger's instead of a ring. The daughter's also mine now," - he says, - "I won't leave her now." And then I hear their boss laughing. "And I won't leave her either," - he promises, - "I'll be her Godfather..."

The pain's getting worse and worse... I screamed. I opened my eyes. There's nothing there . Only my hand twitches. I felt for the switch. Here it is... It's my finger festering. I injured it yesterday when we were carrying the TV. I closed my eyes. Good Lord... I must have listened to too many of those stories. Oh, Yevdokia, I think...

I pull myself together. I should get up. I can't go back to sleep anyway.

Only then I realised: the living man talked cunningly. You couldn't always understand it. But this one talks like everybody else. Like they do in our village...

It's all black outside the window - not a light, not a star. I feel so sick... "It's no accident," - I think, - "this finger, and the dream..."

We had our walk and had dinner. We put Sofia to bed, and sat down to spool the yarn. They sit there and steal glances at the TV from time to time. Ogling it. Glikeria is the first to dare to speak:

"Maybe we should turn it on? What if they're showing something important..."

It looked like Yevdokia was waiting for that. She put the knitting needles down immediately:

"Turn it on."

It came on. People inside the TV are marching and swinging their arms. Ariadna looked closer:

"Good Lord! Look, they're sportsmen... A sports parade."

Cheerful, festive music's playing. Glikeria looks at them in amazement:

"It's February, it's winter outside. How come they have a parade now?"

The lens runs, moves. Balloons are dancing. There are portraits on poles and banners. People are happy: they shout and laugh. You can't hear words though – it's all music, as if they were mute. Ariadna says:

"It looks like a holiday. The First of May, I think..."

Glikeria looks carefully:

"It's a holiday all right," - she agrees, - "Only they're wearing striped shirts like before the war, remember?"

"Good heavens," - Yevdokia stopped short, - "look at the banner, look..."

The guys are happy, healthy – they're carrying a banner on two poles. The cloth is wide. The poles are decked with flowers. There are numbers written in the middle - "1941". The camera lens goes higher and higher – it skims over the people's heads, as if taking wing.

Ariadna closed her eyes:

"I remember. Mine also wore them. They left the younger kid at home – and the three of them went with the people from the Institute."

"Good Gracious..." - Glikeria checked herself, and brings her arms together on her chest.

Ariadna sits there, her eyes fixed on the screen.

They walk and laugh...

Then comes a woman in ringlets, who takes up all the screen. Ariadna's not listening to her:

"I'll go and lie down."

They nod their heads: that's right, go and lie down.

She goes. Glikeria moves her lips:

"At those parades... Did they film everybody or pick certain people out?"

Yevdokia thought for a minute:

"You can't film everybody, can you?.. How many cameras would you need? There can't be that many."

"What if there were?" - Glikeria whispers.

Yevdokia understood her and covered her mouth with her hand.

"That's right," - Glikeria can't calm down, - "they filmed it and hid it. So *they* still have it. They showed these people this time, and the next time they'll show somebody else."

"If it was in forty-one, you can count them dead then... Some died in the blockade, some at the front... When did they start? Before the war? They used to make movies before the war, didn't they?" - she remembers. "Oh," - she grabbed the table. – "I feel sick..."

"They hid them," - Glikeria's whispering again, - "they've been hidden since the Civil war. They built storehouses for them."

Ariadna comes in.

"No," - her eyes are dry and dark, - "I can't. When I think that my own are marching there. Alive..."

Yevdokia says:

"Sit down."

She listens to her and doesn't say anything.

Glikeria puckers up her face, she's about to cry.

The knitting needles are not clicking, and a strange voice is speaking. I get up and creep on tiptoe. The guy's muttering something – his voice is hoarse, it's a bad voice. I can't hear the Grandmas because of this voice... I peep in through the crack: it's the TV talking...

"It's as if they were alive," - Grandma Glikeria rejoices, - "neither wars can hurt them, nor diseases. They stayed the way death found them – young and healthy. They're waiting for their turn: to get on TV."

"You're talking a lot of rubbish!" - Grandma Yevdokia glares at her. – "Everybody's the same, you mean, and has the same rights? They died and they're all in the same place: both the sinners and the righteous... And they're waiting their turn in the same queue?"

"Now that they're dead," - Grandma Glikeria says sadly, - why shouldn't they sort themselves out in the interim...

"No way!" - She got up, with her hand holding her back. – "They didn't sort things out in this world, and no one's the wiser? It's not like that. The Lord sees everything. Death's not war: it won't write off your sins. If you didn't get things right here, then you'll answer for it *there*."

The finger's black and sharp – it points at the TV. That guy's all scared now – he's stopped talking.

Grandma Yevdokia glances at him from time to time:

"I don't believe it! Why would they keep things like that? They're tracks. If anything happens, it'll be turned against them... Good heavens! There she is. Barefoot. You," - she threatens, - "off to bed right now! And don't think about getting up…"

I ran and jumped into bed – I pulled the blanket over my head. Then I heard her shuffling. She came and sat down on the edge of the bed..

"Don't listen to everything people say," - she says. "To all this adult talk. And if you do hear some – don't believe everything. People are all different... A person's face is deceitful. Some are sly like foxes, some are like crows. When you grow up you'll learn to tell them apart..."

She left. I threw the blanket off my head. I can't understand – what were they talking about? Is everybody dead on TV, and that guy too?

Zoya Ivanovna passes me by. "Can I congratulate you on your purchase, Bespalova?" And she looks at me sharply and steadily. I don't say anything. And I think to myself: it must be Nadka who squealed. That bitch just can't rest.

"I bought it," - I reply. – "My daughter can watch it. Didn't you tell me yourself that she's got to go to school?" - "I did tell you, that's right, but there's one thing I don't understand. Who did you swap with?" - "Why?" - I ask, - "Isn't that allowed?" - "It is," - she says, - "everything is allowed here. But you've got to come to the local committee first. Let us know, make a note of it on the list. The queue's for everybody." - "But I didn't know..." - I say, - "And then, what's the difference? We're both on the list." "There's a huge difference. There should be order in everything. This way everyone will decide to swap places ..."

I was going back to my shop and remembered. I told the girls it was someone from the assembly line. What if they ask for the surname? So I went to the galvanizing section and peeped in. He noticed me. I waved to him surreptitiously to show him I wanted to have a word.

He comes out wiping his hands on a rag. I tc˙ ˑ him, and first he frowned. Then he says: "Well... S̃ was me." And I don't know his surname: just tha͠ Nikolai... And I can't ask; what if he gets offeˑ

I went up to Mikhalych after the shift. "What's Nikolai's surname?" - I ask, - "the one from the galvanizing section?" He laughs: "Choosing a husband by the surname? He's got a good one: Rucheinikov. Well," - he squints, -"do you like it?"

Zoya Ivanovna is leafing through her papers: "Here's the assembly line, in a separate folder. Everybody who was on the list got one by the May holidays". Oh, I think, isn't she a bitch, that Nadka: she reported every detail. "I don't understand – it looks like everybody has got one..." Of course, I think: the people on the assembly line are nobility, no match for us. They're always first on the list. And the job rates are no match for ours either.

"So," - she asks, - "who did you swap with? Under whose name should I make a note?" - "Zoya Ivanovna, I lied to the girls," - I explain, - "I don't even know how it happened. The assembly line has nothing to do with it. I swapped with Nikolai Rucheinikov from the galvanizing section. He doesn't have a family, and he doesn't have a room either. We agreed that I would take a TV now, and he'll do so later, towards autumn. They should give him a room by the May holidays. He says it's about time."

She doesn't say anything, just leafs through the papers. "Funny how you and Rucheinikov understand everything... He should get a room, then? Lots of guys with families can't get one, but he should. He shouldn't have put his name on the list if he didn't need a TV. There's no lack of people who need one more." – "So," - I say, - "what do I do now? Shall I take it back?" – "What for?" - She became thoughtful. – "It's over now, all the money's paid anyway. Use it for the time being. Here," - she says, - "it says on my list: Rucheinikov N.N." - "Could you write my name instead of his?" – I ask, – "so that there's no confusion later." - "We will," - she promises, - "There won't be any confusion. We'll write everything we need to."

She took a separate sheet of paper, scrawled something on it and attached it to the top of the list with a paperclip. She looks at me: "You're a shrewd wench, Antonina, but stupid, I see. It's all right to do these things when you're young. But you aren't an innocent girl anymore. You gave birth to one little bastard already, and it looks like you're thinking of having another one. Do you want to keep spawning fatherless kids? You take advantage of the fact that the government's so kind to you – the nursery, the kindergarten, it's all handed to you on a platter. So you can have as many babies as you like, any gutter will do... "

"Why are you saying these things, Zoya Ivanovna?" - I say and my hands are trembling. – "Am I burdening anyone? I work two shifts to support her. And she only was at the nursery for three months, and she doesn't go to kindergarten". - "You should be grateful the foreman lets you work two shifts. And mind you: in America they drive people like you into the street. They don't stand on ceremony with mothers like you. Go and think it over," - she says, - "Or it'll be too late".

I go out. It's all dark in front of me. Only I only see something swirling. Like little snowflakes falling, tiny, golden. I went to the galvanizing section and called him. "Well," - he says, - "did you make a note in the list?" - "I did," - I say, - "Only she's very angry – she gives me such evil looks." - "Never mind," - he waves his hand, - "she'll look and she'll stop. Who cares if we swapped our turns: it's no great sin! I'll finish in a minute," - he says, - "will you wait for me?"

We went out. "What are you so worried about?" - he asks, - "Are you scared of Zoya?" - "I don't know... I don't feel all right... And it hurts inside." - "Come on," - he comforts me. – "Zoya doesn't bite. She must have forgotten all about it already. They have plenty of other things to do... Come on," - he invites me, - "I'll buy you a cup of coffee. There's a bakery. They have coffee and buns."

The tables are high, and there aren't too many people. "Well," - he says, - "take your pick". There are buns and pastries behind the glass. I'm lost: I don't know what to choose. "What will you have?" – I ask. - "I prefer pastries," - he says, - "those rolls with cream." I looked at the price – twenty two kopeks. He prefers them, does he? It's easy for people who live on their own to prefer pastries. "I'll have the same then." And I think to myself: at least I'll try one.

The coffee's nice and sweet. Not like that black coffee... I took a bite out of the pastry. It's nice too. It would be nice to take it to Suzannochka, I think. She'd be so happy. For me it's just an indulgence... And why not, I think. I can wrap it up and put in my bag. No, that would be rude now.Today I'll eat it myself. Tomorrow I'll buy one for her...

"Why are you frowning?" - he asks, - "don't you like it?"

"Is it true that in America they give the sack to single mothers at factories?" - "The things you worry about!" - he's surprised, - "What do you care? We aren't in America, thank God..." - "Still, it's hard to believe... They can't be that heartless, can they?" - "I don't know, - he says, - maybe they're not heartless, but they don't take care of their workers. They certainly don't give them any apartments – you've got to buy one yourself.". - "What do you mean, you buy it?" - I say, surprised, - "What, in a shop?" He shrugs his shoulders: maybe in a shop.

We go out into the street. "Thank you," - I say, - "for the treat. I've got to go now". He wipes his lips: "And how old is your daughter?" - he asks." - "She's five." - "That's good," - he nods, - "that means she'll go to school soon. Who does she look like?" - "I don't know. I think she takes after me." "Well," - he looks at me, - "you're pretty. I noticed a long time ago." "Oh, stop it!" - I laugh. – "Maybe I used to be when I was young..."

Then I see that he's looking away from me.

"So where's her father?"

My heart skips a beat. "I don't know, maybe he's dead already... Or maybe, - I whisper, - "in prison." I blurt that out and get scared myself. Where did I get that from? It was only a dream...

"Yeah," - he agrees, - "that happens... It's like my father. He lost his leg in the war. He didn't mind much at first, he was happy to be back, but then he took to drinking. It all happened at the district centre. He and some other guys broke into the granary: they were looking for vodka. They only took two bottles. But that jerk of a police inspector was walking past the granary at the time.

Dad's buddies all ran away. And where could he go, with his crutch?... So the inspector got him. When my mother found out, she ran and grovelled at the inspector's feet: 'He's a veteran, we'll pay for the vodka...' But the skunk said: 'Let the court decide.' He even mocked her: 'Veteran, you say? The law's the same for everybody. You'd all steal if we let you.' And the son of a bitch never went near the war himself – he sat it all out behind women's skirts. My father, fool that he was, took all the guilt on himself... When they brought him to the court, he was even winking and saying: 'It's all right, I'll get through it, I'm a guard, aren't I?...'

"They allowed him a visit in the end. So mother went. She came back and told everything to my grandma. I lay there and listened to everything, small as I was. 'He's very cheerful,' - she says, 'I haven't seen him like that for a long time. He says it's better to slave away in the camp rather than waste away here in the village. "Once I've served my time – all the roads are open to me: I can go anywhere I like then..."' Maybe, it was the same with yours. Was there a trial?"

"I don't know," - I hung my head, - "maybe there was, but they didn't tell me – we weren't married, you see." - "So," - he puts two and two together, - "the kid's also illegitimate?" - "Yeah, I just had her." - "What's her patronymic?" - "I registered it after him: Grigorievna. They allow that at least". - "Nikolaevna," - he winks at me, - "isn't so bad either, is it?" Good Lord, I think, what on earth does he mean? "All right," - he says, - "I'm kidding. It doesn't matter if she's illegitimate. Let her grow up. As long as she's healthy…"

Oh, I think to myself, what if... Shall I tell him? No. I remember the Grandmas: they told me not to say anything. So I don't.

"And what about your father?" - I ask, - "Did your father come back?" – "He wrote at first. Mother would send him parcels. Then he stopped writing. Not a word from him. We all thought he died in the camp... Then there was a rumour that they saw him in the district centre. But they might have confused him with somebody else. There're a lot of one-legged guys around..."

I walk across the bridge and think about America again. How can that be – apartments sold in a shop? Then everybody would want to buy one. Where would they get so many? There must a queue too...

I came out into the square – it's windy. It burns my face. I covered my mouth with a dry mitten. What if it was possible? It's scary even to imagine... I almost felt feverish. "I'd buy one too," - I whisper. It must be expensive, though... I don't care if it is, I think. Your own room, and your own kitchen. Linen curtains in the window – with blue stripes. And your own toilet: walls painted a light colour... Good heavens, I just realised: who would I leave Suzannochka with? They don't have either kindergartens or nurseries in America. However nice your apartment is, you can't leave a kid alone in it. No, I think, never mind your own flat. We'll stay with the Grandmas...

We sat down to dinner.

"Well," - I ask, - "how is it? Did you turn it on during the day?"

They sit there, not daring to look up at me.

"What?" - I say, frightened, - "Did it break down?"

Yevdokia says:

"It works all right. You can see everything."

"The news is at nine," - I remember. - "Go," - I say, - turn it on. We'll at least see what's happening in the world."

Suzannochka gets there first. She's quick, and presses the button herself.

The music's powerful and menacing: they sit together, as if they were a family.

"Hello, dear comrades," - they announce.

First they talk about a factory. The shop floors are clean, spacious, with glass partitions. Where is it, I wonder? It must be in Moscow. They're having a meeting – during a break, by the looks of things. They rounded up so many people. There's nowhere to sit. They're standing together with their heads almost touching.

Some guy, who looks like a foreman, is delivering a speech. I listened carefully: no, that's not the way things are at our factory. Mikhalych, when he has to talk, always mumbles like a sexton. And the workers are also half asleep: because the political information lecture is usually before the shift...

A woman who looks like Zoya Ivanovna comes along. With her hair in a bun. Women from the Trade Union always wear buns. She takes out a piece of paper and reads. Something about art. "The word 'artist' comes from the word 'bad'," - she says. What do the guys in the audience care, they just listen to her. They raise their hands.

I sit there watching and I can feel my finger pulsating. It was all right during the day, and now in the evening it's there again. Infection gathering right next to the nail. Yevdokia has a look:

"Go bathe it in potassium permanganate. Make the water extra hot."

Glikeria says:

"See that the nail doesn't peel off..."

Grandma Ariadna looks at the TV:

"And when exactly did they film that?" - she whispers.

Grandma Yevdokia gets angry with her:

"Can't you see that it's now... Look how fat-faced they are, the guys... Especially that one. He stuffed his cheeks so much that he's wider than he is taller. It all went into his gob."

I come back with the little jar of potassium permanganate. They've started on the foreign countries now. What if they show apartments, I think. No, they're having a strike. They're waving their arms, shouting in their languages.

The one wearing the tie says: "Cutbacks in manufacturing are taking place at present. Workers are fighting for their jobs. The bosses don't stand on ceremony. Those who are made redundant are literally thrown out into the streets."

What a bastard that boss is, I think... He needed them while they worked for him, and now that he doesn't he throws them out... Women are also there: ones without husbands. They are no doubt the first to be got rid of... Oh, I'm so sorry for them, my heart aches. They'll get up tomorrow and will have nothing to feed children... And it's not the children's fault, is it?... You don't choose where you're born...

I can still feel my finger twitching.

"Well," - I ask, - "Is that enough or what?"

Yevdokia says:

"You should squeeze the pus out first."

"How can I do that if it's under the skin?"

"You take a pin," - she tells me, - "make it red hot on the stove."

"It would hurt," - I screw up my face, - "to pierce through the quick..."

"It's dead if it's festering... It's necrosis," - Ariadna explains, - "mortification of the tissues. If it's dead it won't come to life again. And if you don't pierce it, it will kill the living part..."

I found a pin, and held it above the gas-burner. I jab and jab at the finger – the pus doesn't come out. I only scratched it raw.

Grandma Glikeria says:

"Why don't you sit up straight?... You've perched yourself on the edge, and your back's all crooked. Look out that you don't grow up lop-sided..."

Grandma Yevdokia waves her hand at her:

"Why bother talking to her... She can't hear you. She's glued to the TV... Girl, you'll ruin yourself with that TV – you'll wear your eyes out."

"Where is this?" - Grandma Glikeria asks, surprised. – "In what country?"

"They told you, didn't they? In America."

"America..." - she sighs. – "I can't imagine..."

"What's to imagine? They're people like everybody else. Remember, in the war – they had canned meat. And those cars, what's their name, Studi.. I can't remember. Now I see they have different ones. They must have sent those here and made new, better ones for themselves."

"I remember," - she brightens up. – "Studebakers. Oh, they were good cars!"

"How do you know? Did you ride in one?"

"Of course not..." - she laughs. – "Solomon Zakharych told me."

"Good Lord!" - Grandma Yevdokia shakes her head. – "Your Zakharych seems to be an expert on everything... Both on vinegar and cars. Why didn't you marry him? – He's as safe as houses. How old is he now?"

"Yes, well," - she looked thoughtful, - "he's about our age: he fought in the First World War... He went to the front as a student, from the medical faculty..."

"Look," - Yevdokia interrupts, - "they're showing something from here again... See: that's the Nikolaevsky railway station."

"The Moscow station," - Grandma Ariadna corrects her, - "now it's called the Moscow station. Look, Sofyushka," - she says. "All the streets are decorated for the holiday. When you grow up, you'll go to Nevsky. It's very nice to walk there on holidays..."

The dead are all cheerful. They walk the streets and laugh... Their streets are wide, decorated for the holiday. There are garlands hung across the streets. Cars are everywhere. And their children are dead. Here they are: walking to the music – they're not talking either...

As spring comes nearer, the sun shines brighter. Ariadna says: "The air is quiet and alive..."

When I go outside I really do feel that the air is cheerful. In winter it's dark – I go to work, than go back home. And that's it. And now I come out into the street after the shift and I sort of feel happier myself, and everything around me is brighter. Nikolai also noticed: "It's going to be summer soon. In summer everything's easier – working and partying." I nod in reply and think: maybe we'll go to the park, I'll get a chance to put on that new dress.

I can't wear it to work. The hell with those girls – they'll make a laughing stock of me. They're already teasing me: "Go on," - they say, - "your fiancé is waiting for you." Especially that Nadka: "Aren't you smart, Antonina? You went and got yourself a man on the sly, he's got goodness coming out of his ears, only short of being a party member." And sometimes she comes up to me, gives me a sly wink and says, "The toiling masses here are wondering if he's any good in bed. If he is, you could share him with the people, couldn't you – it's not nice to have it all to yourself. " And the women laugh with her.

I wave my hand at them: "The hell with you!", but I don't feel like laughing. For guys it's no big deal — he'll ask you out a few times and then he'll get tired of waiting. He's asked me to his place at the dormitory so many times... And I've always said "No, I can't do that". "Well, then," - he says – "take me to your place. Your mother will understand, won't she?" - "She will," - I say and still think to myself that I can't take him there. How? The old women are always around. And the kid...

"Don't be afraid" – he says – "I'm not fooling around. I mean it in a serious way. We'll talk and get to know each other first."

We were having dinner and I ventured to talk about it:

"I want to invite a friend over. He's a good man, he doesn't drink... We work together. What do you think?" - I ask them – "Do you mind?"

Yevdokia pursed her lips:

"What's that now?! What do we have to do with it? If you want to invite somebody over, then do it."

"Well, aren't we like a family?" - I say.

139

"That's just it," - she replies – "No one brings guests like that to the family – they find a place elsewhere."

"Bless you, Yevdokia Timofeevna!" - Ariadna comes to my rescue. – "What are you saying?..."

"If I say something, it means that I know what I'm talking about. I wasn't born yesterday. Just remember, children see everything, she'll understand it when you start leaving her with the old women so that she doesn't get in the way."

Glikeria wipes her hands on her apron with her eyes cast down.

"Maybe" – she says, - "she's right, it's not worth bringing him here..."

"See," - Yevdokia chimes in, - "listen to her. She's our expert on stuff like that."

I swallow. There's a lump in my throat. Tears are dripping from my eyes. Glikeria glances at me and waves her hand.

Ariadna moves her cup:

"I don't see what the problem is...The man will come and have tea with us."

Yevdokia jerks her shoulder.

"See for yourself…" she says. – "Remember me when you start shedding tears of blood... Where does he live – at the dormitory?"

"For the time being," - I explain, - "at the dormitory. They've promised to give him a room before the May holidays."

"Well, what will he need you for if they give him a room?"

I'm at a loss for words. Glikeria flings up her arms.

"You're mean, Yevdokia," - she says, - "You're always so uncharitable with people."

"Why am I uncharitable?" - she sneers, - "He's free: what he needs is a free woman or an unmarried girl. You didn't want a man with kids yourself, did you? And ours is a mute... People abandon their own invalid relatives – who'll pity someone like that?"

Ariadna isn't listening:

"If he comes to visit, we'll have to receive him properly, have a festive meal, and get sweets for tea."

"And a bottle," - Glikeria moistens her lips.

Yevdokia slams her chair against the floor and leaves.

I lie in bed at night and turn her cruel words over in my head. Especially this one: invalid. What if she's right? I've shed enough tears – and I'm looking for more sorrow... And not even for myself, but for my daughter... I close my eyes: and I'm afraid that the old dream might come back. What will I say, how will I explain everything?

I wake up: No. I didn't dream anything, I didn't imagine anything. There's only blackness. I go to work and think: shall I invite him or not. While I walk, I decide that I won't. If he's not willing to wait — that means it isn't meant to be.

He comes up to me during lunch, smiling. His eyes are cheerful. "Well," - he asks, - "have you thought about it? I've already bought her a present – as a way of saying hello. Kids like me. I'm the youngest in the family – my elder sisters have nephews of mine. We played together. I'm an uncle to them, but also a friend."

I went to hide the milk: what does this cursed life do to us?... Yevdokia is so fierce. Glikeria said it right: it's just not humane. As if she were living in America. Her life is not easy, of course, she has buried everyone, but to think like this – and what about Ariadna? All of her people are also lying in the ground, their bones have rotted away, but her heart is still alive…

Never mind, I think. Suzannochka can come out for a little while – she can come out to say hello, and accept the present. There's nothing for her to do at the table anyway. I'll explain that she's a shy child, and isn't used to guests. I'll tell the old ladies to keep quiet. Maybe he won't even notice. And then perhaps he'll like her – she's a smart girl and knows French. I'll say that a doctor examined her, but didn't find anything. God willing, she'll start talking one day.

Glikeria instructs me:

"You should put on your new outfit."

"OK," I say. "But make sure you ask Yevdokia Timofevna to keep quiet about the fact that she's mute."

"Why don't you do it yourself?" – she asks.

"She'll get angry," - I reply. "And she's more likely to listen to you."

I see that Glikeria is hesitating. She stands there and doesn't leave.

"You shouldn't be angry with her," - she says. - "Her life's like that – it's like a washboard: ridges and ridges... She thinks that if life around her is heathen, then all the people are heathens. But God is merciful. There are still more pure souls than not. Perhaps you'll be lucky..."

"Thank you, Glikeria Yegorovna. For your kind words, and for your wishes. You know yourself, and tell both the others – whatever happens, I won't forget your kindness. You're like a family to me. I made a mistake because I was young – it won't happen again. Don't even doubt that."

"There you go," - she says. God be with you. "You're also like family to us." – She raises her hand, and pinches her thumb and first two fingers together. – "Lower your head," - she commands. She makes the sign of the cross over me: just like my mother. She sometimes did that when I was young...

She went to the door – and turned around:

"If something does happen, don't panic – don't forget about the vinegar..."

It all seems fine: herring, pickles... I bought a bottle of "Kagora" wine. We'll boil potatoes. Fry onions in vegetable oil... I don't think I'll make a vinaigrette salad – it's not a holiday. Maybe if it was the May holiday, then I would. I'll make some pancakes. Suzannochka likes pancakes. It's all fine – but I still don't feel right. I imagine the meal: the old ladies sit and scowl. And how do I explain to him? I'll say that they're my mother's relatives, distant cousins. I'll say that I didn't know them to begin with, but now we're all one big family.

I go into the hallway – and then I remember: my dress. I was so worried about these pancakes that I completely forgot. But it's too late now...

I open the door, and there he is:

"Hello."

His voice is dignified, but he winks his eye – he's happy.

"This is great! I could smell the pies from out on the staircase. Well, where's your daughter?"

Then I notice that he's holding a box. "Suzannochka," I call. "Come out."

She looks out of the room. Her eyes are round. Yevdokia also comes out – and freezes by the door frame.

"Let me introduce you," - I say. "This is Yevdokia Timofeevna. And this is Nikolai..."

"Nikiforych is my patronymic," - he says.

"And this is my daughter, Suzanna," - I turn to her.

He holds the box out to her. She looks at me, and takes it.

"This is called a spinning-top," - he explains. "Do you know how to play with it?" – She shakes her head to say she doesn't. – "Let me show you."

He takes the box back and opens it. The bottom of it is red, and the top is transparent glass or plastic. Under the glass there is a horse and coachman in a driving box. He puts it on the floor and takes it by the handle. It turns and spins – it plays some gentle music. It starts moving… Suzannochka opens her mouth in admiration.

"Well," - he asks, - "can you do that yourself?" - The spinning-top falls on its side. – "I can see you're not very talkative. Are you scared of me? Don't be. I'm not the grey wolf."

"She doesn't talk at all," - Yevdokia says. –. "She's mute. She's been mute from birth."

I stand there and my heart pounds.

"Come off it," - he smiles – "mute. Mutes can't hear. But she can hear everything, and understands it."

"Yes, she does understand," - I cut in. – "She even understands books in French. And radio broadcasts…"

I talk and talk – my voice hurries, as though I am afraid of being late. Suzannochka picks the spinning-top off the floor. She scurries back to her room. That Yevdokia is a nasty piece of work, I think, or Glikeria forget to tell her… I look into the room.

"Stay here for the time being," - I say. – "I'll bring you some pancakes."

He moves his chair to the table.

"We had a boy in the village, a bit older than me" – he looks at the old ladies. – "He never said a word. People also said all sorts of things about him: he was mute and so on. He kept silent until

145

the age of seven, and then he started talking. He grew up and become a pioneer. He was killed in the war, true. But he was quite a lively fellow. He was scared as a child: they came to dispossess the kulaks. They drove them out into the snow in winter, but then they sorted things out – they were found to be middle peasants. So I say: it happens: the child can get scared, but later it recovers."

Yevdokia gets excited:

"What should she be scared of? No one drove us out. We live quietly."

Glikeria sits there and looks away. I shake my head – never mind, I think, I'll deal with you later.

We drink and eat – I serve the pancakes. Glikeria takes only one – she can sense something…

"What's wrong with you," - I say, - "Glikeria Yegorovna, or don't you have any appetite?"

"What appetite can I have at my age," - she replies.

"Oh," - Nikolai shakes his head. – "Delicious pancakes," - he says. "They don't cook meals like that where I come from. The people are stupid and superstitious – they say that pancakes are for funerals."

"In the country," - I say, - "of course. Where I come from they're also for funerals. It's a different matter in the city. People don't observe traditions."

"There, Yevdokia Timofeevna," - he turns to her. "You've brought up a good daughter. She's hard-working and modest, and people respect her at the factory. So do I…"

Good gracious, I realize what he means. He thinks she's my mother. I look at Yevdokia. She nods and says nothing. Never mind then. Things are better that way. What's the point in wasting my breath… I call the others by their name and patronymic, but I don't call her by her first name: I just say "you" to her.

"This boy who was silent, when he started talking, he forgot what happened before — well, while he was mute. And when he was an adult, he seemed to have forgotten it completely. And so I think: is that how being mute works? When you're silent, you have no memory?… That's probably how it is… Oh, - he remembers – they used to tease him afterwards: 'Well, Minka, how were you dispossessed as kulaks? Do you remember?' He got angry: that never happened, he'd yell! I don't remember! We're middle peasants. And that's what they called him to tease him – Middle peasant."

"What about you," - Yevdokia can't help herself. – "You must be from the poor peasants?"

"Yes," - he says. – "My father was one of the first to sign up".

"Why didn't you stay at the collective farm? It was probably good there."

Ariadna gives a curt look and shakes her head.

"What's good about it," - he frowns. "In the city things are better. Pyotr, my neighbour, served in the army and ended up in Moscow. He came to visit. He brought presents with him – calico for his mother, and a scarf. And shoes for his sister. He boasted that he had his own room, and was paid his salary in cash. My mother listened and listened to him – it was time for me to go into the army…. Never mind," - he furrows his eyebrows. "Here I am babbling… Let's drink to your health: live long and don't fall ill. And may your children be healthy, and bring you joy."

Yevdokia looks straight at him.

"That's a good toast," - she says. - "It would be a sin not to drink to it."

Nikolai drinks and puts the glass down carefully. The others don't drink. Only Glikeria takes a sip.

"Oh," – I say – "I'll go and take her some pancakes – I promised."

Suzannochka is playing with the spinning-top. She turns it, and the horse runs. I look at it and think: that's clever, the horse gallops, as if it were running over hillocks.

"Well," - I ask, - "did you like the present?"

She looks at me: her eyes are sharp and understanding. Will she really forget about this spinning top? I wonder. Let her forget then – the main thing is that she starts talking…

We finished eating. Nikolai got up.

"Thank you," he says. "It was all very delicious. Perhaps you can show me your room — just to take a look."

Yevdokia purses her lips.

The child is in there. She goes to bed after dinner. You can talk in the kitchen. We'll go and lie down too.

I take away the dishes and sit down at the table.

"Yes," - says Nikolai. – "You're mother is strict – like a general. You can't let yourself relax with a person like that. Are the others her sisters? They look very alike."

How do they look alike? – I think:

But I reply:

"Yes, something like that."

We sit and he takes my hand. I'm pleased, but I hear someone shuffling. I snatch my hand away and sit there. Glikeria comes into the kitchen. "I need some water," - she says. "I'm thirsty after the wine." She takes it and leaves.

Things quieten down. As soon as he reaches out his hand, there are steps again. Yevdokia opens the door.

"I put her to bed," - she said. – "But she won't go to sleep – she's restless. I'll go and sit beside her."

"Well," - Nikolai stands up. – "It's time for me to go. I've got work tomorrow – I should get to bed early."

We say goodbye in the corridor.

"I do miss my mother sometimes. She's strict. And then I think, no… It's more fun to be free…"

He leaves. I start washing the dishes. They're allowed to have fun in freedom… But here you rush around like that horse. Up and down the hillocks… I brushed away a tear.

Glikeria is watching television, and says in surprise:

"In the morning I thought they showed… This guest."

"The morning report was from Poland," - Ariadna corrects her, - "and that one is from Hungary."

"Who can tell them apart," - Yevdokia snorts angrily, - "for me, they're all the same…"

"What do you mean! The Poles fought for us. But the Hungarians fought for the Germans."

"Now I see, they go places…. They should have done it during the war."

"Here's what I heard," - Glikeria says timidly. - "People abroad lived better than we did – before the war."

"That's no surprise," - Yevdokia replies. "They didn't have a revolution or a civil war – why shouldn't they live well?"

"There you go…" - Glikeria gets excited. – "Vasily with no arms told me, who used to hang around the Nikolsky Cathedral."

"I remember him," - Yevdokia nods, - "he played dominoes…. His arms stopped at the elbows, and so he made artificial limbs. He also used his teeth."

"That's right," - she said. – "The war in Czechoslovakia was coming to an end. And he was full of praise for the way they lived. There were shoe factories there – Bati. I don't know if that was a nickname, or a surname. 'They made decent shoes,' he said. 'The officers, who were quicker about it, stocked up with them – but I was an idiot. I lost my arms in the war, and they would have been so useful.' After the victory…"

"He really is an idiot who talked too much," - Yevdokia agrees. – "Those people were sent out of the city. Now he's probably dead…"

I'm on my way to the storage area, and Zoya Ivanovna comes towards me: "Oh, it's good that I ran into you, Bespalova. Come to the Committee office after the shift – I've got something to talk to you about." - "What is it?" - I ask, - "We made a note on the list". - "And you're some kind of innocent, aren't you? You think we haven't got better things to do but to make notes of your TVs. Don't you sense any of your other sins?"

Her lips are bright red – she puts lipstick on them.

I found Nikolai: "Don't wait for me today after the shift. Zoya has summoned me – she's on to something. I'm sure she'll tell me off again for not sending the kid to kindergarten. But what's there for her at kindergarten? Children are nasty: they'll do her in. It's like handing her over to be tortured."

"Well, talk sense into her," - he knitted his brow, - "Explain things properly. It's different if the kid doesn't talk." - "Don't even mention it!" - I wave my hands at him. – "She doesn't know anything. Not a single person does. Just you."

"I guess that's right," - he says, - "'Once our women start talking there's no limit to what they can say." - "That wouldn't bother me," - I say, - "Let them talk. I'm afraid of something else: they'll drag her around hospitals, and mess up her life." I told him the story of the boy with dropsy. "Yeah," - he says sympathetically, - "Doctors are all different. There are some who harm you on purpose... Take the Jews," - he says. "When they found saboteurs among them, I was one of the first to vote." - "But they acquitted them later, didn't they?" - I say, frightened.

"They acquitted those". - he looks at me, - "But others may still be harming people." - "Well, it's kind of hard to believe," - I say. – "They're doctors after all..." - "What's hard to believe? The Germans were no fools, were they? They built special camps for them. I reckon that they didn't do so for no reason. Anyway," - he concludes, - "you're right to be scared. You should be."

I go to the Committee room, and I feel cold inside my heart. As if there were somebody's fingers on my throat.

In the Committee room, workmen are bustling about, mounting scaffolding. They've obstructed the whole floor with it. I pull and pull at the door handle – it's locked. "Go round to the other side," - they shout, - "It's locked here".

I go round to the other side. I open the door, and the hinges creak. They're happy to paint, but don't bother oiling the hinges... I go in. There's a strong smell of oil varnish, but it's so nice there – it's hard even to recognize the place...The walls are painted green, and the table is large and new. There are some women sitting around the table, and Zoya Ivanovna's at the head of it.

"Come in, Antonina," - she nods to me. "We've gathered a female council here – to have a talk about you. We'll talk and think about your life. Since you don't listen to me." Her voice is soft and quiet like an autumn fly. It buzzes.

I listen and can't understand what's happening to me... My hands are wet. I wipe them on my smock and look around. They have tea and cookies set out on little plates – they sit and sip their tea. They've all changed into dresses. So they must have had the time to shower too. I came dressed as I was, in my smock. I'm afraid that I smell of sweat. I found a vacant chair and perched on it in the corner.

Zoya Ivanovna tidied her bun. "Well, Antonina," - she begins. "We have received certain signals about your dissolute lifestyle. I've tried to warn you in many ways -   I'd say I took a motherly interest in you – but it didn't seem to bother you: you stick to your old ways. It's not good when a woman doesn't look after herself when she has a kid growing up, especially a daughter. What kind of example is that to her? A woman is first and foremost a mother. And everything else comes after that. As women," - she looks around, - "we understand you, but we can't let it slide – we haven't the right. So answer us: how are things between you and Nikolai Rucheinikov – are they serious or not?"

I nod my head, but I can't say a word. It's as if a stake has been driven into my throat. I can neither breathe nor speak.

"And if they're serious," - she continues, - "you should marry him. And if he starts being obstinate, we'll find a way to show him what's right. Just look at him, sitting pretty – he's found himself a woman. Now, he says, we owe him a room. That, as far as

I understand, is so he can have a place to take her. It's more convenient in a room. At the hostel you can barely turn around."

I see Valka Parmenova raising her hand asking for permission to speak. She's all smooth and wide, and has enormous tits. "You know what I think," - she starts, - "It's not really Antonina's fault. A guy, whatever he's like, is never keen on going to the register office. He'll keep changing his mind."

Zoya Ivanovna listened to her and sniffed. Only then I noticed that she had a nose like a duck's bill, and that she looks like a duck – she moves her elbows around on the table, and smartens herself up. "That's all right," - she says, - "we'll find our own justice for him. We know all about that sort who can't make up that minds."

Here everybody laughed. And I laugh with them, as if I too think it's funny.

"A woman is the guardian of the domestic hearth." - Zoya Ivanovna said, straightening her strap. - "What's that?" - Sytina asked. "Well," - she explains, - "it's a saying. The protectoress of the oven or stove," - she moved her hands as if she was shovelling coal. – "That means order in the home. Because a guy's like a little calf. If he falls into the hands of an intelligent and handy woman – he becomes like that too. All the folly goes out of him... Take mine, for example: at first he used to drink... But now I don't even bother keeping an eye on him after payday. He'll have a mug of beer sometimes, of course, but otherwise — all his pay comes home. You're a good woman, Antonina, but you give in too easily – you can't make a life like that. Only dissoluteness comes from that. And also,

I've noticed you're stand-offish. We're all in the same boat as a collective, but you keep to the side. I've told you so many times: don't ruin your kid's life. Send her to the kindergarten. But it's like talking to a brick wall. You refuse. As if the kindergarten is full of enemies..."

Verka Buragova raised her hand: "That's unheard of, to deprive a child of a happy childhood! That's not a mother, that's a stepmother!" - "Don't push it!" - Zoya Ivanovna comes to my rescue. – "Anybody can label a person – that's easy. We haven't gathered here to label one another."

She's kind after all. Thank you, I say to her, in my head. If you give women free rein – they'll peck you to death. I should have told her everything. It's too late now anyway, and it's not the right time either – I can't do it in front of everybody.

I can see that Buragova's sulking: "What's it to me?" - she pouts her lips. – "I'm worried about her kid. The child has no way to protect herself." - "Now you're talking," - Zoya Ivanovna agrees, - "It's time for you, Antonina, to come to your senses. Well," - she dismisses me, - "go now."

I went out. And I walk without knowing where I'm going. I go one way and it's locked, then another, and I come to the scaffolding again. There are bags strewn about on the floor and you can't climb over them... And my legs are weak. I lean against the wall. And there's only one thing I can think of: I've got to save the child...

I see someone coming. I look closer – it's him. "What are you doing here?" - he asks. And his eyes are kind and sympathetic. So I feel better. And indeed, what did I get so scared for, as if they were already taking her from me?... That boy with dropsy, he was really sick.

"Yes," - I complain, - "they've heaped up so many bags here, the bastards." - "That's all right," - he holds his hand out to me, - "Let's go..."

We passed the guard house, and I didn't even think about the milk in my bag. They've put one fear into me and I forgot all about the other one...

"Why did they summon you?" - he asks. "It was a female council about me." - I explain. - "Some council," - he shakes his head, - "Generals. So what's the disposition at the moment? Where's the major attack going to strike?" - "They've started in again about the kindergarten." He nodded.

"And I," - he hesitated, - "was waiting for you here, and you know, I was thinking. They'll find out anyway – sooner or later. And in the kindergarten they're small children – they'll just laugh at her. At school it's worse. They're brutes there."

I feel pain. And I nod: that's right... "But you never know where it'll be worse." - "That's true," - he agrees. - You never know. Sometimes you think – this is rock bottom. And then, you see, it all turns out to the good. There are so many stories like that! Like our Pyotr, the one who came back with presents... We had a few drinks, and he told me – I remember it well...

"It was before the war. He came to the city and didn't hope for anything at first. He thought he'd have to wait a long time yet. But they soon summoned him and told him to go and choose. They gave him three addresses to choose from – he had made his mark by that time: he was a branch manager. And the rooms were all big, spacious, even furnished. He looked at one, then at another. Then he came to see the third one and there was an old woman there sitting on a chest in the hall. As frightful as death.

"He walked past her. He didn't even say hello. He thought she was as deaf as a post anyway, and wouldn't hear him. But the old lady called him herself: 'Are you going to move in with the engineer, dear?' Pyotr was surprised: 'What engineer?' He took the scrap of paper out, - 'They gave me an order to view it, they said it was free.' – 'It's free,' - she mumbles, - 'it's free. There comes a new lodger every year like clock-work – there have been three of you so far.' – 'So where do they go?' - he asks. And the old woman looks at him, shakes her head: looks like she's either nodding or shaking because she's so old: 'Well, go ahead and move in – you'll find out for yourself...

"He looked at the room – oh, it was a good one. He said good-bye to the old woman – and went out into the courtyard. There were boys kicking a ball around. He called to one of them: 'Do you know by any chance what happened to the engineer who lived in such and such a flat?' and the boy, little chap as he was, 'Why not?' - he laughs, - 'Of course, I do... Everybody knows. He was shot.'

"So he came back to the dormitory feeling ill at ease. 'What do I care about this engineer?' - he thinks. And it's as if he hears the old woman's voice: 'Move in,' - she says, - 'move in...' The room's good and there's a lot of furniture: a wardrobe and a dinner table, and chairs. It's the best one of all three.

So for a few days he thinks about it. 'What does it matter if there was that engineer... I'm not an engineer myself. And then,' - he thinks, - 'the little chap could have got it wrong. So many people left for other places – say, for the Urals, to work on construction sites...' They were building everywhere before the war - so a lot of housing space was freed up. And then he decided: no. I won't move in there. Thank God, I can choose – there are another two.

"He went to look at them again. And the rooms were good, and there aren't too many neighbours, but his heart isn't in it. He can't help thinking about the engineer's flat. His own legs are taking him there. All right, you devil, he thinks, I'll just take one more look – for the last time. And he's already scared... And he's an upright sort of guy – not timid at all... But this time he's frightened: he feels as though he himself is the murderer. They say that they're attracted to the scene of the crime...

"He turns up, but nobody's there – just a young girl. She opens the door to him and goes to the kitchen. He looks at the chest out of the corner of his eye – there's no old woman. He goes to the kitchen. The girl's by the stove boiling something. So he asks her: 'Where,' - he says, - 'is your grandma? The one who sat on the chest?' – 'What grandma? We don't have any grandmas here.' And she keeps stirring the linen. She stirs it, snags it up and looks at it. And the linen's dirty – with spots on it. Like it's rust or blood... 'What would we want with a grandma?' And she's back to stirring the linen again. And the smell from the basin's disgusting, rotten. He stood there, smelled it and turned around to go. He didn't even have a look at the room. As if he had forgotten all about it.

"He goes out into the courtyard again. He pulls himself together – and comes to his senses. 'Well, who knows, she might have been a beggar.' There were plenty of them the village, weren't there? Especially during times of hunger. Mother told me about it.

"They dispossessed one family and loaded them onto a cart. And their Grandma was in the wood picking mushrooms. So they took them all away and left her behind. The neighbours told them: 'Their grandma will be back soon." So these city people waited a bit, then gave up and went. 'What's the use,' - they laughed, - 'in waiting?.. She'd only die on the way – and we'd have to deal with that. She'll die herself – when she comes back." They'd taken all the bread...

"So Pyotr thinks to himself: who cares about linen. He's used to dirt. The stink will air out. So he moved in in the end.

"That old woman never turned up by the way – she must have come there only once. And the rest of the neighbours were fine. They got on well. And the girl was good too – she was looking after some old man: a distant relative. He promised to leave her something so she did his washing. He turned out to be an honest old man. He left her some coins of Tsarist mintage. He kept them aside when everybody was giving up their gold. Pyotr found this out later, when he was hitting on her. They'd almost got to marrying, but the girl contracted tuberculosis – and burned out in three months. Before she died she showed him her hiding-place: right in the room, under the floor. Once they buried her, he went to check it out. It turned out to be empty. One of the neighbours must have found out about it and got there first. The house was old and the walls were thin. He squirmed about a bit, but it couldn't be helped — he couldn't prove anything, could he?.. And he had no rights. It was also dangerous to start any talk. And then the war started.

"They didn't call him up to the front – they issued an exemption for him at the plant. So, all the men from that apartment were killed and he survived. 'So,' – he said, - 'I was scared for nothing. I thought it was all for the worst. But it turned out to be for the best. It turned out to be a lucky apartment. So these prejudices, they're all superstitions,' - he explained, - 'nothing but superstitions. Who cares who lived there before? They lived there and now they don't, what of it?'..."

"How long, - I ask, - have you been in Leningrad?" - "Since I came back from the army," - he says, - "since '49. At first I'd hope and think: they're about to give me a room. And then I stopped hoping. I must have turned up too late – right after the war there were a lot of rooms available, and then the evacuees started to come back to their old places. So I've been knocking about since then. It's going to be 15 years soon... Later, they started to build but there was this queue again. They provide for those with families, or for those like you – with children. Well," - he says, - "it's all right. It won't be long now. But maybe I should have gone to Moscow – they must be building more there..."

"It's good in Moscow," - I agree, - "And their doctors are good. Our doctor here said there's one who treats muteness."

"How?" - he says, surprised. – "With pills?" - "I don't know," - I say, - Maybe with pills... Or maybe he knows some spells. They used to treat it that way in the country."

"Well," - he advises me, - "Why don't you go to the country. There're a lot of old people around: there must be some healers among them."

There's no way I can do it! - I think. The grandmas won't let me...They're church-goers. Especially Glikeria. I can't even mention something like that in their presence...

We said goodbye, and I thought: I never told him about the other thing. I had forgotten all about it. Evidently he distracted me, talking about this Pyotr of his. And then, I think, what can they do to him? They might call him up at a pinch, and tell him off... What are words, after all? They don't break bones. Especially, not for a guy... If only I could reach an agreement with the grannies: how will they look on all this?...

Everybody had gone to bed – I went to see Glikeria, and knocked on her door.

"Can I come in, Glikeria Yegorovna? I'd like to talk to you."

She gets up but looks away from me:

"It's not my fault," - she says, making excuses, - "I warned Yevdokia."

"Never mind... that's all in the past. It can't be helped now if she blurted it out. That's not what I wanted to talk about. How would you look at it," - I ask, - "if I married Nikolai?"

"He's got a nice name," - she says, - "in honor of our defender and miracle-worker."

And she crosses herself before the icon.

"That's what I say too: he pities me."

"That may be true," - she says thoughtfully, - "although it's dangerous."

"What's the danger? Because of Suzanna? But he's good with children."

"No, that's not what I meant," - she hesitates.

"Well, please, explain," - I plead. – "I have nobody else to ask."

She sits down at the table – and motions me to sit opposite her.

"See for yourself," - she whispers, - "they don't say for nothing that there's no harm in getting married as long as you're happy afterwards... You're young yet, you don't remember everything. And when I was young I lived with a count."

"What do you mean with a count?" - I say amazed, - "Are you a countess then, Glikeria Yegorovna?"

I ask her, but I don't believe it myself. Countesses must be different, I'm sure. I saw them in a book: they have dresses like church bells and hats with feathers on their heads. I've gone through her wardrobe so many times – it's all rags.

"What countess..." - she laughs quietly. – "We just lived together. My mother was one of their serfs. He was good and kindly and loved me a lot. He proposed to me. But I didn't dare: there was no way I could do it! I didn't have any manners. So I told him. And he laughed: 'You're the most beautiful of all, my girl!' And he said it in such a way that I made up my mind. Then came the revolution. So he begs me: come away with me. We have a house in France – we'll sit it all out there.

"And I'd had a daughter just before that. And they sent her to the country – to Chernigovskaya province. They had an estate in those parts."

"Why did they send her there?" - I ask, surprised.

"Well, I told you we weren't married. The child was born out of wedlock, illegitimate."

Good Lord, I think... They were monsters back then. Now, thank God, it's not like that.

"So did they send all of those children away?" - I ask.

"Well, yes, they tried, of course. They tried to hide the shame. They sent some to the orphanage, some to other families. Poor families would take children in for money."

Oh, I think to myself, it's worse than in America. They only give them the sack there. They don't make them send their kids to an orphanage. Thank God for the revolution... They would have taken Suzannochka away, God forbid...

"I felt sad for a while, but then I was all right. I didn't really see her. They took her from me straight away. And baptised her without me. He

told me later they called her Serafima. So I said:
'We'll go, but I'll fetch the child first. So that we're
together – and then come what may...' And he says:
'Why move the child? We'll come back in three
months at the most,' - he said. And I said: 'No.' I
dug my heels in. So he let me go. The trains weren't
running as regularly as they used to. It took me a
while to get there, and when I did, they told me she
was dead. I grieved and I cried for some time, and
then I couldn't get out of there. There were a lot of
gangs roaming around. I only came back in a year
and he wasn't there. And other people were living
in his house. So many of them in each room! There
was no place for me. I met our yard-keeper. He
occupied a place in the third floor. And he used to
live in a closet... So he told me: "His Excellency, the
count, has gone abroad". He must have waited and
hoped till the last. But then they started to shoot
them, and so he fled...

"I missed him, and cried a lot. And now I
think: say, we'd have got married... Then what?
A lover is one thing. They don't wait for them all
that long. But a wife... One's got no choice but to
wait. So he'd have waited until they shot him and
me together. There were many of those wives
who died because of their husbands... They take
him first, her after... It looks like God saved me.
Look at Yevdokia's family. They took the elder
son and then the wife too. And she was such a
fine lady... No match for me. And the younger
one too. He worked for the NKVD. Then came
their turn – and they both vanished, him and his
wife."

"Whose turn?"

"The ones who worked at the NKVD. Only it was later. They let them live a bit longer."

She sits there, sad.

"What do you think? That I've always been an old hag? Well, there was someone during the war, proposed to me: a good man, a Jew."

"A doctor?" - I ask.

"Yes," - she nods. – "How did you guess?"

"There were a lot of Jewish doctors back then." - I say, looking away from her.

"That's certainly true," - she says happily. – "Jews are good doctors. And Solomon Zakharovich especially. They'd seek his help in all situations. And he was so impressive himself. He resembled my count. Not by his face, but by his manner. He was also a widower. He had two girls. I almost made up my mind. And he says: 'If the Germans take the city, they'll shoot me and the girls among the first...' So I thought: I'd be shot together with them. I'd wait, I decided. We'll see when our guys get the better of it, I thought.

"After the war he started on it again – marry me, he kept saying. We won, so, I thought, it was my destiny to marry him. But I was still biding my time... And I didn't even know why I was doing it. It's like some evil spirit was telling me to wait and see how it went. And something did happen. They planned to deport the Jews. And I thought that if I were married to him they'd take me with him. It turned out all right, thank God. But then I decided that I'd had enough. God had saved me twice, and there might not be a third time. So I had no business getting married. It would have been different if it had been a great love, where it doesn't matter if you live or die, as long as you're together. But with a cool head, you're better off scraping by alone. Well," - she says, - "I've told you everything. It's up to you, though. We're old, we won't last long. And if anything happens, they'll put her in the orphanage."

"They had a female council today. They said they were going to take measures to make him marry me."

She beckons me closer with her finger and whispers into my ear:

"They aren't just doing that for nothing. They say they want to protect you, but all they can think about is how to tie you to someone so that it's easier for them to ruin you..." - She got up. – "Otherwise," - she says, "marry him, if you're ready to sacrifice everything. Both your life and your daughter. And now," - she asks me, - "I want to be alone. I need to pray."

I left her, and sat in the kitchen. I thought about her bitter words. I sat there and sighed for a while. I needed to do some washing. The linen had been put to soak a few days ago – it would soon start stinking. I tried to lift the basins, but my hands wouldn't hold them: I couldn't stop thinking about what she'd said. I try to understand if I'm ready to be ruined... No, I decide, I'm not. I feel too sorry for my child...

I lay down and I didn't wash anything in the end. My head is full of gloom. I'm almost afraid to think. I drew the blanket over my head, pulled myself together and asked myself: "What if it was my Grigory – would I be willing to die together with him?" And the minute I thought that I felt so light-hearted, as if my heart were a lark. "I would," - I answered myself, - "I would..." And I was so full of joy, as if I were about to get married. I nuzzled into the pillow.I'm crying and thinking: in the country, brides always cry...

Yevdokia pulled on a strand of yarn:

"They go to the Mausoleum... Why do they go? To look at the deceased? They don't have enough of their own. So they need to look at someone else's... Well, so?" - she put the skein aside. – "Did she come to talk to you? Or did I imagine it?"

Glikeria looks away:

"She did."

"What about?"

"Nothing, just a dress." - she says, - "She wants another one for summer."

Yevdokia screwed up her left eye:

"Aren't you good at it?.. You shouldn't have said anything. Your lies stick out a mile."

"She wants to get married," - Glikeria admits, - "To that Nikolai."

"Here it comes,' - she knitted her eyebrows. She's as black as thunder-cloud. – "That's the end of our quiet life... It'll be the same as it used to be. They'll forget about Sofia and have screaming babies."

"Well," - Ariadna looks away from the TV and turns the sound down a bit, - "we'll stick up for her if anything happens..."

"And they'll listen to you, of course. You've got some hopes! Did she ever listen to what you said – that Sytina woman? You sat with your tail between your legs when she was here. That Nikolai's a night cuckoo... So what did you say? What was your advice?" - she asks, - "to marry or not?"

"Well what can I do..." – Glikeria moves her finger.- "I said it was up to her – that it was her life."

"Well, aren't you great," - she praises Glikeria. – "Gave a good piece of advice, didn't you? Only keep it in mind for the future: Nikolai will count every nickel and look into your mouth to see how much you've eaten. With your retirement benefit you'll be nearly starving..."

"We managed to live on it before..." - she answers.

"Yes, before their reform. Your 370 rubles used to count for something. And now? Don't forget how the prices have gone up. Antonina talks, and I take note. You'll live like a dog: on bread and water. Don't you lick your lips at wine and herring?.. You got used to living in clover in the master's house."

Ariadna looked and listened – and slammed her fist on the table:

"It's embarrassing even to listen to you". - she says, - "This might be Antonina's only chance... One that only comes once in a lifetime. What if it's love?"

"Love..." - Yevdokia turns her nose up. – "She should have thought about it when she was by herself... But with a kid, and one like Sofia... In any case," - she sums up, - "my opinion is: when the child's of age then she can marry. Whoever she likes, even five guys at a time. As for this love of yours... It would be much better if there was no such thing..."

"You're so coarse," - Ariadna shakes her head, - "and love means such happiness..."

"That's right... They made your heads spin in those grammar schools. Come on, tell me, so that we can rejoice together, if you got much happiness out of that love of yours. You must have married for love... But I didn't. My parents arranged it. And now look how it ended for both of us. That's right. And listen what I tell you. Remember in the war there was this song about the dugout? They used to play it on the radio.

"I was sitting in the reception ward, and the doctor comes in, Klavdia Timofeevna... She had a little son who was born just before the war. And her husband was at the front. He fought here near Sinyavino. One month he doesn't write, two months, There hadn't been a letter from him for two months and then they started to play that song on the radio nearly every day... She listened to it and heartened up: 'This song '- she says, - 'is about me. I can't even tell you how much I want my husband to come back. Every night I think about where he is and how he is... And this song's like a prayer. I don't believe in God, of course,' - she says, - 'but I do believe in love... That's the only thing that gives me hope'..."

"Near Sinyavino?" - Ariadna asks.

She nodded.

"Did the kid survive at least?" - Glikeria felt for the ball and started to draw the yarn between the fingers.

"They took him away. It was her mother who looked after him until she passed away. She didn't last very long, she died in the first winter. So the doctor would bring him to the hospital with her. Then later she couldn't do that any more, she was too weak for that. It would have been all right in the summer... But in the winter... She even lived close by, but it was still too hard to carry him across those blocks of ice... The chief doctor watched her for a while, and then ordered for the kid to be sent away with the orphanage. She tried to leave together with them. But they wouldn't let her, as she was liable for service... Don't you remember her? Fair-haired – very thin... Rich long plaits – she used to arrange them around the head... What was it called?

"The wreath of peace?" - Glikeria suggests.

"No," - Ariadna wrinkles her forehead, – "that was after the war..."

"When she packed his things she embroidered letters everywhere. What do you call them?.."

Ariadna whispers:

"Initials."

"That's right. She would come talk to me about it. 'Who knows,' - she says, - 'They keep a record of the children, of course, but mine's so small, he doesn't remember his own name. But they'll put it together if they look at the letters.' She'd ask me: 'What do you think, Yevdokia Timofeevna?' And how could I tell her what I thought...'

"Did they bomb them out on the ice?..." -Glikeria pulls at the thread and rips it.

"No," - Yevdokia comforts her, - "they got over Ladoga all right. They went as far as Ulyanovsk. That's where he disappeared."

"Really?" - Ariadna says, amazed, - "Without a trace?"

"What do you mean? There was a trace. They sent her an official paper."

"So, did she go to see the little grave?"

"She went after the war, but not right after... It was three years or so later. Don't you remember how it was at first? People were afraid to leave: you could leave all right, but they'd only let you back here with a pass."

"I remember that," - Glikeria says. – "Marya, the matron from the hospital, went to the country – her mother was dying. And she couldn't get back by hook or by crook. She tried everything. And then the time was up. They registered her at the collective farm. She did come back later, but her room was taken. The story was that the neighbour moved into her room, and took it over. She tried to get in, but he wouldn't let her pass. And Marya was even stupid enough to beg him: 'I'd just like to pick up some things.' And he says to her: 'There aren't any. Go away – you country trash. Look for your things in the scrapheap.' – 'What do you mean in the scrapheap?' - she asks, - 'There were good dresses, and pans too.'

"Oh, how could that be?" - Ariadna says sadly. – "She should have gone to the house-manager..."

"What for? That neighbour of hers worked with food supplies. All through the blockade . He exchanged food for gold. Some woman would come and bring him a ring or some earrings in a piece of cloth. She'd unfold the cloth and cry. He'd give her half a loaf of bread, and she'd cry even more: 'The child's dying,' - she'd say, 'I'm giving you the last things I have. Couldn't you add another half a loaf...' And he pouts his lips and says: 'The prosecutor,' - he says, - 'will add some for you. Take it or leave it.' So who could she turn to for help?..."

"Why didn't Marya inform you know who?" - Ariadna's surprised again.

"Well, he used to feed her too from time to time so that she wouldn't talk. He'd give her a piece and say: 'I can always buy off the authorities. They're people too. They serve the country all right, but they still get hungry...' How did they manage to carry stuff out? They searched everybody at the bread factories..."

"Well," - Yevdokia says, - "he wasn't just anybody then, the neighbour. He must have been someone with authority. What did they care? They didn't have to take anything through the guard-house. War or no war. It was even more convenient..."

"That's right. He must have bribed the house manager. So he took the order out for him."

"Oh," - Yevdokia shakes her head, - "those people got rich all right. They searched other people's apartments. They'd get in as soon as the owners died... Just like rats. They'd take everything: furniture, crockery, all the home utensils... There used to be rich apartments around, they looted them all in the war."

"You make it sound as if was only the house managers who robbed..." - Ariadna says angrily, -

"There weren't any of them after the Revolution, but still... And furniture was chopped up for firewood."

"Of course it was," - Yevdokia pursed her lips. – "the master's furniture. And why not?"

"So did that fair-haired woman find his grave?"

"Fair-haired..." - Yevdokia mocks her. – "Klavdia Matveena is what you should call her. She was very strict – you have to remember her."

"Well, I don't," - Glikeria throws up her hands, - "it's been such a long time."

"Of course, you wouldn't" – Yevdokia sneers, - "you were having your little affair back then: how can you remember...

"She got to Ulyanovsk and went to the police to make inquiries. She asked them: 'Where's the orphanage? The one that was evacuated from Leningrad.' She showed them the slip of paper. It had a number and a stamp on it. They checked it by the number, and didn't find anything. The orphanage must have passed through their city. They would have taken the dead off the train and gone on their way. 'Maybe in some ditch,' - they said, - 'by the railway. They'd take a lot of bodies off the trains – no one had time to register all of them.' She walked back and forth, and stood on the embankment – she bowed her head down to her son. So she went away empty-handed..."

Ariadna wiped her eyes.

"Good Lord..." - she said sadly. – "Poor, poor things. They're still lying in ditches..."

Nikolai comes towards me, grey in the face. His lips are dark and chapped.

"Come with me now, - he says, - Did you go running to them yourself, or did someone give you the idea to do it?" - "To do what?" - I say, surprised. - "What? To go to the factory committee. I treated you fairly," - he sounds hurt, - "and that's how you pay me back..." - "How do I pay you back?"- I say, frightened." "Don't you play the fool." – His eyes are boring a hole through me. – "They gathered a female council, did they?.. And why exactly? The guys explained it all to me: you went to the factory committee and the committee went to the female council. And that lot is only too happy to help... Well, why aren't you saying anything? Did they raise the question? "

"What question?" - I still don't understand. - "To make me marry you," - he says, not looking at me. "They started it themselves," - I say hurriedly, - "I didn't even mention anything." - "That's right," - he wrinkles his face. – "So they did raise it. That's the truth then..." - "What does it matter if they did raise it... Let them. They'll talk about it a bit, and then forget it." - "As for forgetting it, I'm not so sure, and as for talking about it, they already have..."

Good Lord, I think...

"So what?" - "So what do they care?" – he smirks, - "They don't mince words. They took me off the list." - "What list? For the TV? Don't you worry: I'll give it back to you."

At that he clenched his teeth and groaned: "What TV! They took me off the list for the room... They promised I'd get one by the May holidays... Now they won't give me one."

I hear his words, but still my head's empty.

"What do you mean? You've been waiting for so many years..." - "Easy," - he's almost crying. – "They decided to give me a separate apartment if I get married. An apartment for the family. And the foreman took their side too: 'Watch it Nikolai,' - he said... 'The women on the female council have got really wound up this time: they say that they'll make you if you refuse.' But mind you: I'll talk too. Don't you think I won't," - he looks at the wall. – "I'll tell them everything if it they call a meeting. I'll say that there was nothing between us. That you're trying to hang a child on my neck. An invalid. That you kept it secret till the last. I didn't even know..."

It was only then that I understood. Everything darkened before my eyes. I tottered.

"And when is this meeting?" - I whisper. - "In a month. They give us a month to sort it out between ourselves and then the community will interfere. Damn them all..." - he swore a dirty oath.

I grab on to him: my back has gone weak. That's it, I think, they'll take my daughter away. I didn't even notice myself sinking.

"Don't ruin her," - I say putting my arms round his knees. – "Don't ruin the child..."

He tries to wrench his legs free. "What's come over you?..."- he mumbles, - "Get up, get up."

He's pulling me up... But I can't get up. I'm grovelling at his feet. He breaks away finally: "Get up off the floor right now." - He lifts me and puts me against the wall. He's red all over. – "Stop making a monster out of me... You did it all yourself. You think I'm not sorry for the kid? You've got a month.

Think of something – it's none of my business what it is. You'll explain it to the women yourself."

"What can I think of?" - I say, crying. - "That's up to you," – he looks away. "Say you've got some disease – some women's thing. Say that's why you can't marry."

"Oh, thank you..." - I hurry to say. – "Don't you worry: I'll do whatever it takes to make them leave you alone."

He turns round and walks away.

I run home, barely able to feel my legs: I need to talk to the grandmas straight away. They didn't work in hospital for nothing, did they? They'll advise me about diseases.

I open the door: Suzannochka meets me there smiling. She's holding the spinning top. I squirm when I see it.

"Don't you dare play with that rotten toy!" – I shout.

I snatch it away from her out. She starts crying. Yevdokia looks into the hall.

"Good Lord!" - She cries out. – "What's going on here? What are you scaring the child for?... Let's go, my little dove," - she calls, - "Let your mother calm down..."

She takes her away. And I think: what's wrong with me? It's as if I'm possessed. The kid has nothing to do with it. I go to Yevdokia's room and hold the toy out to her:

"It's all right, darling," - I say, - "Go on, play with it..."

We had dinner, and sat down in front of the TV: the news was on. My eyes can see what's on the screen, but I can't understand the words. They talk, but for me it's as if they're speaking some foreign language. There's only one thing in my head: how to make up some kind of disease...

Well, that's all for now, I think. They started on the weather. And there weren't any strikes: they must be having a break from them... And maybe the previous ones had an effect – made the owners think...

Ariadna put the kid to bed:

"Shall we have tea?"

"Let's," - I reply, - "Especially since I've got something to talk to you about."

"No doubt you have," - Yevdokia put the knitting needles together and stuck them in the ball. "You've got only one thing to talk about now – we know what."

"Good Lord," - I say, - "Yevdokia Timofeevna, - I'm in trouble..."

Glikeria gasps:

"You didn't protect yourself? Didn't I tell you what to do?"

"It's not that,"- I lower my head, - "There wasn't anything between us."

I can see that they're completely at a loss. Yevdokia's as white as death. She looks around at the door:

"Have they taken him away?"

"Who?"

"Well, that Nikolai."

"Taken him where?" - Then I realised what she meant. – "On what charge?" - I say, surprised. – "A plague on that tongue of yours."

"Thank God, then," - she crosses herself. – "If it's not that, then it's hardly trouble, is it?"

I explained it all to them in detail: about the factory committee and the female council. And I mentioned the room too, of course. I only didn't tell them how I grovelled at his feet. I was ashamed of myself.

"Well," - Yevdokia chews her lips, - "what's your trouble then? Serves this dog right. That'll teach him how to do those kinds of things."

"But you don't know why they're making him," - I explain, - "They say they'll give him an apartment if he marries."

"Now I'm totally confused. So what do the bastards mean?"

"Never mind them," - I say, - "He doesn't want it himself. He says he doesn't want to have anything to do with a disabled child."

"I see," -Yevdokia shakes her head, - J"ust look at that brute. He doesn't want a disabled child, does he?.. I'll show you who's disabled! She's ten times smarter than any talkative one...What are you so sad about, you fool? There are no suitors for you, and this guy isn't a suitor either."

Then I feel my heart getting faint again.

"It's not about me, though... You know what he threatens? He says he'll tell them the truth. He'll say I hid it from them that the child is sick... If they find out, they'll drag her around hospitals or put her in a boarding school. He only gave me a month to think of some disease. Some women's disease with means you can't marry."

"Pah! And that's it?" - Yevdokia spits into the corner. – "Just that? Well, think of something then. There's no shortage of diseases... Barrenness, tumours. All you've got to do is choose."

"Tuberculosis too," - Glikeria helps. – "Or prolapse of the uterus. After the war so many women suffered from that – they lifted too many heavy things."

"They'll ask for a certificate, won't they? They won't just take my word for it."

"You go and check with the doctor," - Glikeria suggests, - "Almost everybody has something wrong with them. They'll be sure to find something if you go to them. So you'll get your certificate. And I don't think they understand much at that factory committee. What do they care what kind of disease that is?"

"Oh!" I cheered up. Why not go indeed?... "My stomach gets all twisted anyway every time I lift something. I'll give them a piece paper and they'll leave us alone."

I cheered up so much that I even started with the washing. I lifted basins happily: doctors find something as soon as they look at you... They've got whole books full of diseases. Perhaps they'll find one for me...

I went to bed: there was some spotting again. But that only comforted me even more.

I worked until the lunch break, and went to talk to the foreman. "I need to go to the women's health clinic." - I say, - "Is it all right if I leave a bit earlier?" - "You've chosen a fine time, haven't you? It's the end of the quarter. Couldn't you have done that a bit earlier, or wait a bit? Have you got a temperature or what?" - "No," - I look away, - "it's a woman's problem." - "Well, surely that you could do after the shift!" - he gets angry. - "I can't." - I say. – "There's a queue there. They won't see me if I come late..."

I go to the doctor. She's a nice young woman. And she's got curls like they do on TV. They've got a nice job, I think to myself. Not like us in the shop. We've got our heads covered – you can't see our hair under the headscarf.

"When was the last time you were here, Bespalova? I haven't got your patient chart."

"Well," - I say, - "I haven't been sick really. I came when I was pregnant, of course. Only it was a different doctor here."

She asked me all about the child and the labour. She filled in a form.

Have you had any abortions?

"No," - I say, - "I haven't."

"Do you have sexual relations with anybody?"

Good Gracious, I get scared...

"No," - I say, - "Of course I don't."

And think: well, in my dreams...

The doctor noted something in her paper.

"All right. Do you have any complaints?"

"Well," - I say, - "I don't know... My belly hurts sometimes... After lifting things at work and at home too... It sort of pulls at the bottom."

"All right," - she gets up from the chair, - "undress, please."

I started to take my clothes off: Good Heavens, my tights have patches sewn on them. I didn't notice it in the morning. I crumpled them and stuck them under the clothes. I climbed on to the examination chair. And I made a note to myself: she's tidy, she's washing her hands under the tap.

"Fold your hands on your chest, please." - she orders.

She felt around for a while and frowned.

"I'd like to get a certificate to show to the factory committee," - I say.

But she doesn't listen to me.

"Do you often have discharges? With a lot of blood? Have you been spotting for a long time?"

"It happens" – I admit. "It's been going on for a year now."

"So why" – she screws up her face, - "didn't you come to me earlier? How old's your child?"

"She'll be six soon. She starts school in a year."

"You'll have to have an operation." - She goes back to her desk and looks into the form, - "And it's urgent. Start looking for someone who can take care of your child. Have you got family?"

What operation, I wonder? There was nothing between us...

"I had a mother," - I say, - "She died."

"You've got a tumour, Bespalova. A tumour in the uterus."

"But isn't there any other way?" - I say confused, - "Must I have an operation? Can't I take some pills or use some ointment?"

"What pills!" - she shakes her head, - "You should have come earlier. Now it's very advanced."

"And..." - I remembered what my business was. – "With this disease... Can I marry?"

She puts her papers aside and scowls:

"Are you planning to get married, Bespalova?"

"No," - I reply, - "I don't mean... I was just wondering. Who knows what the future may hold, what if things work out... Once things didn't work out."

"You can," - she looks away. – "It's all possible. Just don't admit to your husband that your uterus has been removed... So, take your tests and come to me. But don't delay now. The sooner the better."

"But what about the certificate," - I recall, - "the certificate?"

"You'll get the certificate after the operation, at the hospital."

"What about tomorrow?" – I ask, flustered. – "Do I go back to the shop floor?"

"What shop floor!" – she shrieks. "Home, go home. You're bleeding..."

I go out, and can't collect my thoughts. How is that going to be? An operation... I go into the courtyard and sit down on a bench. I think to myself, I lived decently... Some girls really sleep around, and nothing happens to them. Take that Nadka Kazankina... She can't even remember who she's been with. She has one after another.... Every year she has an operation. She recovers and off she goes again. So many men have been with her...

"It's my right," she says. "It's not prohibited by law anymore…" But why did this happen to me, I wonder…

I felt so bitter. I sat there collecting my thoughts. "What if it also counts if it happens in your dreams… I wonder… We did commit a sin…"

I get to the baker's, and it's hurting down there. The doctor poked around: why did she have to press so hard…

The old ladies greet me: "So, did you get a certificate?" – "No, not yet," - I reply. "But they found a disease. I've got a tumour in my uterus." – "Lord," - Yevdokia flings up her hands. – "What do you have that from? You're still young… A tumour in the uterus is something you get when you're old."

"How do you feel, then?" – Ariadna intervenes.

"It aches now and then, and there's sometimes spotting. The doctor also said: go home, you're bleeding." – "Oh well," - Ariadna reassures me. – "Bleeding happens for many reasons. Maybe you've got a polyp…. Did they schedule treatment?" – "What treatment," - I reply. "They said they were going to cut it out."

I see that she's shaking her head.

"Perhaps everything will all be fine," – I say.

We sit down, and Yevdokia complains again.

"I've been feeling bad since morning. I sat down to knit, and the yarn gets tangled up. And the loops are crooked – I can't work out where's the front, and where's the back."

"You should have taken a simpler pattern," - Glikeria suggests.

"What do you mean, simpler: it's all tangled. I've knitted it so many times, but today I can't control my hands... And I dreamt of cats..."

"Were they black cats?"

"All kinds," – she replies. – "It's like I'm sitting down. And around me are balls of wool. The cats play with them, and roll them with their paws. I want to get up and shoo them away with a broom, but I don't have the strength... I used to dream of these balls of wool. But this is the first time I've dreamt of cats... Things look bad for her," - she says. "At that age *processes* happen very quickly...

"I remember one woman had it in her breast: they cut and cut her, but she still died after half a year. And she was hopeful, the poor thing – she looked into everyone's eyes. What did the doctors do? They reassured her, of course. But among themselves they talked differently. She died and left two children behind. For her husband to look after."

"What are you saying!" – Glikeria says, frightened. – "There are different sorts of tumours: maybe there is no *process*... And the doctor's so young. At the hospital, the doctors are experienced – they'll take a good look at her. I was told about a man who was brought to the oncology section right before the war."

Yevdokia interrupts.

"To us, you mean?"

"No," - she replies. "To some other one. At Mezhdunarodnoye, I think."

"So? What happened?"

"They cut him open. They found metastases. Terrible ones – in the liver, and the kidneys. They didn't tell him, but he read it himself, on his patient's chart."

"How did he do that?" – Yevdokia asks, doubting. "They keep the patient's charts locked up in the doctors' rooms."

"He had an affair with a nurse," - she explains. "She showed him."

"An affair!" – Yevdokia shakes her head. "Metastases – at what stage? Hardly the time to have an affair…"

"Oh," - Glikeria sighs. – "In these matters all kinds of things can happen – I've seen it for myself. The person seems to have one foot in the grave, and then… We had one tuberculosis patient…

"Stop it!" – Yevdokia interrupts. – "Must you go on about that?"

She falls silent, offended.

"Well," - Ariadna says, - "what happened next?"

Glikeria sighs.

"Well, the war broke out. They let him go home. To die. But he went to the military enlistment office. He thought that if he was going to die anyway, he may as well do so usefully – at the front. And they had a quota to fill at the enlistment office, for volunteers. So they took him. Those men are going to their deaths anyway, they thought…"

"The enlistment offices also had their own boards," - Ariadna says, doubting. – "They checked people's health."

"But that was in forty-one," - she says anxiously, - "remember what it was like…"

"That's for sure," - Yevdokia sighs. "They didn't know what to do…"

"So, off he went. To start with, of course, he felt pain and weakness. He was looking for death. He'd seen how cancer patients died… For every mission, he was the first: for an attack, or reconnaissance… He saw that death was avoiding him: it was mowing down the healthy, but missing him. And then they started sending paratroopers by Sinyavino. In the morning, they'd drop 200 men, and count them in the evening. They were lucky if 10 were left, and they'd be crippled. He decided to ask if he could join them. He thought he'd give death one last test. What would they care, if he wanted to go himself? 'All right, off you go,' they said. He got ready, he wrote a letter to his family, and set off. No one knows what it was like there. But he was the only one to come back. He was delirious, he didn't recognize anyone. He only saw the dead people who he had gone on the mission with. But a while later, he recovered.

"He felt that the pain had gone away. So had the nausea, and the weakness. He made it to Berlin. He came back, and thought that he should go to hospital. For a check-up. The doctors looked at his chart, and were amazed. He should have been dead already. But he was alive, and decorated with medals. They examined him, and found that he had no metastases – all his tissues were healthy."

"How did that happen?" – Ariadna gasps. – "Where did they go?"

"They disappeared," - she replies. – "As if they had never been there. They vanished of their own accord. He must have been religious. Miracles happen to the faithful…"

"All sorts of things can happen with cancer," - says Yevdokia. "I've also heard it's like fighting fire with fire. If a person experiences fear, or grief. But not just any grief, a deathly grief. The worst kind there is… Death fights against death – like dogs. Sometimes one dog wins, and sometimes they both retreat: they wound each other…"

"I've read about that," - Ariadna recalls. "But the book put it differently: Good against Evil."

"I don't know about that," – Yevdokia muses. – "I've seen death fight against death. Fear against fear. But good against evil… When was this written?"

"A long time ago," - she waves her hand. – "Before the revolution."

"Well, if that's so… In those times, life was different, and so was death. And evil and good were different. Their powers used to be identical – it wasn't certain which would win… But I say that perhaps it was a special case," - she frowns – "and evidently he had a good surgeon. He cut out everything properly. Things aren't like that anymore. I'm not sure about the doctors today. The old doctors studied in Tsarist times: those would be the ones to see…"

"They also studied before the war," - Glikeria says. "They'd send students and Solomon Zakharych would teach them – they'd be rushed off their feet. They'd follow him around, making notes. He'd ask them sternly about what to do, and how…"

"Wait a second," - Yevdokia recalls. – "That Solomon of yours is a gynaecologist."

"You're clutching at straws!" – she raises her hands. – "Never mind about him now… I haven't seen him for 20 years or so: perhaps he's dead."

"But these days they just get out the knife without thinking," - says Yevdokia. "They don't care if it's a person or a dog. But then what? How are we going to cope with the child by ourselves?"

"Good lord," – Ariadna is the first to think of it. – "If something happens, she won't stay with us. She'll be taken to an orphanage. We're no one to her…"

"What do you mean no one?… We've brought her up since she was tiny… Is she really better off at an orphanage?"

"Quiet, now" – Yevdokia snaps. – "Ariadna is talking sense. There've been so many cases when children weren't allowed to stay with their real grandmothers, and who are we… Oh," - she groans. – "I'm a hopeless fool. I didn't think things through myself, and here comes grief. It's come to our home and is banging on the gates. That's it" – she says. "Zakharych is our only hope. We've got to hunt him down, at any cost."

"But where?" – Glikeria is frightened. – "Shall we look for him around town, knock on people's doors? How much walking would be able to do – with legs like ours? And what if he's dead? We can't bring him back from the other world…"

"Even if he is in the other world," - Yevdokia's face is mournful, and every bone is visible. – "He's our hope and salvation. There's no one else we can count on."

She crosses herself. – "Your words are blasphemous," - she says. – "Salvation is from God."

"Don't frighten me with the Lord," - Yevdokia says, pursing her lips. "I'm no less of a believer than you are. But God has backed away from our life. Did he used to allow such things to happen? I've been on my knees all my life: did my prayers make any difference?... Never mind – we are damned. But I'm not giving up Sofia. Up yours," - she gives the finger. – "That's for those bastards. That's all I've got to say."

"How is that?" – Glikeria sits there, pale. – "We're nothing against them. They'll crush us without noticing …"

"Well, I don't hold on to their version of life," - she says. "I've lived and seen plenty, thank God. I have something to tell them in the next world. You can't even imagine in hell the things that have happened on earth. So there's no point trying to frighten me. I've trembled all my life – at least I'll stand up before I die… But if you have your doubts, then sit and think it over…"

"There's nothing for me to think about," - she says, offended. "People are used to making a fool of me. This is what I say: if someone's alive, they can always be found. I saw it in a film: before the war. There was this guy who fell in love, but the girl vanished…"

"Pah," – Yevdokia spits, – "what's that got to do with it?"

"He found out her name and went to the register office. He has a rare surname – Rafulson, or Rifalson. I mixed it up when I was young," - she blushes, - "and I was embarrassed to ask a second time… Their people are very easy to take offence."

"So, you're frightened too," - Yevdokia shrugs.

Ariadna looks at them. - "Where is this register office?"

They don't say anything – they just look at each other. They haven't gone any further than the church for so many years.

"Never mind," - says Yevdokia. – "My tongue hasn't gone numb, thank God. We'll find out from others. We'll ask at Nikolsky, or at our office. We have to go there before the May holidays anyway – to stand in line for flour…"

"What about Sofyushka," - Ariadna remembers. – "Where is she?"

"In her room. She's cutting snowflakes out of paper. Glikeria taught her, and now you can't tear her away from it. She's used up so much paper."

"They're quite beautiful, as if they're made of lace. She'll cover the whole earth with them, I tell her. And then we won't need winter. Spring is coming soon, I say. What do we need snow for?"

They look out the window, and it really is snowing. As if there isn't going to be any spring.

IV

GLIKERIA

Glikeria takes down the tea service from the shelf – what's left of it. There are five cups, and four small plates. There are just three saucers. "Don't bother with the saucers," Yevdokia orders. "Last time there weren't enough to go round, and that was no good. Better put the plates out instead. Ariadna will provide the ornamented spoons."

Glikeria fusses and looks around. "Let's sit in your room," she says. "Solomon Zakharych is well-off: he's not used to the kitchen." – "What do you mean, in my room?" – "Oh," she remembers. "Antonina is lying there."

"That's how things happen," Ariadna rubs the spoons. "We've been living near each other for so many years and never met. But we used to walk past his house..." – "He's been there for ten years now. He exchanged with his elder daughter. They live in separate apartment now, all on their own." "How about that," – Ariadna says in surprise. "I didn't even think there were any left. I thought that there were only separate apartments in the new districts." – "What do you mean!" Yevdokia throws up her hands. "We have ballerinas living in apartment two. Also by themselves."

"And he recognized you straight away," Ariadna is happy.

"I rang the bell. He opened the door. Hello, Glikeria Yegorovna, he says. As though it was only yesterday that we said goodbye."

"Yes-s," says Yevdokia. "You've been successful with that. Another person wouldn't remember you a year later. But this one did after so many years. You were really stupid – waiting for the count. You should have married Solomon: he's respectable and independent. And a doctor, what's more…"

"You can't tell your heart what to do," she says.

"As I was saying, you're stupid."

"Oh," Ariadna remembers. "We forgot the tea. Tonechka won't remind us herself. And where's Sofia?"

"She's sitting with her mother," Glikeria replies. "She's been with her for two days now. She can sense something, evidently…"

"You'd have to say that," says Yevdokia. "You like reading the funeral rites. Solomon doesn't even know, and you're already prophesying ill. As if someone were making you say that." - "He said: it's the liver." – "So what if it's the liver… He'll go and find out. He'll talk to her." – "Let's hope they don't make him go away," she says, worried. "No, don't worry," Glikeria reassures her. "A doctor won't drive away a doctor – they respect their own kind."

"Well," Grandma Glikeria asks, - "are you still sitting here? You should let you mother rest."

"Let her stay," – the mother moves her hand. – "I rested enough in hospital. – Did you buy milk and bread?" - she asks.

"We're not in the blockade," - she puts the cup down and covers it with gauze – "we've still got bread. We won't be hungry, thank God."

"But still," - she whispers, - "I should go. For supper... I try to remember the people at the factory," - she complains. – "but I can't. All I can remember is the hospital. I wake up and don't know where I am..."

"You're not used to it yet. Yevdokia also complains that she can't get used to your room."

"You shouldn't have put me here. I would have been all right there." – "You'll get better," Grandma Glikeria comforts her, "and you'll move back. It's more enjoyable to be ill when you have a television..." She turns to me – "Don't bother your mother."

Mama looks at me:

"She's smart. She draws her own pictures."

"That's good," - she strokes my head, - "draw, then."

In the middle is a room. Mama lies in the bed. The grandmothers whisper: they've cut everything out of her. How is that possible – everything? Her arms are still there, and her legs. She takes a cup and drinks water. They've got it wrong again. They don't know anything...

There's a television in the corner. A man is on television. They've cut everything away from him. Only his head remains. He's quite happy about this: "why do I need a body," he says. "Just having a head is better. Then you don't need to wash..."

Up above is a cloud. The father sits on the cloud and looks at us. Mama looks at him, and the dead man gets angry. "Look at me..." he calls.

Elena Chizhova

Mama takes the picture. "There," - she says – "good girl, you've drawn it well. And who's that at the top? Is that our neighbour, Pyotr Matveich?"

No, I shake my head. But Mama closes her eyes – she doesn't want to look...

Solomon sighs, and drinks tea. "Things are bad. The process is well underway. A pupil of mine works at the hospital. He did the operation. He said they cut out what they could. But the liver is affected. On the whole, it's a matter of time. You need to get ready." He took out his handkerchief and wiped his forehead.

Yevdokia froze. "What if her liver is cut out?" – "That's impossible," Solomon Zakharovich explains. "It's a single organ. If it were a kidney or lung – but then there's still no guarantee. But you can't cut out the liver."

Glikeria just stood there motionless. "How can this be?..." – she whispers.

He shrugs and spread his hands. Ariadna was the first to recover: "She has no family. And she has a small child. We've brought it up, but we're strangers..." Glikeria starts sobbing. "Shush!" – Yevdokia hisses. "You can cry later. How much time does she have?" – "It's hard to say," he says, thinking. "Maybe half a year, maybe less. You can't guess these things." "So she'll last until the

Assumption," – she closes her mouth with fingers pressed together to make the sign of the cross.

"What will happen to the child?" – Ariadna persists.

"Try to register guardianship," he advises. "Gather the necessary documents. First, go to the housing association. They should write down that you've brought her up from early childhood." His voice is weak and hoarse. He doesn't believe in what he is saying.

Yevdokia is listening. "Do you really think they'll give her to us even if we have the papers?" she scoffs. "If they want to take her away, the papers won't stop them." – "We'll try," Ariadna says hurriedly. "Of course, we'll go there and try. On your advice."

Yevdokia looks at her and waves her hand.

"Where's her husband?" – Solomon knits his brow. "The child's father. He should take her, at least formally." "How does that work?" Glikeria asks. "According to the documents," he explains. "But she'd live with you. He only pays alimony." "There is no alimony," Yevdokia curls her lip. "We're raising her without a father."

"That's no good," Solomon frowns. "That means the loss of a breadwinner. Not only will she be sent to an orphanage, the room will be taken away. Is she registered here with her mother?"

Yes, they nod.

"Minors aren't entitled to rooms. A commission will meet to decide."

When Yevdokia hears this, she turns grey. "If they do it by the law, then that's the end."

Glikeria looks into his eyes. "Solomon Zakharych," - she clasps her hands together. -, "Please help, don't abandon us." – "But how can I…" – he frowns. "While I was still working, I had some connections: I had *wives* under my care" – he points to the ceiling. – "But what about your pupils," Glikeria wonders. – "you taught so many of them…" – "There's not much hope from them," – he scoffs. "It used to be different. But now there's very little hope."

"How will we tell her?" Glikeria thinks ahead. "Or do we keep silent about it?…" – "Usually people hide it," he says thoughtfully. "But our case is special. She may remember how to find the father, or relatives… Who knows, maybe there's someone left in her village. Brothers or sisters… Talk to her," he advises. – "See if you can find out tactfully."

He writes down his telephone number, and leaves. Glikeria sees him to the door. "Look at this," she whispers, unfolding the piece of paper, - "he not only has a separate apartment, he even has a telephone…"

Yevdokia sits and holds her head in both hands. "No. We'll keep silent for the moment – there's no point in driving her into the earth before her time. This especially concerns you. You're a real chatterbox – you say whatever comes into your head. When the day comes, we'll tell her. Or she'll realize herself, when the pain starts." "But I," – Glikeria protests, - "do I really…"

"As for us," Yevdokia ignores her, - it's time to get busy. Ariadna, you go to the office. They won't put up with me. I've argued with them so much… But you're educated and cultured. That will be useful. Talk to them politely. If they don't register all of us, let them at least register you. You may not be a godparent, but still, you're responsible." – "Lord," Ariadna says in despair. "What do they care about that? … Do you think we should tell them?"

"We shouldn't tell them," Yevdokia says. "I'm not saying it for them, but for you. Things really are more convenient with a certificate. Maybe there are some decent people on the commission, and they'll listen. Just don't tell them anything you shouldn't," she warns. "I wouldn't put it past you. You might say something stupid… Sometimes I think you're quite foolish… I'll talk to Antonina myself. I'll try to find out about the father, about that stud. Perhaps some trace of him can be found. We found Zakharych…"

"Also through the address book?…" – Glikeria says hopefully. Yevdokia thinks it over, and shakes her head.

She went to the office. She comes back. "Well?" – Yevdokia asks.

"Oh, I can't take it," she groans. Her lips are trembling. – "What are these people, what are these people?' "Cut that out," Yevdokia snaps. "All that groaning. You're not at a ladies' finishing school. Get to the point."

She drinks some water.

"I went to the office, and there was a queue. Everyone was sitting waiting to see the head woman. I also took my place. I walked in, and she didn't even look at me. As if she were looking through a wall. 'Forms aren't my business,' she says. I explained that our case was special, and sensitive. We brought up Suzanna Bespalova, and wanted to receive papers about this. 'Why do you want that?' she squints at me. 'You brought her up – not just for nothing, I expect. Her mother's been working for you for years now – you live like duchesses. I've been watching you for a long time now, and we get signals about you. You're exploiting a person. It's a tsarist regime you've got there. And now you want this document…"

"What did you say?" – Glikeria freezes.

"What did I say? You couldn't tell her about the illness. She says: 'I see! You probably wanted to register her, and get a room for her. It won't work the way you want it. Not with a form, or without one. Our rooms belong to the state. They're distributed according to the law.' – She looks into the office book. 'The Bespalovs have nine and a half meters for two people. And you've got 12. And you want to exchange it, but they won't let you. Because of the worsening of conditions.' But things will improve for them, I objected."

"There you go," Yevdokia nods. "That's what they're afraid of. What did you say, then?"

"We don't have much longer, I said. 'Then die, by all means,' she replies. 'The Bespalovs can wait in line. If they're allowed. The queue, for your information, is for four and a half meters. And they have four meters seventy-five – which is in fact too much.' I went towards the door, and she said to my back: 'They're shrewd ones! One foot in the grave, and they're still up to all kinds of tricks.'"

"What did you say?" "What did I say…" - she's tormented. - "I didn't say anything."

"You should have," Yevdokia's eyes glint. "You should have said, thanks for your concern. The Bespalovs live very well. And indeed, they have too much. There's two meters set aside for them in the other world, but you have far too much – four and a half…. So," she calculates. "That means they're duchesses. Well, countess," she says to Glikeria. "Get ready to go for a walk. Buy milk and millet. I'll cook kasha this evening. If Antonina wakes up, maybe she'll have some too."

We got to Nikolsky, and Grandma Glikeria looks in:

"It seems to have dried up. Look how tidy the paths are. Let's walk there, my little dove. The lawns are muddy, but the grass is fresh and thin… It lies there like smoke on the ground…

"Don't tramp through the mud" – she says. "If you take a step, you'll tread in something. There are all kinds of things hidden under the snow: dog turds, rotten stuff. They think that the dirt has gone into the ground. But the ground is firm and frozen – it doesn't accept their dirt. You need to remember everything while there's still time" – she says, looking around. "Our house is over there. And this is the Cathedral. We've taken so many walks, you must remember now. If you forget, the bell-tower is tall. You can see it from everywhere. Let it be your guide. But if you come from the canal, things are different: you need to go across the bridge, past the lions. The lions are stone – nothing will happen to them. But don't ask people" – she warns, shaking her finger. "Who knows what they might do… They may lead you astray, or take you away. I'll embroider your letters" – she comforts me. "So rely on yourself – walk by memory."

I look around: where will she embroider them? On the buildings or something? You can draw on the buildings, or even better, on the pavement. I took a stick: the letters are large and crooked.

Grandma Glikeria looks. She nods, that's right, good girl. Write it down, remember…

And she wipes a tear away and says:

"We'll go for a walk tomorrow – we'll go in the other direction. You need to try going from Ofitserkaya. *They* will think: she's small and doesn't know anything. Let her walk, she won't remember anything. But you keep silent. 'That's right' – you should nod. I'm just going for a walk. I'll take a walk and come back to you.' And remember: whatever direction you come from, everything is familiar to you. The Cathedral, this theatre, and the bridge…"

Ahh… I get it. When I wake up… One hundred years will pass – and I'll go home. And they will be sitting in the cellar. They look out and stand watch. Other children also go, gathering their letters. But those ones have sharpened their nails, and threaten to eat them…

Grandma Yevdokia comes into the room:

"What are you drawing, Little Red Riding Hood? Is she wandering around the city? And who's that? The grey wolf?" – She looks at it. – "I don't understand this at all" – she says. The flowers are strangely shaped – they look like letters. Do these letters of yours grow out of the ground?..."

But Grandma Glikeria is hiding in the corner. She has laid out my dress and embroiders it. Then Grandma Yevdokia notices her. She goes up to her and looks under her hand.

"Come on," - she says – "lets go out."

Grandma Glikeria is scared, and follows her...

"So then" – she stands opposite her – "that's what you've thought up... You'll embroider letters, and let them take her away. That's not going to happen. You should know, it's not going to happen." – "Maybe just in case..." – Glikeria pleads.

"In what case? They'll dress her in state clothes. They'll burn hers." "How is that?" – She folds her hands and presses them to her throat. Yevdokia gives a sob and turns away to the stove.

Ariadna comes in and sits down to the table. "Where can we find out if parcels are accepted, or if that is also prohibited?" – "It happens that they accept them." Yevdokia hunches over. – "What about visits?" – "That's up to their discretion. It depends on a lot of things, on behaviour..." – "But she's an obedient girl," Glikeria says quickly. "She's well-behaved."

She closes the door.

"This is what I'm thinking," - she whispers. "We're very old. If they take her away, our hearts won't hold out. It's all right for us... But she has to stay here. What if," - she looks at the door, - "we took her with us..."

Ariadna looks at her, and her eyes stop moving: "What do you mean, with us?"

Glikeria is frightened herself. "Forgive my sinful soul, may the lord protect me, I don't know what I'm babbling..." Yevdokia goes to the tap and turns the water on. "I know what she means: some sort of medicine... That would do it..."

The water rushes and splashes. "In the war," - Glikeria whispers, - "one of Hitler's henchmen, what was his name? His wife poisoned all the children, so they wouldn't fall into the enemy's hands – there were five, or six of them..."

"Come to your senses!" – Ariadna shrieks. "You want to behave like animals?!"

"Oh," - Yevdokia gets up and turns the water off. – "It's hard to tell who are people and who are animals. As if we lived in the forest. Our sins are heavy... These thoughts come along – who knows where they come from..."

"Antonina is better today..." - Glikeria gathers the cups, and changes the subject. – "She ate kasha, a couple of spoonfuls." – But her voice is shaking. – "She walked to the toilet herself. Perhaps we should buy her something nice to eat – fish or cheese? She asked for chocolate yesterday. I'd like some, she said..." – "The money's running out,"

- Yevdokia frowns. "When we get the pension – then we can…"

"I was thinking…" - says Glikeria. – "Do they give an advance on sick leave? Maybe we should go to see them?" – "They won't register it to us in any case," Ariadna says. "They do it all according to documents there." –"Why not…" - Yevdokia supports Glikeria. – The suitor took me for her mother. I'll go there and pretend to be the mother. 30 rubles, or maybe 40." – "It's far," - Ariadna doubts. "Do you think you can find it?" – "What, am I some sort of idiot…" she's offended. "I'll ask Antonina…"

They've gathered for supper, and Solomon Zakharych turns up as they are sitting down to eat. Glikeria is happy to see him and invites him to join them. "I've only come for a minute," he says, breathing heavily. He stands there and crumples his hat.

They take him into the kitchen.

"Guardianship is a lost cause…"

Ariadna turns to Sofyushka and calls her in French. "We'll have supper later," she says. "We're in no hurry."

Solomon sits down and hunches over. "A former pupil of mine has connections in these cases. You can't do anything without the father. That's what he said: it's a lost cause. The child either goes to the grandmother, or the stepfather. And there are also problems here: a statement, references from work…"

"Well then," - Yevdokia looks at the black window, - "thanks at least for that. Their law is written so that it is more convenient for them. They didn't ask us when they wrote their laws…"

Solomon gets up and leaves. Glikeria looks at him as he leaves: he is very old. And can hardly walk. But he used to run… Up and down the stairs from early morning. Either making his rounds, or flanked by the students …

Sofyushka runs out into the corridor – she has a picture in her hand. "Show me," Solomon Zakharovich asks. "What's that you're drawing?" She isn't afraid, and shows him the picture. "Good girl!" - he admires it. - "You've done a fine job! You should take lessons. There's a special group," he explains. "An artist's circle. At the Palace of pioneers. My grandson went there, but didn't learn anything," - he waves his hand. - "He didn't have any talent, I suppose." "Our girl is talented," Glikeria says. "As soon as she has a spare minute, she draws. And where is this palace of pioneers?" she asks. "On Fontanka. By Anichkov Bridge. It's a bit far from here, of course…" – "That's OK," - she says happily. "The three of us will manage… We'll take it in turns…"

Yevdokia scowls. Her face falls…

Solomon leaves.

"Let's gather our strength," Yevdokia calls. "You feed the child, Ariadna, and I'll put her to bed. Antonina needs to be washed. She hasn't been washed in days. If things go on like that, she'll get bedsores. We'll rub her back with camphor spirit, and change the sheets: she could use some clean ones…"

Glikeria says: "Boil some rags, they've run out already. She's bleeding a lot – you can't have enough of them"...

Grandma Yevdokia tucks in the blanket and sits down next to her. She takes the headscarf off and strokes her hair.

"You know," - she says, "whatever happens, remember your name. Not Suzanna. That's for people. For God, your name is Sofia. She is the heavenly intercessor. She is a virgin white as snow, the glory of God. She is the wisest of all, there is no one wiser than her on earth. God whispers to her, and she speaks to good people. She passes on every word of His messages. And those who do not listen have nothing in them but despair and stupidity. But Sofia does not look at them: she knows herself and looks around. She looks around during the day, and in the evening she sits down, and takes up paints and pencils – and draws everything as it is. Green forests, blue seas and cities of different colours. In a word, she's an artist...

"You know what," - she bends down and whispers into my ear. – "Listen to me. Who knows, perhaps you will be taken away... All kinds of things happen in this life. Sometimes children are taken away. You may be locked away, and we won't be able to see you. You'll have to be alone. But you should know that wherever they lock you up, I am with you. Every day behind the fence. I'll go there as long as the Lord gives me life. Perhaps you won't see me, but remember one thing – my grandmother is there. She walks back and forth. She sits down, rests, and then walks again. You understand me?"

I understand, and nod. That's when I will be asleep. And then I will wake up.

V

YEVDOKIA

That Zoya of theirs recognized me immediately: she's well-built and independent. She came out to the watch house – they didn't let me in without her.

She looked at my pass: "Hello, Yevdokia Timofeevna. I've wanted to meet you for a long time, and talk." – "What would you talk to me about," I said in surprise, "an illiterate old woman? You've got a huge factory here – plenty to do." "What does it matter that you're illiterate," she says. "In the olden days they didn't used to teach people how to read and write much. Wisdom doesn't only come from books." – "That's for sure," I nod. "Life teaches us in its own way…"

And I think to myself: why is she delaying things?

"I would like some money, an advance for Antonina," I say. "My pension is small, and the child needs this and that." – "Yes, of course, - she waves her hand. – I'm a grandmother myself – I have two grandchildren." – "Really," - I pretend to be surprised. – "But you look so young. You wouldn't say that, looking at you…"

"Don't worry about the advance. If the bookkeeping department doesn't issue it, I'll take it from the local committees. We'll put it down as welfare assistance. There's just one thing… These operations aren't particularly encouraged… But I'll talk to the women, and explain things to them," she promises.

"Thank you," – I nod.

But I'm amazed: why are they opposed to operations? People don't choose to have diseases of their own free will.

"And how does Antonina feel?" she asks. "She's been ill for a long time. I hope there are no complications..." – "Yes, it varies," I reply. "Sometimes she's fine, sometimes she's worse. She lies huddled against the wall". – "Yes-s," she nods. "It's not easy to exterminate a child – with your own hands..."

What child, I think... Good gracious! Then I realize the operation that she was taking about... I think I should explain things to her. Why carry this shame...

I'm about to open my mouth, and she says: "We don't condemn your Antonina among ourselves. And truly, now is not the right time. When she gets married, there will be time. They're young – they'll have more children. Does Nikolai visit?" she asks.

"Yes, he came to look in, and had some tea". – "Did he come to hospital?" – "No," - I say. – "He didn't go to the hospital."

"Oh, these men! They're always the first to screw us, but if they have to take responsibility, they vanish. Nikolai and I have talked separately," she explains. "Although we didn't know then... And if we had known, we wouldn't have treaded so delicately. Where would he go, the bastard? And now we think that they should sort things out amongst themselves. If he makes a decision, why would our group interfere... And if he tries to get out of it, then we'll order him. We'll remember everything. So," she explains, "prepare for the wedding. And there'll be a housewarming, you'll see... The factory won't stand aloof – it will provide a separate apartment."

I listen, and my throat contracts – I can't breathe in or out. Our wedding would be in a funeral shroud, and the mother would be the damp earth.

But she smiles at me. "That's enough crying," she says, "when life is just starting to work out." I cope with my tears, and say: "I want to talk to you about something, Zoya Ivanovna. It's quite important!" – "Is it about the girl? – she asks." "Yes," - I nod. – "It's about her."

"Actually, I wanted to talk to you about her myself," she says. "But can you reach an agreement with Antonina?" she waves her hand. "The child is six years old, but still sitting at home. Children at her age sing songs and tell stories. My younger grandson isn't even five, and he remembers everything about Grandpa Lenin. He has stories read to him: about heroes, and about the war. But what about your girl? You can't make up for it later. A child's memory is tenacious. Whatever is put aside, that is for life."

"But we don't just sit around twiddling our thumbs," I reply. "We read her books. Stories." – "Well, it's one thing to do it yourself. But there are teachers who instruct them specially. These seven years are the most decisive. The things that we give them, that's the way they will be. There's a kindergarten at our factory, and a children's camp..."

"Oh, is there a camp?" – I ask.

And I think to myself: you're a fool, Yevdokia. And your tongue is wicked – you shouldn't have opened your mouth... They're just trying to humour you... But if they find out about the illness, you'll never hear the end of it.

I cross myself mentally, and say: "Right you are, Zoya Ivanovna. How can we teach her wisdom... I'll talk to Antonina, but after she recovers. She's a sensible woman: she always listens to good advice. Why not agree to do something worthwhile?..."

She cheered up then, and took me by the arm. "Let's go to the bookkeeping office," she said. "We'll sort the money out. The main thing is that we've made a decision. Well, where's the form?"

"I left it at home," I said, afraid. "It didn't occur to me to take it, for some reason." – "Never mind," she said. "We'll register it some other time. I'll allocate it from the local committees now. I'll have it registered by tomorrow."

I walk back, and things are black before my eyes. I don't remember how I got home. I lie down for a while, and then go into the kitchen. I tell everything the way it happened: about the operation, the children's camp and kindergarten, and about that... husband. "So," - I conclude. "There's nothing to hope for. Nothing but a miracle. So start praying," I say. "The Lord doesn't listen to me. Perhaps he will heed you."

"But I already pray every night..." Glikeria says, defending herself.

Ariadna gets up. She's white as a sheet. "There it is – the miracle . The Lord himself is showing it to us..."

I look at her: "What are you talking about, you

idiot! Have you completely gone out of your mind? Your tongue won't stop wagging."

"How did they intimidate Nikolai? If he didn't get married, he would never receive a room. They think that she got rid of the baby. But they don't know about her illness…"

"So?" – Glikeria stands there and blinks.

"So he doesn't have any other choice if he wants to receive a room. The only option is to marry Antonina. And as soon as he marries her…"

"Right," – I clenches my fist. – "I understand the rest. You should think of something else. What if he refuses? If he says he doesn't know where the child is from…"

"But we are witnesses, says Glikeria. "He came here, and stayed here for a whole night."

I thought and thought.

"No," – I say. – "That won't work for us. As soon as he looks at her, he'll realize. The way that she looks now… Better-looking people have been buried."

"Let him realize then," Glikeria gets excited and looks at Ariadna. "It will be better for him."

"That's right," – Ariadna nods. – "Especially as it's advantageous for him. She'll die, and he'll get the whole room to himself." – "What do you mean," - I say, surprised. "What about Sofia? She's registered there, thanks heavens." – "Well, what difference does it make? She's going to live with us. Not with him."

"Oh, I can't decide – what if they get to the bottom of it? What about the operation?" – "We won't show them the certificate," Glikeria says. "What about the money? They don't give you

Elena Chizhova

a kopeck without a certificate" – "Oh well," - Ariadna straightens her back. – "we'll just have to go without the money somehow…"

Yevdokia crosses herself by the window.

"A miracle, you say?... Yes-s, you're smart… You didn't study at grammar school for nothing. I wouldn't have thought of that…"

"And really," - Glikeria whispers – "we are witnessing a miracle…. The Lord has rescued us before death."

Ariadna sinks down her head sadly.

"We'll have to deceive them… We are taking sin on our souls."

"But we don't have any choice," - Yevdokia replies. "We must be thankful for whatever miracle we are given. Have some respect, a straw is being offered. It's up to us to grab it. Let it at least work out for us. If only to save this girl…. And the sin can lie upon me. My soul is already ruined. By my children."

I opened my eyes. It was dark all around. I didn't know if it was night or evening… Everything was confused within me. And I couldn't make anything out.

Yevdokia looks in. "Aren't you asleep?" – she calls. – "I feel sick, Yevdokia Timofeevna." – "Oh…" She shifts the blanket. – "God has a plan for everything. For misery, and for sorrow…"

She sits on the edge of the bed. – "I have something to talk to you about. I don't know where to begin."

"Do you think I don't understand..." I say. "It's hard for you to do everything yourself. To do the washing, cook, and go to the shop. I'm trying to get up, but I'm weak. I'm all shaky. Just be patient for a little while longer," I plead.

But she wipes her eyes and replies: "Get along with you... Who's blaming you? I'm not talking about that. All kinds of things can happen in life... Take these operations... It's good if it's successful, but if something happens, your daughter will be left by herself. She doesn't have a grandmother, or even a stepfather – before the law..." – "I don't understand," - I reply. "You should get married," - she looks at the floor. "Even to that Nikolai. Zoya also advises that you do. She says you'll be given an apartment..."

"I'd make a good bride," - I say, shaking my head... "With these rags to soak up the blood. I don't whether to laugh or cry..." – "I'm talking to her about something important," - she says, angrily – "and she talks about this... She's a second Glikeria, really... Lord forgive me!"

"And when did you plan this for?" – I turn my head towards the wall. – "The sooner the better. Why delay? Your Zoya is also hurrying it." – "I'm not talking about myself. How do we explain to Nikolai? And you can't explain... about this sickness".

And I think to myself: I crawled on my knees before him, I begged for my daughter... How can I live with this, if we both remember.

"We'll take that on ourselves, she promises. We'll explain it somehow. And if not, we'll call Solomon: he'll explain." – "I'm tired." – I turned to the wall. – "Do as you know best…"

Yevdokia leaves the room – she closes the door behind her. The others are waiting in the kitchen.

"Well, how was it?" – Ariadna stands still. – "Did you talk to her?"

"Yes, I talked to her. But I don't have the strength to tell the whole truth to her. My tongue couldn't get around it. All I could manage was to talk about this marriage."

"What did she say?"

"She seemed to agree."

"Oh well," - Glikeria breathes out. – "Thank God for that. She can be ill in peace… We didn't buy chocolate again. She asked for it…"

"How can a sick person eat chocolate," - Yevdokia avoids the question. "She can barely eat kasha. And Solomon said she shouldn't."

"When was that?" – Ariadna says in surprise. - I don't remember anything like that."

"No? He said himself: dietary food."

"But that's what chocolate is," - Glikeria says.

"Go ahead!" – she holds her sides. – "Dump on him like he's dead. Solomon here, Solomon there – like an angel. You can't take a step without Solomon. All you do is bow down to him…"

"Chocolate gives you energy," - Glikeria looks at Ariadna. – "In the war, the Americans… There were thick, crunchy bars…"

"That's it," - she waves her hand. – "Now there's no distracting you… If you aren't trying to cheer her up with men, then it's food… And chocolate is from the devil."

"What nonsense! You can eat chocolate during Lent…"

"That's for people who don't go a day without meat," - she replies. But for other people like us, even fish means breaking the fast."

"Sick people aren't forbidden to eat meat or fish," - Ariadna cuts in.

"Pah," - she gets up. – "Christ refused even bread… Ah! Have it your way. Forgive everything at once – even the fasting."

"The saints didn't think about tomorrow," - says Ariadna. "The day will come, the food will come."

"Aha," - she shakes her head from side to side. – "Where the horse puts its hoof, the crab sticks its claw. The saints didn't live on our pension. They were given bread, or brought gold…"

"That's enough," - Ariadna gets up. – "I can't listen to this crazy talk anymore. Wait. I'll be back shortly."

She brings a box and places it on the table. Yevdokia opens it.

"Oh," - she gasps. – "That's beautiful… How much could that cost?"

"The stones are good and pure. They were given to me at my wedding – my father chose them himself. In old money they could even be worth two thousand…"

"Really, are you sure?..."

"My father knew the value of everything, - Ariadna is offended. He ordered these earrings in advance. They were old. He was proud: it was a royal gift…"

Yevdokia admires the stone.

"Look at that! You lived well, in your parents' home. They sent you abroad, and gave your diamond earrings. Others counted their pennies…" - She closes the velvet box. – "We'll ask Solomon. He should know. He's a Jew."

"But how?…" – Glikeria defends him. – "He's worked in hospitals all his life."

"Well," - Yevdokia softens. – "Let him find someone to advise us. We'll be swindled if we try to do things on our own."

VI

THE STEPFATHER

Zoika, the bitch, is bothering me: go visit, go visit.

"And stop those tricks of yours!" – she threatens me.

I wonder if I should tell her where to go... But then I realize: Zoya is friends with the bosses. I need to be easy with her. "OK," - I say politely. – "I'll go." – "If you're going," - she sticks to me like glue – "don't go empty-handed. Buy some present."

I returned to the shop floor, and I felt sick. As soon as I remember her, how she crawled at my feet, I feel as if I'm in a noose. What did I do to her, I think, what did I bring her to? Perhaps she didn't go running to the management. Those women are shrewd themselves, they found out. And that present for her... What shall I take with me? If it was for a man, I'd take a bottle, but what do I get for a woman? Something sweet, some sort of pastries, then...

I decided to see Vasily. He's a guy who's been around, he's experienced – he's got three kids.

"Are you going to see Antonina?" – he winks. "You're taking a long time... It's the fourth week now."

God, I think, he counts the weeks too...

"You're a son of a bitch, Kolya," he says. "The woman went under the knife for you, and you're worried about a present..." – "What do mean, for me?" – I say, angry. "I've got nothing to do with it." – "Damn it," - he spits on the floor. – "My daughters are growing up. When I think about you studs – I'd strangle all of you."

The men stand around eavesdropping.

"You can't strangle everyone," - they laugh. "Leave someone – for the tribe… You're angry," - they say – "because you had daughters yourself. If you'd had sons, you'd be singing a different song. You'd teach them to go to whores yourself…"

I drag a piece of iron and think: nothing happened between us. Well, I think, I'll tell them, say. Nothing happened between us. They'll just start laughing. If she'd been a virgin, but she's a woman. You didn't break down a woman's defences, they'll say. OK then. I know I'm right. They can say whatever they want.

I finished the shift, and Zoya came along again. "Don't go there today," - she says. "Go tomorrow. You can take 20 rubles with you, welfare assistance. But look here," - she waves her finger threateningly – "don't drink it."

"I don't drink," - I said. "Only on holidays." "We know!" – she waves her hand. "You can tell your wife about that. I know all about these things… If you had your way…" - she thrusts out her fist, - "this is where you should be held."

I went back to the dormitory, and Seryoga, my neighbour, invites me:

"Is Zinka interested in you?" – he winks. – "What Zinka?" – "Shurka's friend. From the packing shop." – "What's it to her?" – I ask.

"Yes," - he laughs, - "you're famous now: the whole factory knows about you. Remember my words: the girls will start hovering around you like flies." – "We know what flies hover around," - I say, really angry now. "That's what I'm saying…" he winks again.

I grab him by the chest: "Repeat that, you bastard!"

"Idiot," - he pushes me away. – "I'm setting him up with a girl, and he comes at me with his fists. You could say I'm finding you a wife." – "If I need to," - I calm down – "I'll find one myself." – "Aha," - he shakes his head. – "First you sat like a crayfish under a rock, and now you've found a wife – it's ringing through the factory…" – "Why is it ringing? You're ringing yourself, I'm sure." – "And you've made a kid. But you stay away…" – "Where's that coming from – a kid?" – "What?" – he's surprised. – Is it a state secret? Everyone already knows about it."

Christ, how about that, I think… They all know – except me.

"Well then?" – he turns to the mirror. – "Maybe the wind blew her up? Or it was an immaculate conception?" – he laughs. "I remember the lecturer told us… There are cases." – He blew on the comb and stuck it in his pocket. – "So, are you going?"

I lie there. I stretch out on the bunk.

"To hell with you then, if it was the holy spirit."

What have I got myself into, I think. No… I need to go. To sort things out. She can explain it herself.

I sit there, and think to myself: what is she going to explain to me? Will she show me her man? That will be to her disadvantage. She planned to get me involved. And Zoya is behind her – they'll hang it around my neck… And then I think: who? She got rid of it…

I sat there for a while. And then it dawned on me.

She arranged things specially to make me marry her. It didn't work the first time – but now she's smart. She has proof. And I'm an idiot: think up an illness, I say. But she doesn't need to think – she thought it up a long time ago.

Oh well, never mind. I raise my fist threateningly. They'll remember me. Antonina and her mother. The old women no doubt came up with it. They'll remember me!

I sit there seething with rage. Seryoga runs back.

"So, you're still sitting here, are you!" – he says. "I forgot the most important thing, the bottle. I got it yesterday – for the trip to the cinema. Maybe you've changed your mind?" – he takes it out from under the mattress. "Yes, I have," - I say. "Let's go".

"There you go," - he says. – "Get some fresh air. Before they put the clamps on you for good." – "We'll see about who puts the clamps on who! They might get tangled up themselves – in the stirrups…"

We got to the cinema, and Seryoga pokes me in the side. "I took the last row," - he said. "There weren't any others," - he winks.

The girls giggle as if someone were tickling them. We start to sit down, and Zinka squeezed in – she sat next to me. The film started, and she moved towards me. She grabbed my hand and put it on her knee.

I squeezed and squeezed, but didn't feel anything. She was quite cold. As if it weren't her leg, but an artificial limb… What is this, I think? Have they sent me some curse or something – damned witches…

We go out of the cinema. Zinka screws up her face. Seryoga says: "We should finish the bottle. Or shall we drink it at home?" – he winks to Shurka.

They started talking among themselves how to get into the girls' dormitory more easily. There's a fire escape there. The girls will go through the door and open the window.

I listen and listen. "Drink it yourself," I say. "I'm going home." I hear them laughing at me as I walk away. And Zinka is the loudest of all…

Never mind, I reassure myself. What did our company leader say? The main thing is not to panic. I'll go there and look into her eyes – her conscience should wake up. She'll confess, I expect…

They open the door. Her mother is on the threshold. I don't remember her name. It's all gone out of my head. She nods.

The room is large, with furniture set out around it. There's a lampshade above the table.

"I've brought you assistance," I reach into my pockets. "Zoya Ivanovna sent it."

She reaches out her hand, and conceals the money under her apron. The others sit there like stone statues. I sit there too, but don't know how to begin. When I walked there I thought that Antonina would open the door herself.

"I'd like to see Antonina…" I say. "How is she? Is she better?"

Her mother turns her eyes away. "No,"- she replies. "She's dying."

That's it, I think: the old women have gone mad. So she's dying then...

"And she's only got six months to live. Maybe even less. But she doesn't know – she still hopes."

I remembered her name in my fear. "Don't grieve, Yevdokia Timofeevna. She'll be ill for a while and then recover. People get ill." – "People," - she replies, - "get ill. But cancer isn't illness, it's death."

What death is she talking about? Where did she get this idea?...

"If it weren't for the child," - she says. "It will become an orphan. So you have to marry her to save the child."

I listen, but don't understand. As if my ears were full of cotton wool. What does she mean, the child? Didn't she get rid of it? So she has cancer, and a child?

"This child," - I explain, - "isn't mine. I wouldn't reject it if it was. You should go to the real father. He should marry her." – "The father is dead. You can't call him back from the other world. So you'll have to marry her – there's no other way out. But don't get too upset," she comforts me. "You'll fill out the documents, but we'll look after the child. She'll live with us. And you'll be given the room. She'll die, and you can move in by yourself. It can't be any other way," - she looks at me.

"Right," - I say, stalling for time – "I need to think about that... I can't decide right now..." And

I have one thought in my head: to run away from there. Now they're staring at me...

Then she gets up: "Think about it." She digs around in the chest of drawers and takes something out of it. – "We'll die, and you'll get this." She opens a box and shoves it under my nose. I look at it, and there are sparks in my eyes. Then she shuts it. "Not now. After we're dead"...

I don't remember how I got out of there. I walk out and stand by the streetlight. There they are, I think, the wooden idols... I remember Pyotr: there was also an old woman... Will that also repeat itself with me... And the gold, and the stones... That's it, the evil power! Pyotr said something about this...

I returned to my room. I lay down and drew a blanket over my head. Seryoga brings the kettle: "Have you caught a chill or something?" – "My body's aching," - I moan. And really, I do feel dizzy...

So I walk along. And I'm holding an order to view an apartment. But without any choice – I have to take what they give me.

I approach, and the door is open. They seem to be waiting for me. The room is large and spacious, but without any furniture in it. There are just three chests. Her mother and the other two – her relatives. They sit there and move their needles. And on the floor there are balls of wool. There isn't any room to step.

I show the paper. "Where is the free room?" – I ask. – "There it is," - they reply. "Move in." They show me the door. "What do you mean, move in?" I say in surprise. "Antonina is there…" – "She's moved," they say. "You could say she's moved for good. This is her cardigan."

I look, and see that the cardigan is whole, but without any arms. And the torn thread dangles down to the floor. "What about the child?" I ask – "She lives with us," they say. "This is her cardigan."

So, I have a daughter, I think. I look and see that this cardigan is striped, made of different-colored yarn. "What are you knitting?" I ask them. "How can she wear that?" – "It's made of the remains." – They point to the floor. – "There are so many torn pieces… That's what she'll wear."

I look around, and the balls of wool have gone. The strands are torn and twisted. The entire floor is covered with them.

I want to run away, and it feels as if something is pulling me by force…

I scream, and open my eyes. It's dark.

The men are snoring in the corners. Seryoga, my neighbour, sits up: "What are you yelling for?" I get up and feel my way towards the window – there are empty bottles everywhere. "Ah," - he turns onto his other side. – "We finished them yesterday. Fedka Kostyl came here."

I lay down, and felt sick. So I thought, I'll have a daughter. It's a shame that it's not a son…

Yevdokia looks at the door: "It's OK... The main thing is they talked. Although he didn't stay for long. And she's keeping silent... She's weak. I don't know how she'll go there. They require people to go in person when they file and application, don't they?" - "That's all right," – says Solomon Zakharych. "Gennady Pavlovich rang them. They promised to make allowances for them. The groom should go and hand in both passports."

"Oh," - Glikeria says admiringly. "How well you organize everything! We're so grateful to you..." – "Not you. I should be grateful to you." He sits there, hunched over.

"So many years have gone by, and I still dream of it. I don't dream of my late wife, but this..." – he coughs. – "I open my eyes, and once more I see the meeting: there's a forest of hands. And voices... I hear their accusing speeches." "Most of them were probably forced to," – Glikeria frowns. "Those were bad times."

He shrugs his shoulders.

"Of course," - Ariadna says. – "Everyone knew you..." – "And what was the point?" – He catches his breath. – "Yes, of course I understand. And I understood back then. But I stood there and thought: they're my students... Will none of them stand up? Not to say they were *against it*, of course, but at least to *abstain*... But not a single one of them stood up. I thought that I would die with this... And now," - he breathes heavily, - "I know: they remember me."

Yevdokia looks at him: "Drink some hot tea." – She rinses a saucer. – "You've got a tickle in your throat." – "And the weather," - Ariadna says hurriedly, "it's bad, and changeable. When has there ever been snow at this time of year?" – "It's the bird-cherry tree," - Glikeria says. – "The bird-cherry tree is blossoming. Every year it gets cold…"Ariadna looks out the window: "Of course it gets cold… But it doesn't snow…"

"Yes…" - Yevdokia turns to the window, and admires the snowflakes. "And I see that your scarf is all bunched up." "I'll knit another one for you by autumn," Glikeria says cheerfully.

He controls himself: "We still need to live until autumn… Yes, another thing… Gennady promised, of course. He'll do everything in his power. But he advises you to think things over. Nikolai is young, sooner or later he'll get married…" – "And what does that matter to us," - Yevdokia raised her eyebrows. – "This is what,.." – he raised his finger. – This is the whole problem. While you're alive, the girl won't end up on the street. But what happens next?... I talked to Nikolai. He's not a bad person, but he's weak. As they used to say, without an inner core. He'll do whatever his wife tells him to… And orphans at least are given rooms. Not very good ones, but it's still a roof over your head… How old is she? Oh dear!" – He shakes his head. – "Children today aren't like us. There's still helpless at 16… I can judge by my grandson. The idiot is 26, but if something happens…"

"That's all right," - Yevdokia gives a curt look, - "we have our own calculation… If God grants, we'll hang on. We'll live."

"Well then," - he gets up. – "You know best. So call Gennady Pavlovich. He'll do everything he can for you. But the main thing... Nikolai is no help to you. Count on yourselves... Yes-s," - he shakes his head, - "you scared him... He thought that she was pregnant. 'What child are you talking about?' – he said. 'There was nothing between us...' He swore..."

"Antonina is getting worse," - Yevdokia lowers her eyes. "She completely refuses to eat. She can only suck on a bit of chocolate. Maybe it's bad for her?" – "No, it's not. Let her. Give her something to drink. Compote or something..." – "We make that already," - Glikeria nods. – "With that dried fruit. It's left over from last autumn." – "When the pain starts, I'll talk to the right people. We'll find a doctor. Only she'll have to be paid," – he says in embarrassment. "She's not from the clinic."

"Will they inject her with opium?" – Glikeria frowns. "Well... With some drug." – "Do we have to pay her a lot?" Yevdokia says in alarm. – "I don't know..." - he shrugs. "It used to be five rubles, but now...". – "Perhaps it's stayed that way," - she moves her lips. "Fifty kopeks then. And if the nurse is from the clinic, is it free?"

"It's free from the clinic. But they may not prescribe medicine. That is, they prescribe it, but not a full course. And she will need it every day, and then twice a day." – "Lord," - Glikeria throws up her hands, - "do they grudge opium? For patients like that..."

Yevdokia doesn't listen to her: "It costs one ruble, then?" She fishes in her apron, and takes out a box: "Here it is." – She opens it. – "We've thought about selling these. The earrings are good, and old. Perhaps your daughter would like them"..." He looks and shrugs, as if to say, where could I get this money from.

"At least offer them to someone," Yevdokia does not back down. "We'd be swindled if we tried it ourselves." He shrugs: "I'll try…"

He turns the box in his hands, and puts it in his pocket.

"And you, Solomon Zakharych, we would like to invite to the wedding," Glikeria says. "Thank you," he smiles. "If I'm feeling up to it… Yes," – he recalls – "when you decide on a date, Gennady has a car. I told him," – he puts on his hat – "That you were my relatives. So we've become related…"

"Solomon," - Yevdokia says. – "He's a smart man. So, we're relatives…"

"Well," - Glikeria purses her lips, - "people aren't family only by blood."

"By blood", - Yevdokia gets angry, and her face turns dark –"it's only blood… We weren't the ones who said that a person's enemies were the people in his house."

"That's about something quite different…" - Ariadna corrects her. – "*Who does not leave their father or mother and does not follow me…*"

"That's it!" she raises her finger. "Me, and not the devil…"

She turns to look out the window.

It's dark. Evil spirits are raging outside.

The sky is low and grey. If only it would snow, at least…

"Oh," - she sighs. – "I'm frightened. Solomon is right. What we're doing is stupid. And now Nikolai is scared. And when he moves in, he won't forgive anyone, or forget: not us, not Sofia... Where is she then?" – she remembers.

"She's reading a book," - Ariadna sits proudly.

"By herself, really? The Lord is wise... Some live out their entire lives, and it's they couldn't care less about that... But she's reading by herself..."

Glikeria looks at Ariadna.

"Quite independently. And at 16, imagine what she'll be like... No one will catch up with her."

"Go on," - Yevdokia teases. – "Make up stories. Comfort yourselves..."

"In the old days," - Glikeria recalls, - "in the country, this cancer didn't exist. No one had even heard of it. People used to suffer from tuberculosis, dropsy, or toothache..."

"No one ever died from toothache," - Ariadna chides her.

"What would you know!" – she becomes excited. – "In our village..."

"But cancer," - Yevdokia doesn't listen – "is it actually a disease? I thought back then: they give people radiation treatment, for example. Everyone seems to be the same, but some recover, and others get worse. What sort of disease is this, if everything depends on the person? Not on the medicine."

"What do you mean, it's not a disease? It affects the liver, or the lungs... Or the uterus..."

"If it is a disease, the bastards invented it themselves. Other deaths are not enough for them..."

"Never mind," - Glikeria mixes the dough. – "If necessary, we'll find someone to sort him out... But maybe," - she wipes her hands on the cloth, - "he is a good person…. Solomon liked him. He said he was good, but weak."

"I've seen people like that," - Yevdokia puts the pan on the burner, - "both good, and weak… Take my son. A friend of his came around. He sat at the table with us. He was also good, but he stopped coming around. I didn't understand to start with. I then realized that he had been taken away. He was from the orphanage. I thought, who would bring him a parcel? I put one together and took it there…"

"Did they accept it?" – Glikeria says in surprise.

"Don't interrupt, first you listen to me. Time went by, and I ran into him. He was walking down the street… I was happy to see him. Hello Volodya, I called. But as soon as he saw me, he jumped, as if he'd seen a rat…"

"Well," - Ariadna disagrees. – "I guess he was just like that. A good person is always good. My brother also had a friend. They served at the regiment together. Only my brother was an officer, and Sergey was a volunteer. The famine began, and he often came to see us. Father completely lost the use of his legs. And I was left alone with my son. Sergey helped us sometimes: he'd bring us herring, or sometimes a chunk of wood. And he had a family of his own. Although he didn't have any children, he wasn't married. And my father had some gold rubles left. "Take them, Sergei Nikolaevich," he pleaded. But Sergey just laughed. 'Forget it!' He disappeared in '21. They found him out, evidently."

"But volunteers were more or less protected," - Yevdokia frowns.

"But he was an officer by then," she explains. "He passed an examination to become an ensign…"

Yevdokia comes into the room. "Who's there?" I ask. "I thought I heard the doorbell ring…" – "Yes, that was our neighbour, Nadezhda Karpovna. She met Glikeria on the staircase. Glikeria is like a radio…She'll broadcast everything. The neighbor brought you some preserves. Let Antonina eat it, she said. It's made of paradise apples. Her relatives sent them to her, from Krasnodar…" – "Where is that?" – "In the south, I suppose… I don't know my cities very well. Here it is." – She holds a saucer. – "Try it. We've already had some."

The apples are small and wrinkled… I took one by the stem and chewed it. I don't notice any taste at all. They must be delicious when they're fresh…

VII

ARIADNA

Solomon unfolded the piece of newspaper. He counts the notes. Yevdokia can't take her eyes away. "Oh," - she complains. "I lost count. My eyes are terrible. There's too much here. You count it yourself."

He gathered up the notes and straightened them out around the edges. "There you go, 800 exactly".

Yevdokia stretched out her hand. She froze. "How much? How much?..." she asked.

"I didn't expect it myself. It's all Gennady. It was a patient he was operating on. And it wasn't a difficult case, actually. Her husband turned out to be an antique dealer. And he valued them..."

"May God give him health," - Glikeria crosses herself. – "Imagine that, an honest man…" – "Who? Gennady?" – "No," –she's frightened. "That guy, the husband… Another man may have deceived us." "We are rarely deceived," - he laughs. "We doctors".

Yevdokia takes it, and gives it to Ariadna. "Go and hide it," - she whispers. And she fusses as she looks At Solomon. "Have some tea," - she offers – "With paradise apples."

Ariadna sits there, not moving – as if stuck to her chair. Yevdokia looks at her.

After they finish the tea, Glikeria sees Solomon off.

Ariadna looks on after him: "That seems a lot…"

"Oh, it's a lot," - Yevdokia repeats. – "Now we have enough for everything – the injections, and God knows what else… We've been lucky." She squints. "I immediately realized, but I didn't say anything when Solomon was here. How did that husband think, I wonder. The doctor showed him earrings."

Glikeria returns and listens in to the conversation.

"And the antique dealer was happy. He's rich, and it's not as if he's giving him any money… And here the doctor makes the hint himself. Just don't tell Solomon anything," - Glikeria waves a threatening finger.

"What am I, completely stupid!" – she says, offended. – "I won't say a word."

Ariadna sits there.

" It's shameful. As if we're taking something from someone else."

"Pah!" – she bursts out. – "When one of them isn't being stupid, another idiot comes along. What were you planning to live on? Off you go, take it back. What do we care, we're rich. There," - she points to the wall – "we'll sell the television. I don't need it. You're the one who likes watching it. You sit glued to it."

Ariadna gives a sob and leaves the room.

Glikeria looks on, feeling sorry for her.

"Why did you say that, Yevdokia Timofevna… Don't you have a heart? She is hoping for her loved ones – to see them someday, even for one fleeting moment."

She falls silent, and sulks.

"Ah!" – she waves her hand. –"Do what you want. Sell everything. Take it to the flea market. Even for three rubles…"

Glikeria follows Ariadna – she sits by the head of the bed.

"Don't cry," - she comforts her. "He didn't earn his money by hard work. What hard work? He got it in the blockade, no doubt. And God sent it to us – for our poverty."

"But I don't want this sort of money," - she raises her head from the pillow. "If God sent it, I won't accept it from him."

"Lord," - she crosses herself. – "Subdue your pride. It doesn't become our rank…"

"That's my business," - she says. "I'll meet the Father in the other world… What will I say to him? It was earned in the blockade, from the blood of others…

"Oh," - Glikeria gives up. – "You're smart, work it out for yourself. What can I say…"

Yevdokia walks into the room. "It stinks of medicine. The room needs an airing… Perhaps you'd like some compote?" – "No thanks." – She turns to the wall. – "I don't want anything." – "Maybe some milk or cake cheese? Cake cheese is good, it's soft. Don't be like this, Antonina. How can someone survive on just chocolate…" – "Turn on the television," - she whispers. – "Lord!" She throws up her hands. "You watch it all day… Where's that from?" – "Suzannochka brought it."

The little toy apartment is glued together, right by the bed.

"Did she do that herself?" – "Yes… And she cut out the snowflakes – she placed them all around…" – "Yes…" - Yevdokia looks around the room. – "It's become beautiful. Like it's winter…"

"Don't forget about my debt," she asks. "Two hundred and fifty rubles are left. I gave him 100." - "But he'll be your husband," she says, flustered.

"No." – the patient's eye flashes. – "Give it back to the last kopeck. And the television will go to Suzannochka. She can have it."

Yevdokia goes to Ariadna – she closes the door. "What can I say…"

Ariadna listens. "Well…" - she nods. "If that's what she wants." – "So, just kopecks will be left. We'll pay the money back, and how will we live after that?" – "Perhaps," - she thinks, - "he'll be embarrassed. He won't take it…" – "Him?!" – Yevdokia gets up, and walks out.

Grandma Glikeria looks into the room:

"How are you then, Tonya? Aren't you cold? We decided to heat up the apartment. We'll turn on the stove in the kitchen. We'll leave the door open, and it will warm you up a bit. Gather up your snowflakes," – she turns to me. "It's going to get warm, they'll melt."

Mama beckons her with her hand.

"Sit down," she says. "I feel ill, Glikeria Yegorovna. I'm going to die, and it's like I haven't really even lived."

"Then live," - she sighs. "You have a daughter."

"I close my eyes, and I see vats, and vats... Those bars of iron... People die, and no doubt dream of other things... I also used to dream: I'd get married, and my husband would give me a ring. There's never been a gold ring for me."

"Maybe you will be given one."

"Not anymore," - she gives a laugh. – "Maybe in the next world... I watch television," - she whispers. "They have things good there... It's all easy and kind there. Not like here."

"Who is 'they'?"

"I don't know." – She turns her eyes away.

Grandma Glikeria calls:

"Come and sit by the stove. Let Mama sleep in peace. She should rest."

"I'm frightened, Glikeria Yegorovna... It's forever. And then I think, what if I just fall asleep? And then I wake up... I'll see Grigory," she whispers. "That one," - she whispers, "in the little apartment, looks a lot like him... I lie here and imagine: this table is in our room. We've come home from work, and sit down to eat. Borshch, meat and buckwheat... I see it so clearly, it's as if I can even smell it. And I breathe in the smell, and feel sick. I suppose my soul can't take it – this human food..."

"Don't think about that," - Glikeria tries to comfort her. "The Lord himself will sort everything out. In the other world things are quiet and peaceful. In the green pastures... You see everyone who you have said farewell to. What sins can you have... Let those tremble, whose path lies to hell."

"I dream of living under communism, Glikeria Yegorovna. Just to have a glimpse of it... The people who will live to see it are happy." "Oh!" – she waves her hand. – "When will that happen? They promised it before the war..." – "Before the war they were just guessing... But now they know for certain: in 20 years. They say that everything will be different. Machines will do the laundry..." – "What do you mean!" – She's stunned. "Will that be outside? Like street-washing machines?... The laundry will get all mixed up. They'll never be able to sort it out afterwards."

"No, why do they have to be outside? People will install them in their homes." – "Good gracious! How will they put them in their homes? Where will they go?" – "Well," - she looks at the little apartment– "maybe in the kitchen." – "Where will people cook then? Or," she smiles, "Will there be a magic table-cloth? Like in the fairytale." – "Why will they need that?" – she's serious, and doesn't smile. "They'll boil potatoes, maybe soup... And they'll have chocolates. They'll have everything – and they won't need to cook."

"For everyone?" – she is surprised. "Yes," she nods, "for everyone."

"What sort of pensions will they have, if they can afford chocolate every day?" – "There won't be any pensions." – "Not at all, you mean?" – she's scared. "Like in the old days, on the collective farms? Oh!" – she crosses herself. "Have they planned that again? I hope God does not let me live that long..."

"There won't be any money at all. It will be completely abolished." – "How is that possible?

What about groceries? Will they be issued by cards? What about dry goods?" – "They promised that everything would be given freely. As much as people want... For them," she looks towards the corner, "everything is planned differently. I think," she whispers, "that they show it beforehand on television. They have money, but the people are completely different. I look at them, and can't stop admiring them: they're not like us. They're kind and cheerful. They go to work, and everything is fine there. And things are decent at home..."

"Is everyone kind?" – Glikeria turns towards the television. "What about the bad people?" – "There won't be any bad people at all." – "That only happens in heaven, I'm afraid..." – "That's right," she nods. – "I think that's what paradise is like. Just the way it is on television. I didn't use to believe that. But now I think that this is what it is like. I dream of going there..." "Well," - Glikeria rubs her eyes. "You will... Believe me... Who else, if not you. It will be just like it is on television. They probably don't just show these things – they know about them..."

Ariadna crunches up the newspaper. The fire doesn't burn without newspaper. She bends over to throw in the match. The newspaper crackles, and then bursts into flame. The fire has started...

Yevdokia takes the poker and stokes the fire. Steam comes out of the oven, and the logs crackle.

"Oh," - she says, "I like the stove so much... When I was young I used to sit and look at the flame..."

"I like it too," says Ariadna happily. "My father used to get angry with me. 'What are you staring at the fire for?'" – he said. "'You'll encourage the devils.'"

"Nonsense!" Yevdokia waves her hand. "Do you think devils hang around in ovens?"

Sofia sits and listens.

"I saw one once" – Ariadna says, looking around. "Just like I can see you now."

"How's that?" – she says in amazement.

"Just imagine, it really did happen. I was coming home from school, and my brother had guests over. He was studying at university at the time. I went to my room – the wall was thin, and his room was next to mine. I could hear them: they were laughing!... And our janitor, Arkhip was there. He was putting logs into the stove, and also listening. 'Hey, the young masters are laughing... They find something funny...' He left. I opened the little door and warmed myself...

"I looked and saw a tongue of fire. It crackled as though a piece of coal had jumped out. It was *Him*. He was small and nimble. His arms were wrinkled – he rubbed his palms... I was frightened, but I was also curious. He rushed around my feet. He laughed, and threw his head back..."

"Well then?" – Yevdokia asks impatiently. "Then what?"

"Then what?" – she seems to come to herself. – "Nothing. It vanished."

"Maybe you imagined it. You should have said a Hail Mary."

"We weren't believers in those times. I liked poetry, and my brother was interested in philosophy. He was always carrying books with him – he hid them from our father. He went to the war with Germany and put some books in his bag. 'Who knows,' - he said – 'maybe there'll be a calm spell – I'll do some reading'…"

"Was he enlisted, then?" – She puts the poker against the wall.

"No. He volunteered. He was awarded a St George soldier's cross. Father was proud of him. He came back on leave and said: 'I don't live in the barracks, but the soldiers still like me. And I'm on good term with them.'"

Yevdokia snickers:

"What about your father?"

"We were sitting down at the table to have a meal. My father threw down his napkin. 'You idiot!' he yelled. 'You studied that all at your universities. You've found yourself an amusement – the peasant! The peasant will sell himself for a kopeck, and sell you for less than half a kopeck!'"

"Well?" Yevdokia listens. "What did your brother say?"

"He argued: 'You are wrong, father. The peasant believes in God. And his morality is child-like, and natural – you need to treat him kindly.' And father looked at him and replied: 'I didn't go to university, and didn't read your books. I'm from the peasants myself. My father was a serf – I bought him out. And I bought you out, you idiot – in 1905.'"

"How is that?" – she said in surprise.

"He participated in the protest. With the

students. Father went to the police station to talk to the officer."

"Did he buy him off, then? Yes," – she says dreamily – "those were good times..."

"We sat down to drink tea, and my father started again: "I know those peasants of yours. I've seen plenty in my time, and this is what I can tell you: the yids at least sold God for money, but this peasant of ours, if it comes to that, will sell him for nothing. Out of bravado or drunkenness. And he'll even boast about it, how cunning he was... And all because he doesn't believe, but he's afraid. And he takes his fear for belief. And so fear and bravado mix together. Whichever triumphs will remain. So far," – he says – "they're held back by fear. But when the fear goes away, everything will collapse. And it will all crumble: watch out!

"And my brother said: 'Fear degrades a person, father. But the peasant is also a person. This is the law of logic,' he says. Father moved his saucer aside. 'Eh,' – he sighs –'It's going to be bad for you. The peasant knows one truth: this is what our fathers and grandfathers did, and this is what we're going to do. But perhaps their grandfathers were highway robbers... They killed innocent people...' He raised a finger: 'This is what it says in Scripture: they reject the word of God for the sake of the traditions of the elders. This' – he says – is about them.'"

"And what did your brother do?" Yevdokia asks.

Ariadna takes the poker. She stokes the stove. The flames are lively and high. There's a dry heat. The tears dry up by themselves.

"They dealt with him. In 1917. There was a disturbance at the barracks. The officers stayed in their quarters – they were afraid to go out. But he said: 'I'll go and talk to the soldiers. I'm not a stranger to them.' He climbed on a barrel. 'Brothers! Brothers!' he shouted. And they grabbed him by the legs. We weren't informed immediately, only later. When father found out, he didn't sit still all night, he paced around the room. 'I told him, I told that idiot,' he mumbled. And in the morning he took to his bed: his legs failed him. 'I can't feel my legs,' he said."

Glikeria came into the kitchen. "Antonina is saying something about money being abolished. Very soon."

Yevdokia turns away from the stove: "Abolished?! Is this another reform?... When was it announced? I went to the shop yesterday... All the grain would have been snatched up..." – "No," she explains. "That's what they were told at the factory..." – "What factory is she talking about?" she clutches at her heart. "She doesn't go to the factory. She hasn't gotten up for three months..."

"My God," - Ariadna turned pale, - "our money... You can't exchange that much. One to ten again..."

"But, it's just..." - Glikeria tries to tell them.

"That's it then!" Yevdokia threw down the poker. "The antique dealer didn't give a bribe. He was just getting rid of worthless paper. But we... That's it." – She sat on the stool. – "The end. So." – She tried to get up – "Prepare the bags. We can buy cans of some sort, if any are left. There was probably a run on them in the morning. Maybe at least some cans of fish are left... What are they called, those crabs..."

"No, no," – Glikeria is almost crying. "There isn't any reform. It's supposed to be their future: paradise… They show it on television… Antonina, in her suffering, dreams about it…"

"What!?" – she freezes. "What paradise can there be for them? We know the road they are on…" – "But they don't believe it themselves," Ariadna says. – "How is that?" Glikeria objects. "Everyone believes in paradise. At the demonstrations, they bring their rags with them, the demons. I thought that they were meant to replace church banners."

"So what?" – Yevdokia frowns. – "Demons are demons. So they are devils then, and their banners are devilish." – "But devils also remember paradise," she says triumphantly.

"Pah!" – Yevdokia sits down. "You'll have a stroke. What do we care about their paradise? Or maybe," - she says – "maybe I should go? It's not far." – "It's seven o'clock," says Glikeria. "All the shops are closed. Unless we go upstairs to Karpovna?.." Yevdokia scowls: "Are you completely out of your mind! They'll say we're spreading rumours…" – "Well," – she says – "maybe we ran out of sugar. I'll take an empty cup …"

Yevdokia considered. "All right," - she decides. "But you go, Ariadna. Glikeria will blurt out something again."

"There," - she returns, showing a full cup. "Nadezhda Karpovna gave it to me." – "Thank God!" Yevdokia crosses herself. "We were waiting and waiting. We thought we'd sent you to your death. Right then, it's almost eight o'clock. Time for supper."

She drained the potatoes.

"There's not going to be paradise for them," she says. "They shouldn't even dream about it. And as for you," she says to Glikeria. "Remember for next time. First find out about things properly, and then start scaring people." – "But I didn't understand myself," she said, justifying herself. "They supposedly have machines that wash clothes. They say they'll put them in the kitchen. I don't even know how they'd drag them in there". – "What's that to us?" – Yevdokia mashes the potatoes. She pours vegetable oil on to them. "That's for the bosses. They have big apartments. They'll adapt."

"If she starts talking about that paradise, you agree with her," Glikeria lowers her eyes. "Let her be happy at the end. The Lord sees the truth – he will forgive her…" "Don't teach me…" - Yevdokia puts down the plate. "What am I, a beast?... I understand…"

Grandma Glikeria tucks the blanket in and sits down.

"Oh, life is so cruel.. Be happy while you're young. When you grow up, who knows… How will things happen?... All right then." – She wipes her eyes. – "Everything has already happened on this earth. It's only nasty people who live and don't know. But others understand everything. They just keep silent…"

She strokes the scarf on her head. She starts to untwine my plaits.

"We're both so forgetful. We completely forgot to do it this morning. And what about you? You could have reminded me. You could have brought the comb: to say, brush my hair, grandma. Now it's all tangled up... Well, never mind. I'll untangle it strand by strand. And you be patient, and listen..."

As the soul cries, it stretches out. It stands before the icon of the Saviour. How hard it was for the soul to say farewell to the white body – to depart into the heavenly distance, beyond the three hills. And behind the first hill, tar boils – black and sticky tar. Do you want to sit in tar, soul? She cries and struggles.

As soon as the Lord heard it, he cried himself. He sent two angels to meet her. They travel along the heavenly path – they meet her and take her under their arms. Why did you walk past paradise, soul, they ask? You walked past heaven and did not look at it...

The soul is sad and lowers her head. She addresses the angels of God. I would happy to go with you into the cypress paradise. But my sins have not been repented. How do I, sinner, justify myself? Damned, how can I be happy?

The angels of God answer her. Do not cry, soul, wipe your tears away. If it were our fate to live on earth, we too would no doubt be acquainted with sin...

...There is a small creek. It runs playfully, only the water is very murky. I step off the footbridge: that's all right, I think, I'll drink my fill. But as soon as I bend over, I can't believe my eyes. The bottom is sprinkled with rings. I'm amazed, and scoop up a handful. Now, I rejoice, I'll choose a precious gold ring... I open my palm, and they scatter. They jump up and down as if they were frogs. I remember, as a child, you'd stick your hand under a sunken log, and there would be a nest of them. You felt around, and took a whole handful, and they would scatter...What kind of country is this, if there are rings here in place of frogs?

I raised my head: there's a tall mountain. And on the mountain there is a tower. It reaches right up to the sky. And I hear a radio playing – loudly, across the whole land.

So this is Moscow, I guess... And I feel happy. Moscow is where the doctor lives. He will cure Suzannochka of her muteness. I only need to find him – I'll have to ask people. The footbridges are dry and smooth. I walk and look from side to side. I see a pleasant-looking woman. She looks like Zoya Ivanovna.

I walk up to her.

I ask her advice. She listens to me and asks: where is your child, then? She's at home, I reply. She doesn't go to kindergarten, she sits at home with the grandmothers. I came here to get married, I say. And the woman is delighted. Why didn't you tell me right away, she says. I was a bit confused, I reply. And my groom is late – evidently he got lost. And she laughs: that can't be! There's one road to us: you can't go astray. There's the gate, she points. That's where you enter.

I look, and see that there is indeed a gate, but it is made of glass and without hinges. What do we need hinges for? she asks. Our gate is special. It opens by itself. For those who believe.

I see a car entering. The gate ripples, ripples. The car passes through, and it becomes still again. And the car is also special – without wheels. It's a washing machine, she explains. They used to wash corpses, and now they launder them in washing machines...

What about a malignant disease? I ask. They've laundered it, she comforts me. We don't have diseases any more.

Oh, I think, if only I had Suzannochka with me.... I wouldn't let her put together an apron made out of poppy-colored scraps. I'm an idiot. I was scared of death. But death is happier than life...

I hear a rumble from under the ground. The hill is shaking. I scream and open my eyes. Glikeria is standing over me.

"Get up," - she wakes me. "It's time to go. The car will be here soon. What are you going to wear? Shall I give you a skirt?"

"No," - I say. "The poppy dress. Give me that one..."

She goes into the kitchen and says: "Put on the iron. She asked for the new dress. She's not going in the skirt."

No sooner do I close my eyes, but Glikeria calls me again: "Get up," - she hurries me, - "get out of bed. Here are your stockings and tights."

I pull them on somehow over my legs, and started to try to put on the dress. I undo the buttons, but my fingers feel strange to me. I barely manage to pull it over my head. Glikeria looks at me and stifles a sob. "I'm going to clean your shoes," she says, looking away. "I'll wipe them with a rag."

"I can't take it," - she complains. "She's got so thin. She's as pale as death – I've seen better-looking corpses. It's like I'm dressing a dead person. You go in, Ariadna."

Ariadna comes in, carrying a comb. "Come on, Tonechka," she says, "let's brush your hair." She lowers her own head – she doesn't look. She runs the comb through my hair, and it hurts. The skin on my scalp is sore. "Just undo it by the strands," I ask. – "I can't undo them," she says, tearing up. "All right," I nod. "Don't bother. I'll tie a scarf around my head. Let it stay the way it is."

We go out into the corridor. Yevdokia pushes me along. I see a young, pleasant-looking man. "Don't worry," - he says. "Antonina Dmitrievna and I will manage by ourselves."

We walk down the staircase – he supports me. He's kind and helpful, I think. He leads me to the car. "Where will you sit?" – he asks. "Perhaps the back seat would be better?"

The motor roars… I feel warm, festive. That woman is there again. She walks towards me. Did the groom come, then? she says.

And then suddenly it occurs to me: what if he's still alive? After all, I don't know for sure, and I wasn't at the trial. And she laughs: yes, there he is, he's coming down from the other side. He's coming for you...

My heart pounds: it's him, Grigory. He comes, grasping the rail. His eyes are dark and merry. Just like a living person.

He comes nearer. I've got a present for you, he says. He opens his hand, and there's a scrap of cloth in it. Now he unfolds it, and in it I see my cut-off finger, and it has a gold ring on it...

"Did you fall asleep, Antonina Dmitrievna?" I open my eyes, and the man turns to me: "We're here already. Let's get out."

I got out of the car – to meet Nikolai. He took me under his arm. I walk and think to myself: this isn't right. My wedding is on the other side...

The man walks up from the side: "If her head starts spinning, give me a sign. I have medicine with me."

I signed my name in the book. I felt dizzy. I don't remember how I got back into the car. That's it, I think. Thank God... Now I'll see the tower... That's where my life starts, that's where my husband is...

VIII

SOLOMON

Yevdokia opens the door. "Good gracious," she says. "She's completely white. Let her lie down."

Her eyes are dark and sunken. As if they had been drawn with slate. Gennady Pavlovich holds her by the arm. "Is Solomon Zakharovich here?" Yes, they nod, he's here.

They put her in bed, and he comes out of the room. "I'll go and say hello," he says, "and then I'll be off to work." – "Perhaps you'd like to eat with us," - Glikeria invites him. The table is set." – "Thank you," - he declines. "I'm on duty at the hospital. I'm afraid that I'm already late. Don't you worry," he says, pointing to the door. "That's how the injection works. She'll sleep and the effect will wear off."

Nikolai is still standing there, shifting from foot to foot. Ariadna goes to him and beckons him with her hand. "Come with me, Nikolai Nikiforovich," she says. "We have something to talk to you about." Yevdokia looked and thought better of it: she followed Gennady Pavlovich.

Sofyushka looks into the corridor. Glikeria waves her hand, motioning her to shut the door: stay out, it's not your business.

I'm cold, cold. And my head feels as if it's made of glass. Where am I? I think. There are cut-out snowflakes all around. Then I remember… It's my wedding.

Yevdokia bends towards Glikeria.

"Well, that's it," - she says. "He refused. I went on purpose, and talked about it in front of Solomon. He's his teacher: I thought he would be ashamed in front of him. That's a lot of money, I said, for these earrings. The antique dealer meant something else: he wanted to thank you."

Glikeria stares at the door.

"What did he say?"

"He blushed. He refused. That can't be, he said. He didn't take a kopeck."

"Thank God," Glikeria rejoices. "If it can't be, it can't be. We'll tell Ariadna. She'll be reassured. She was very worried."

Ariadna comes back. She has talked with Nikolai.

"Well?" – she says. – "Did he refuse?"

"He took it," she said, ashamed. "Everything, down to the last kopeck. He even re-counted it."

"And what," – Yevdokia smirks – did it work out for him? Never mind." – She mentally tallies the sum – "We'll talk about that later. We're celebrating a wedding now."

They fill the glasses. It's as if the bride and groom are sitting side by side. Sofia also gets a glass – water with jam stirred in.

Ariadna looks at Solomon. "I try and try to wake her up – but she refuses. Go ahead without me, she says." – "So then," Yevdokia raises a glass. "We congratulate you, Nikolai Nikiforovich, on your lawful marriage." He drinks the vodka and puts the glass down.

Elena Chizhova

Glikeria bends over to Yevdokia. "We should remove the empty glasses. It's not quite right," she whispers.

The husband pours himself another drink. He downs it. The rest sip their drinks.

"Have a bite, Nikolai Nikiforovich," Yevdokia says, pushing the vinaigrette towards him. "Here's some herring." He spears some with his fork, and smirks: "Don't worry, Yevdokia Timofeevna. I will do what I promised. I won't refuse.".– "God be with you," Glikeria says, blushing –"As if we…" – "I'm an honest man," - he says, looking at Yevdokia. "And I'm true to my word. Well," – he turns to Solomon, - "where are the papers for the child? Bring them to me, and I'll sign everything."

"Go on", Yevdokia reasons. "Today there's a wedding. Help yourself". – "The wedding," the husband twiddles his fingers. "Perhaps it's a wedding… Did you make pancakes, by any chance?" – "What pancakes," - Glikeria says. "Just potatoes. Wrapped in pillows, so they don't get cold. Maybe I should bring them?" – "Now, why not," - he says, pouring out a third glass… "Whatever…Bring them on.".

Yevdokia looks at Solomon: "We have a prescription, Solomon Zakharovich. You should take a look at it, we can't figure it out ourselves." And she motions with her eyes: let's go out of the room.

The two of them go out into the corridor. "Well," Yevdokia asks. "When will the papers be ready?" – "Gennady Pavlovich is working on it. They promised to have them in two weeks or so." Yevdokia looks at the door: "The sooner the better… Look what's happening. He's playing the odds. You never know, what if he suddenly springs a surprise on us…" – "Well, the man's had a bit too much to drink. He's also upset… We should" – he narrowed his eyes – "get him moved in here as quickly as possible."

Yevdokia stands and nods: "We'll hurry him up now, that's for certain. We've freed up a room for him. Let him live there…"

"Well," - Nikolai has become cheerful, and looks around – "we've drunk to the bride and groom. Now we should drink to you… May your life be rich and happy. So, here's to that."

He leans over to Solomon to clink glasses. "Some music would be good," he says, looking around. "It's a shame there's no music. It would be more fun with music. I never thought life would turn out like this," he says, rubbing his eye with his fist. "How about you? I agreed for the room…But it's not that. What's it to me, this room?… I pitied her as a human being." – "Who's blaming you…" – Glikeria says in confusion. "And maybe," - he isn't listening – "for the room too… Who can tell…"

Solomon Zakharovich gets up: - "I think I'll mosey along now." – "Listen," - Nikolai threatens him with his finger, leaning over the table. "You don't even respect me… What do you think: We tricked this fool, we drove him into a corner. But I say no-o-o.. I decided everything myself. On my own. So this is all the way it should be. According to human law. And no one can order me around…" – "Stop it," Solomon frowns. "No one is accusing you of anything." "Fancy that!" he gets even more upset. "What is there to accuse me of? Am I accused of something? I'm not guilty of anything…"

Glikeria gets up. "Who wants potatoes?" she asks. "They'll get cold."

"Look at you," Nicolai isn't listening. "You've lived out your life. And you're a smart guy, a Jew. Yes," he waves his hand. "Don't be offended. I'm not saying that to offend – I mean it respectfully. But," he raises his finger. "For the truth. Your ancestors crucified Christ, our God. But God didn't take offence. He forgave you…" – "Really?" Solomon smirks. "Where do you have this information from?" – "Where from?" – He frowns. "He left you intelligence. And cleverness." He turns up his fingers. "And you stick together. If one person is in trouble, everyone else comes running to help. Not," he snorts, "like us…"

"What's that?" – Yevdokia pouts. "Are we animals or something?... We're people too no doubt." – "No," he shakes his finger at her. "We're different. We're oh, so scared of each other…" – "That's right," Yevdokia agrees. "And there's good reason for it."

"I'm surprised at you," Solomon lowered his eyes. "You're still a young man, but what you're saying, if you'll excuse me, is from the Middle Ages. As if you'd never been to school…" – "So what?" – he answers, surprised. "School has nothing to do with it. They teach you one thing at school, but life tells you otherwise…"

"We should have tea," Glikeria remembers. "And there's pie – cabbage pie."

"At school" – Solomon is upset – "They teach you properly. All races are equal." – "Really! Equal…" He squints. "If you had been given the choice, you would no doubt have chosen to be born Russian… And that's right. Life's not so sweet for you Jews."

"But it's so sweet for us Russians," Yevdokia puts her plate aside. "You don't even have time to wipe your mouth – from all that sweetness."

"The Russians " – he wrinkled his forehead – "won the war, for all that." "Ye-e-es," – Yevdokia mocks him. "And aren't we all so happy about it." Nikolai looks at Solomon. "But still, I'm surprised at you. You're all as smart as can be…. And you're solidly behind the Soviet regime. But they don't like you. But people like us – respect us – all over the world. On television… Wherever we go…. Even America. They greet us…"

"That's because they admire us from afar," Yevdokia won't calm down. "They should try living here – among us." – "No, no," – he says, looking at her. "We liberated their Europe for them. Without us they would still be living under the Germans. It's dark in here…" he's jerked open his collar. "Could you maybe open the curtains – at least there'd be some light…"

"Well, we're sitting in the kitchen," – Glikeria looks around. "What curtains would there be in the kitchen? Ah" – she points to the window. "She stuck her snowflakes all over it. As decorations for the wedding."

"Decorations…" – he scratches his throat. "Fine, then, let it be… She's a child. How can she understand anything." He gets up, goes to the window, and scratches at a snowflake with his fingernail. "Hey," he says in surprise. "It's really stuck. It won't come off. That must be some pretty tough glue..."

"To listen to you," Solomon says, scowling, "You'd think the Russians had fought alone." – "Of course they didn't fight alone," he frowns, and stops scratching at the snowflake. "Lots of others did too. Only the Russians were the most important. Stalin talked about this... But you," he fills up his glass again, "Explain this to me. You Jews are all so smart – but you went to your deaths like sheep. How many of you died?"

Solomon is silent.

"I'll answer you. A mil-li-on. Why? Because you're smart against us. But against the Germans, you're nothing. Against the Germans we're the only ones in the saddle. That's how it is..."

"Lord," Yevdokia clutches her cheek. Her tooth is aching again. "Where are they then, these Germans! I've lived an age, but I've never met one. And I'll probably die without doing so."

"The Germans," he explains, "are a thorough people. My father fought against them – he told me. They would be an example to learn from... Everything they do is smart." – "We should fight against ourselves," Yevdokia frowns. "That would be something."

Solomon leans against the table: "I'll be off."

"What's wrong? Are you offended, Zakharych? You shouldn't be offended by the truth. It's a sin to be offended by the truth. Tell me about the Russians, tell me the whole truth. I'll never be offended in all my life. Well?" – he leans forward. "Well?"

"I don't know," – he shakes his head. "This whole truth of yours." – "That's right. And no one knows it. Not even you Jews. Because Russians are on their own. They're special. There aren't any people like them, not even if you travel all over the world."

"I can tell you one thing," Solomon rubs his forehead. "This Christ of yours has risen, but my wife will never rise again…" – "That's right," Nikolai says. "But if she were Russian, she would get into paradise. Christ prepared it for the Russians."

"You should eat some potatoes," Ariadna frowns, distressed. "Why discuss these things…" – "Why not," Solomon grins, stopping her. "Perhaps Nikolai Nikiforovich is actually right. Christianity is a religion of charity. If I were Russian, I could hope. But as it stands"…

"Good gracious," – Glikeria remembers. "I need to put the child to bed. She must be completely worn out. Let's go, little dove," she says. "Off you go," Yevdokia nods. "She's sat and celebrated… Why listen to unnecessary talk"…

It smells of pie from the kitchen. I opened my eyes. I could do with a sip of water… My throat is completely dry. I reach out and take off the gauze. As soon as I swallowed, I spat it out. Obviously I can't take it in…

My mother once said that boiled water is dead. In all your life you can never drink enough of it.

Elena Chizhova

I dream of pure water. Oh, for some pure water, for the end. Even just a gulp of living water...

I rise up on my elbows, but can't feel my legs. I should call someone... They won't hear me anyway...

My heads swims, and whirls... I see my mother. She sat next to me and folded my arms. And it was like I'm a little girl again. I move my lips: tell me a story, I ask her. And she strokes the scarf on her head. Sleep, she whispers, close your eyes...

The Raven headed to the thirtieth kingdom. He flew all night. And the steppe is broad and endless. It is covered in white snow: white everywhere.

He came to it and saw: there was a forged iron gate in front of him, and in the gate there was a rock weighing a good three hundred stone. He looked it over. Behind the rock were two wells. They were cut into either side of it, and the water in them was almost overflowing. The water on the right was living, the water on the left was dead. He sat on the rock and thought. He chose the dead water.

He pecked off the icy crust and filled his craw with the water. He wants to fly back but the dead water is heavy. It stuck in his craw. He somehow managed to soar above the clouds. He's flying along, and thinking to himself: why don't I fly a little lower, maybe it will be warmer, and easier to fly. He folded his wings, and looked down over his shoulder. He saw a field. And the field was strewn with human bones. Everything is covered with them, wherever you look.

He was happy, and gave a caw. The water sprayed out of his mouth. It scattered in white snowflakes. It fell on the ground – and all the bones grew together.

They crawled over the field. They should get up, they think, but their arms and legs don't obey. The bones are too heavy. They look up at the Raven, and cry tearfully. But he puffs out his cheeks, and clicks with his iron beak: off you crawl, he squawks. I don't have any living water for you…

IX

THE GRANDDAUGHTER

When the snow falls, I always remember the grandmothers. I stand by the window and think. My grandmothers did not have any illnesses, they just passed away in the same year. First Glikeria, then Ariadna. And Grandmother Yevdokia lived until autumn – I was already studying in the first year at the Mukhinsky Academy. It was just the two of us living together.

My stepfather's family was given a two-room apartment, but no one moved in – that room was turned into a bathroom, and the grandmothers were able to wash properly. They used to wash in their rooms – Zinaida Ivanovna didn't allow them to wash in the kitchen, and they couldn't walk to the bathhouse. I heated up water for buckets, I carried out the dirty water, and Zinaida shouted that we were making the apartment damp, although I put down an oilcloth and never poured it into the sink – always into the toilet.

At the end they started having disorders of the brain. Grannie Yevdokia was happy that she had outwitted everyone, and that now I had the right to move in with Zinaida, because I was registered there: the apartment was given to three people. I didn't want to upset her. I knew that Zinaida wouldn't let me in. She used to say: if I let any old whore in, there won't be enough meters to go around. And Grannie Ariadna threatened to find an authority to deal with her: she said that the world was not without kind people. The factory management would intercede, and if necessary, we would go to Kalinin himself, but Zinaida just laughed: it's long overdue…

Grannie Ariadna also got everything mixed up: she thought they were still alive – her grandchildren, my mother, and even Kalinin. She whispered: there on television…

I remember crying and going to Zinaida Ivanovna, asking her to leave them in peace, and promising that I wouldn't move from where I was. But Zinaida just laughed again: "Just try… You think you're scaring me? I have authority at the factory. Let those witches just try to intrude, and you'll see the feathers fly…"

After everyone had died, they came to me from the municipal and communal services office, and told me that an order had been issued for our apartment, and that I had to go to my place of residence: within three days. Then my stepfather advised me to talk to Zinaida, he said that she wouldn't listen to him, but that I had to try: she was still the head of the trade union, mother had given so many years to the factory, and maybe they would give me a room – even a small one, even in the basement. After the funeral I was completely lost, and Zinaida replied that the factory did not have any spare rooms.

If it hadn't been for the academy, I would have been left out in the street, as I had a Leningrad registration, but I was in fact given a place in a dormitory. My knowledge of French was what helped me.

I went to the dean's office to submit a statement, and they had just received a letter from France, so

Elena Chizhova

I offered my assistance. When the French people arrived, they summoned me from lessons again and asked me to interpret. They had an interpreter, but she didn't understand everything, especially not rapid speech. At first I was a little lost, but I soon got my bearings. And the head of their group came to me and said: "What a surprising combination: a young mademoiselle and old-fashioned language." I explained that my grandmother had taught me French. He smiled: "Now it's clear."

To start with I lived at the dormitory, and then I met Grisha, and we rented a room: his parents didn't let us in, they didn't want me to live with him. His departure cost us dearly, I had no money left. I stayed at other people's workshops. Until I bought this apartment. By then, my works had started to sell. First on the cheap, then it became more and more expensive, especially after the Russian Museum bought one of them. It was even featured in an exhibition, but then it went into storage. Some of the paintings went into private collections – here and in the West. Now it's hard for me to follow the fate of my paintings.

I made renovations and brought furniture to the apartment – everything that was left from the grandmothers. My stepfather had had the idea of taking it all away and hiding it in his village: after his relatives died, an empty house was left. His wife didn't know about this, because the house wasn't registered, and she didn't need it anyway. Some of it had to be restored, but now there is nothing new in my apartment: not cabinets, not sofas, not chairs.

When we met at the exhibition, Grisha invited me to go with him again, and said that nothing would work out here, because life is not arranged according to meaning, but according to the level of human souls. I refused, because I was thinking about my grandmothers. And my mother. I would leave, and they would stay… How would they stay here without me?

Now I understand that Grisha was right. Now I would go with him, but it's too late to talk about that.

Sometimes I get out the damask tablecloth with roses and imagine that we are sitting around the table – my father, my mother, and the grannies. It was for them that I bought such a large apartment. So that thy would have a home in which they would no longer be afraid, because they are our rooms, and no one will take them away.

Now I am always with them, even if they do not see me, as if there were a blank wall between us. But I still walk around. I sit down, stay still for a while and then go to the easel again, so that, turning into that different girl of retentive memory, I may listen to their voices.

Recently I read an old poem called "The Book of Doves," although strangely enough it doesn't have a word in it about doves. This book has a story about Falsehood and Truth, and when I read it, I think that I remember everything. I recognize words that disturb me, and I try to find images to paint this picture. Otherwise, why did I become an artist: why did I sleep and wake up?

Elena Chizhova

A terrible thundercloud appeared in the sky. It brought the dove's book with it. A book that is neither big nor small, but twenty sazhens wide. So the orthodox Christians gathered, looked at the book and pondered. And no one could make a sensible approach to it, no one wanted to stagger up to the book of God.

Then Prince Volodimir steps out and addresses Davyd Yevseich.

"May God bless you, our all-wise Tsar! Read the dove's book to us. Explain to us about Russian life. Why is it that our Sun is beautiful? Why are our winds so boisterous? Why is it that our mind turns this way and that? Why are our thoughts so bitter? Why are our bones so strong? Why does our blood-ore run? It keeps pouring out of our veins – it will never run out…"

The wise Tsar Davyd answers him thus.

"I don't know how to read your books – I don't understand Russian writing. It's hard, this writing, and the book of God is a hundred times harder. The hands cannot hold it, nor the mind take it in. I'll tell you what I know from memory – from my memory, as from a document.

"The Sun is beautiful from the face of Christ, your God, the Heavenly King. The boisterous winds are from the Holy Spirit. Your bones are strong from the stone mountains. Your blood is like ore from the raw earth. And it spurts from your veins and never stops…"

Volodimir the prince bowed to him.

"May God bless you, all-wise Tsar Davyd! You haven't learnt our Russian letters, but you have understood our deadly trouble. Make it clear to us, Psalmist, what our great sadness is – our great and inescapable sadness . Tell us what you know from memory – from your memory, not from writing."

The wise Tsar Davyd questions him.

"May God bless you, Prince Volodimir! Tell me about your sadness. I will settle it as I can, from memory – from memory, not from writing".

Prince Volodimir answers.

"May God bless you, our all-wise Tsar Davyd! I'll tell you what I don't know myself. Last night I slept little, but I dreamt a lot. I saw in my dreams two beasts – they came together in an open field and fought each other. And the first beast came from the underground side, and the second from the daylight side. My heart sank as soon as I looked at them. It was bathed in black blood, like ever-lasting torment. So tell me which one of them is more cruel, which of them is more spiteful."

So the wise Tsar Davyd answers him.

"May God bless you, Sun-like Russian prince! Strengthen your spirit – your boisterous heart. They are not beasts that came together to fight, they're not fierce ones engaged in combat. They are Falsehood and Truth, which came together and fought between themselves. Falsehood tries to overcome Truth. But your Truth is more fierce than fireceness itself. It beat Falsehood, and out-argued it. And it went to Heaven, straight to Christ himself, the Heavenly King. And it *sat on the right of the Father, alongside the Holy Spirit, next to the Mother. And Falsehood walked across the Earth – among all the Christian people. The Earth is shaken by Falsehood, and the people suffer in silence. It is from Falsehood that the people became twisted, twisted and spiteful. And fierce Truth sits up above in Heaven. It will not descend to the sinful earth..."*